"You're a fine nursemaid," Adam told her.

"It's the least I could do. Particularly after you traveled all this way just to be with me." With sudden shyness, Savannah lowered her gaze. "I'm so sorry about what... happened to you. I promise, we don't usually find such ruffians around these parts. You'll be absolutely safe here with me. I'll make sure of it."

It was preposterous—but kind—of her to suggest she could protect him. Adam didn't understand why she thought he'd come to the Territory to be with her, though. Unless she'd found his saddlebags and his journals? Unless she knew about his work for the agency?

After you traveled all this way just to be with me.

A few seconds too late, the truth struck him. Savannah Reed, Adam realized, thought *he* was her mail-order groom!

* * *

Mail-Order Groom
Harlequin® Historical #1019—December 2010

Author's Note

Thank you for reading *Mail-Order Groom*!

I'm so happy to share Savannah and Adam's story with you. It was great fun for me to write, and I truly hope you enjoyed it. If you spotted a few familiar faces, that's because this is my fifth visit to Morrow Creek. I hope you'll look for the other stories in my Morrow Creek series—*The Matchmaker, The Scoundrel, The Rascal* and "Marriage at Morrow Creek" (part of the *Hallowe'en Husbands* anthology, which also features wonderful stories by the talented Denise Lynn and Christine Merrill).

In the meantime, you're invited to drop by my website, www.lisaplumley.com, where you can sign up for new-book alerts or my reader newsletter, read sneak previews of upcoming books, request special reader freebies and more. I hope you'll visit today.

As always, I'd love to hear from you! You can visit me online at community.eharlequin.com/users/lisaplumley, send email to lisa@lisaplumley.com, "friend" me on Facebook, follow me on Twitter, or write to me c/o P.O. Box 7105, Chandler, AZ 85246-7105.

Mail-Order Groom
LISA PLUMLEY

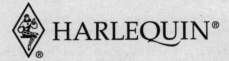

HARLEQUIN®

TORONTO • NEW YORK • LONDON
AMSTERDAM • PARIS • SYDNEY • HAMBURG
STOCKHOLM • ATHENS • TOKYO • MILAN • MADRID
PRAGUE • WARSAW • BUDAPEST • AUCKLAND

Recycling programs
for this product may
not exist in your area.

ISBN-13: 978-0-373-29619-4

MAIL-ORDER GROOM

Copyright © 2010 by Lisa G. Plumley

This edition published by arrangement with Harlequin Books S.A.

For questions and comments about the quality of this book please contact us at Customer_eCare@Harlequin.ca.

® and TM are trademarks of the publisher. Trademarks indicated with ® are registered in the United States Patent and Trademark Office, the Canadian Trade Marks Office and in other countries.

www.eHarlequin.com

Printed in U.S.A.

Praise for Lisa Plumley's Morrow Creek miniseries

The Rascal

"A charming, humorous and enjoyable read."
—*RT Book Reviews*

The Scoundrel

"Will remind you of your first kiss, plus melt your heart. Lisa Plumley's style is the cure-all for a bad day and I dare you not to laugh, and maybe shed a tear, as well."
—*Romance Junkies*

The Matchmaker

"Filled with charming characters, a sassy love story and laugh-out-loud antics. *The Matchmaker,* as creative and unique as Molly's cinnamon buns, will satisfy your sweet tooth. It's a winner!"
—*Old Book Barn Gazette*

To my husband, John, with all my love.

Chapter One

June 1884
Northern Arizona Territory

"For a fella who always gets his man, you sure are spending a lot of time moonin' over that woman of yours."

At the sound of his longtime partner's voice, Adam Corwin jerked his gaze from the blurry photograph he'd been studying.

"She's not mine." Stone-faced, he shoved the photograph in his coat pocket, next to his heart. "She's bait. Nothing more."

"She's the gold nugget in this ol' mining scheme, that's for sure." Mariana Sayles crawled to match his position on the ridge, dirtying her skirts with an aplomb unmatched by any detective—female or otherwise. "But there's no sense looking at *her* night and day. It's Bedell we're supposed to pin, remember?"

"I wish I could forget." Adam reached for his rucksack. Without taking his gaze from his target, he pushed aside his maps and jerky, then withdrew his spyglass. He aimed the instrument at the campsite he and Mariana had identified after days of tracking. He frowned. "Still no sign of movement."

"From you or the mark?"

"Funny." His self-discipline might be legendary, but Adam didn't like to be reminded of it. "You should join up with one of those traveling circuses. Pay's probably better."

"And give up all this?" Mariana gestured at the scrub oak, fallen pinecones, and overall desolation surrounding them at the edge of the mountainside. "Now you're talkin' crazy, Corwin."

"Days of waiting will do that to a man."

"So will days without a bath. I itch something fierce."

"Nobody said detective work would be pretty."

"Nobody said *you'd* be so handsome, but I put up with it."

Mariana gave him a teasing smile—the same smile that helped her charm outlaws and clients with equal ease—but Adam didn't reply. Intent on catching sight of the confidence man they'd tracked across three states and two territories, he scanned the blackened fire pit, the four horses, the empty bottles of mescal, and the trio of canvas military-issue tents—doubtless recently stolen—in the valley below him.

Although the sun had just come up, wisps of smoke still issued from the charred logs—evidence of how late the fire had burned. The bony horses—most likely as pilfered as the tents were—shifted at their iron posts. Otherwise all was silent.

Frustratingly silent.

If Bedell didn't catch up with his four no-good brothers soon, Adam would know that he and Mariana had struck the wrong path. It wouldn't be the first time Bedell had slipped away from them. The man was ruthless, whip-smart and as elusive as a warm bed to the man who'd been trailing him.

"You want me to end all this real quick?" Mariana asked. "I could put on a clean dress, go shake my bustle a little, see if those boys want to come in peaceful for a change."

Adam quirked his mouth. "The day Roy Bedell or his brothers do anything peacefully is the day I sprout wings." He flattened his belly against the gravelly ground. "You stay here."

"Why, Mr. Corwin! Are you *still* trying to protect me?"

"Keep your voice down, too."

"Always the chivalrous one, even after all these years. They warned me about you at the agency, but would I listen?" Her tone as playful as ever, Mariana nudged him. "How do you know I merit defending anyhow? Some people ain't worth saving."

"*Some people* are bound and determined to give up our position." Frowning, Adam tucked away his spyglass. He crawled back from the ridge's edge, then straightened. Deftly he shouldered his rucksack. It contained everything he owned, save his horse and saddle. He couldn't recall the last night he'd spent without it tucked beneath his head. "Saddle up. Let's go."

"Already?" Mariana glanced over her shoulder. "I was just getting comfortable. You're a right spoilsport sometimes."

"Bedell might've changed his plans. He might've decided to meet his mark without his brothers around to complicate things." Adam had hoped to nab the man before it came to that—before the woman Bedell had targeted became even more involved. But just in case… "We should head to her telegraph station."

"Got a *special* message for your secret lady friend? Hmm?"

"I want to make sure he's not already there."

Mariana sighed. "I wish Bedell would get off these phony marriage schemes. Makes me feel sorry for the ladies. Don't they know no better than to believe a man who promises the moon?"

"Mostly, no." All the same, Adam wished the woman in his photograph had. "Bedell's been specially clever about this one, though. Six months laying groundwork, romancing all pretty-like over the wires, sending all those letters—that probably adds up to a compelling case for marriage in most women's minds."

"Humph. You'll never catch *me* being such a saphead."

"Good thing." Safely out of sight of the camp now, Adam tied his rucksack beside his bedroll and saddlebags. He steadied his horse, then swung up in the saddle. "I'd hate to break in a new partner just because you got all swoony over a man."

"Ha! Not while there's breath in my body." Mariana mounted adeptly, her chestnut mare snorting. "Unlike *some* women, I know how to keep my head. Imagine writing down all that claptrap—"

"She didn't think the likes of us would be reading it."

Uncomfortably Adam considered the packet of filched letters in his rucksack. Like all the other missives written by Bedell's lady loves, they started out cautious…then gradually turned more revealing. Intercepting them hadn't been his favorite piece of detective work, but it had been necessary. So had Mariana's part of the job—making copies of the letters in her ladylike handwriting and sending the duplicates to Bedell.

"All I can say is, your lady friend must be sitting on one whale of a cash pile for Bedell to come all this way west."

Adam frowned. "You're forgetting Kansas City."

Instantly his partner sobered. She scanned the ridgeline, her freckled face pensive. "Say…how 'bout we split up? I'll keep watch over the campsite and signal you if Bedell shows—"

"We already talked about this—"

"—and I'll come after you lickety-split if one of his boys takes up in your direction. They're already days late for their meetin', and I'm thinking something's not right. Bedell's done busted up all their plans. I think maybe it's a trap."

"No." Shaking his head, Adam fisted his pommel. Beneath him, his horse shifted eagerly. "If something happens to you—"

"Don't worry." Grinning, Mariana patted the pistol at her hip. When they weren't in town, she didn't bother with trick holsters or short-barreled derringers, preferring to strap an ordinary gun belt over her calico skirts. "I can take care of myself."

Grudgingly Adam studied her. He had the utmost respect for Mariana's detective abilities. With a rough mouth and a plucky demeanor, she'd made her way in a man's world—but was still soft enough to spoil their horses with extra oats. As much as he wanted to shield her, it wasn't his place to hold her back.

"You remember where the station is? Across the valley—"

"And up the mountainside near Morrow Creek. I remember."

At her beleaguered tone, Adam couldn't help grinning. Of all the reasons he liked having Mariana as his partner, her grit stood chief among them—even if it did collide with his own stubbornness from time to time. Mariana was brash, outspoken, and unstoppable. She was the closest he came to family.

She glanced at him. "Oh, no. Don't you give me that grim face of yours, neither. You look as somber as an overworked undertaker." She waved at him. "Git on now. Shoo. I'll be fine."

"You make sure of that." Gruffly Adam cleared his throat. "Let's bring down that double-crossing cuss once and for all."

He touched his hat brim. Mariana offered him an answering salute. Without further sentimentality, he rode away at a clip, leaving his partner a defiant dot on the ridgeline behind him.

Splitting up didn't sit well with him. Despite that, Adam knew it was the smartest thing to do. Every instinct told him Bedell was ahead of him on the trail—not behind, like Mariana thought. She might be a fast and fearless draw, but he wanted her out of the way when the inevitable showdown came.

The moment he met Roy Bedell face-to-face, Adam knew, one of them was going down—and he was deadly determined it would not be him.

For the fifth time in as many days, Savannah Reed stood on the platform at the Morrow Creek train depot, biting her lip while she stared east. Right on time, the 10:12 train appeared on the horizon, trailing sparks as it chugged nearer.

Jet-black smoke poured from its stacks, smudging the clear and sunny Arizona Territory sky. The sound of the train's wheels grew louder, seeming to grind out the words *he's almost here, he's almost here* in a rhythm to match her heartbeat.

Around her, expectant travelers surged forward, tickets

in hand. The portly man to her left bade his wife goodbye, leaving the poor woman sniffling into her handkerchief. A curly-haired youth Savannah recognized from the mercantile ignored the train's arrival, preferring to blush and stammer beneath the attention of a young lady who'd stopped to ask him the time.

Some of these people were setting off on new adventures—most outfitted far more elaborately than Savannah had been on her own journey westward months ago. Others were here to meet someone on the 10:12. None of them had been present on the platform every day for nearly a week. None, that is, except her.

From the depot window, the ruddy-faced station telegraph clerk caught her eye. He crossed his fingers, then held them up to her. He'd been here every morning during her vigil, too.

Most likely, he wondered why she kept returning. Or maybe he'd guessed the reason and now felt sorry for her. Savannah didn't know which. With her belly in knots and perspiration dampening her best dress, she couldn't bring herself to contemplate the matter much further, either. All that counted now was that train—currently squealing to a stop in a cloud of smoke and cinders—and the people about to disembark from it. After all, it wasn't every day that a woman waited to meet her husband-to-be. Especially for the first time ever.

The porter stepped out, setting his movable wooden steps in place and making way for the passengers. Eagerly Savannah raised herself on tiptoes to see. As usual, most of the passengers surged out in small groups, then headed for one of the nearby hotels for a hurried meal. Only a few travelers carried full baggage. Those were the ones who meant to stay.

Her fiancé would be one of them.

Holding her breath, Savannah examined each male passenger in turn. One sported enormously fashionable whiskers. Another held the hand of a shy-looking lady. A third moved with the aid of a cane, his chest thrust outward with an old soldier's pride.

Feeling suddenly uncertain, she sneaked a glance at the written description—unfortunately rain-splattered, thanks to one of her earlier vigils—that she'd carried with her for weeks. A familiar sense of disappointment struck her. He was not here.

None of these men bore the homespun features, sensible suit, and tentative smile described in the letter she held. None of them was the earnest Baltimore telegraph operator with whom she'd struck up a long-distance friendship so many months ago.

Giddy with the freedom and intimacy of the wires, she and her soon-to-be husband had shared their hopes and dreams…and, eventually, a promise to meet here in Morrow Creek. But their rendezvous date had come and gone five times now. Even a neophyte romantic like Savannah had the sense to realize something had gone wrong.

Well, she'd simply head back to her station and man the wires, Savannah decided as she squared her shoulders. It was possible her fiancé had already sent her an explanation for his tardiness. Her helper, Mose, might be receiving her fiancé's romantic, apology-filled message at the station even now.

At the notion, Savannah felt somewhat cheered. She breathed in deeply, then took a final look at the train— just in case, for she was nothing if not meticulous. When her pen pal did not miraculously alight from the car, she turned away…only to find the station clerk's sympathetic gaze pinned on her.

"Too bad," he said kindly. "Disappointed again?"

Mutely Savannah stared at him. For the first time it occurred to her how foolish she'd been. She never should have allowed her hopes to draw her into town day after day.

"I'm sorry," the clerk said. "If you're looking for someone particular on the 10:12, maybe *I* can help you, Miss...?"

Reed. Savannah Reed. He wanted to know her name, she knew, but Savannah had all the reasons in the world not to share it.

At least not until she could change it in marriage.

Thanks to her position at the isolated telegraph station— where few people had cause to visit, much less to wonder about its new operator—Savannah had kept her identity a secret in Morrow Creek...at least so far. She wanted to keep it that way.

Reed was a common enough name, she reminded herself. For now, its ordinariness would likely protect her. Especially in the absence of any other potentially damning information.

"I'm Joseph Abernathy." He gave her a smile—a speculative, curious-looking smile. "I don't think we've met. Why don't you come on over? Maybe I can help track down your tardy traveler."

"Thank you, but I—I'm in a terrible rush." *Why* had she let herself be drawn in this way? The station clerk seemed friendly, but word traveled fast in a small Western town like Morrow Creek. The more people she spoke with, the more difficult it would be to keep her secret. "I'm sorry. Please excuse me!"

Wearing her most harried expression, Savannah bustled away. She heard Joseph Abernathy calling after her, but she didn't dare stop. She wasn't ready to befriend anyone. Not yet.

Her high-buttoned shoes clopped across the platform as

she pushed her way between the few lingering travelers. Once she'd reached a safe distance from Mr. Abernathy, Savannah relaxed. She allowed the anxious look to leave her face. Methodically she let her shoulders fall in their usual position. She eased her steps to a normal pace, then permitted her breathing to slow.

Almost home free. If she were smart, she'd still hurry, despite being clear of Mr. Abernathy's inquisitive gaze. Mose was not as skilled at recognizing the various telegraph operators' signatures as she was. Her beau's distinctive manner of tapping out a message might go by unnoticed if she weren't there to hear it. Raising her skirts, Savannah headed for the street.

She almost tripped over the little girl in her path.

"Oh, pardon me!" Savannah said. "I'm so sorry."

The child gaped up. She stood alone, her blond hair in pigtails and her face wet with tears. She clutched a satchel.

"Have you seen my mama? She was right there—" she pointed with a shaky, chubby finger "—but now she's gone."

"I—no, I'm sorry." Feeling rushed, Savannah cast a hasty glance around the platform. She saw no likely looking adults nearby. Knowing it was probably unwise to call further attention to herself, she nonetheless crouched beside the girl. She offered an encouraging smile. "Perhaps you could describe her to me?"

A sniffle. "Well…" The girl sucked in a breath and attempted a description. Her halting words were interrupted by choking sobs and another mighty sniffle. "M-M-Mama is—"

"All right." Frowning in commiseration, Savannah raised her hand toward the child's face. She flipped her wrist—a move borne of long practice—then brightly withdrew a handkerchief. "Use this, then try again."

The little girl's sobs abruptly stopped. Wide-eyed, she pointed. "You pulled that out of *my ear!*"

Savannah shrugged. "I thought you could use it."

"Do it again! Do it again!"

Savannah smiled. When she'd been a girl, she'd been amazed by that trick, too. "Maybe after we find your mother. Let's—"

"Wait, there she is! And Papa, too!" the girl shouted.

She raced across the platform at full tilt, then threw her arms around a relieved-looking woman carrying a lace-edged parasol. Beside the woman, a gentleman in a fine suit smiled at his daughter. He lowered his hand to caress her pigtails.

At the gesture, Savannah nearly sighed. She wished her mail-order groom were as dashing and caring as that little girl's father. Her fiancé was on the decidedly plain side— at least if his modest descriptions of himself were to be believed—and his avowed affection for tinned beans was hardly awe-inspiring. But he was solid and good, Savannah reminded herself sternly. She didn't care what his outsides looked like, as long as his insides came outfitted with a loving heart.

And as long as he arrived soon.

It wasn't as though she were marrying for love. Not yet, at least. She could afford to skimp on a few of the luxuries.

"…and that lady helped me! She can do magic tricks!"

At the sound of the girl's voice, Savannah brightened. She smiled at the reunited family…only to be greeted by frowns.

They could see. They'd guessed the truth about her.

Savannah's alarm was immediate and unthinking. She stared down at herself, trying to figure out the problem. Was her dress too bright, too new, too showy? Was her manner too forward?

Before she could reason out the trouble, the girl's father disentangled himself from his daughter's grasp. He strode toward Savannah. For one cowardly moment, she considered running away.

But then she lifted her chin instead.

She hadn't come all the way west just to be frightened off by a good-looking man with an expensive hat and an authoritative demeanor. Even if he *did* remind her of Warren, that dastardly—

"Miss, thank you for watching over my daughter."

He pressed something in her gloved palm. Reflexively Savannah tried to give it back, but the man wouldn't allow her to. With a warmhearted smile, he closed her fingers around the object. He tipped his hat, then rejoined his happy family.

For a moment, Savannah could only watch them as they walked away from the platform together. In the warm glow of the summer sunshine, they seemed to embody everything she'd ever wanted—a family, a sense of belonging…a reason to smile that felt true.

Well, soon enough she'd have all that.

She'd have all that and more, Savannah assured herself. If only she stayed faithful to her plan, she could achieve every dream she'd ever had, right here in a sun-splashed territory where no one knew her family or her past—and no one ever would.

Determinedly she shifted her gaze. She uncurled her fingers. In the center of her palm, a silver coin winked up.

Hmm. Evidently she'd erred *too* far on the dowdy side. That was interesting. She'd tried to appear a simple

Morrow Creek woman…and had only succeeded in appearing impoverished.

Before she returned to town, she'd have to remedy that. It was fortunate her costume trunk was deep—and had survived the trip from New York City mostly unharmed, thanks to Mose's help.

Drawing up her skirts, Savannah aimed one final glance at the disappointing train, then headed in the direction of the mountainside. If she were lucky, when she arrived home a telegraph message would already be waiting for her.

A quarter mile from the Morrow Creek adjunct telegraph station, Adam dismounted. With all his senses alert, he staked his horse near a patch of fresh grass, then gave the gelding a pat on the neck. "Behave yourself. I won't be gone long."

The beast nickered. Damnation. He'd done it again.

Talking to the horses was Mariana's province. Feeling beyond foolish, Adam ducked his head, then headed out on foot with only his rucksack for company. Riding straight up to the station was a risk he couldn't take. It was possible Bedell was already there, ensconced in his new "home" with yet another woman who fancied herself fortunate in love at last.

As far as Adam was concerned, the confidence man deserved a special place in hell for taking advantage of lonely women. He deserved much worse than that for what he'd done in Kansas City.

A few minutes' hike brought Adam within sight and earshot of the station. Stealthily he circled its boundaries. He'd scouted the place days earlier with Mariana, learning the lay of the land and the locations likeliest for an ambush. Today, everything appeared unchanged. All the same, Adam felt the hairs on the back of his neck stand up. Frowning, he kept on moving.

Birds chirped, unconcerned by Adam's arrival. A squirrel stopped, stared at him, then dashed up a tree. A few yards away, the station hunkered on sloped ground, surrounded by ponderosa pines and the occasional scrub oak; the mountain loomed behind it. Gaining a foothold amid the fallen pinecones and crunchy dried needles was tricky; so was imagining a woman lonesome enough to accept an offer of marriage from a hard-nosed killer.

Not that any of them knew that's what Roy Bedell was, Adam reminded himself as he crouched to survey the shingled log cabin station and its peeled-log porch. All of Bedell's "brides" had considered Bedell a kindred spirit—at least until he cleaned out their prized belongings, absconded with their savings and broke their hearts. Adam wanted a better fate for the woman in the photograph, but Mariana was right—something was off-kilter here.

Muscles tightening, Adam withdrew his spyglass. He aimed it toward the station's twin windows. Several minutes' patient watching rewarded him with a view of Mose Hawthorne, the man who hauled firewood, repaired equipment and sometimes manned the telegraph. He arrived every day on a sporadic schedule and spent his nights in a cabin closer to the town of Morrow Creek.

Most people did. Those who came out west wanted to be near a town site, where they could find friends and necessities and convivial conversation. Adam didn't know why the station's proprietress had accepted her isolated assignment. The detective in him reasoned that she probably had something to hide. The man in him hoped she liked to be alone...the same way he did.

But that was outlandish. It didn't matter whether he felt a kinship with the woman—whether he thought he understood her. She was a mark. He'd vowed to protect her. Nothing else mattered.

A thorough check revealed that she wasn't at the station. Adam searched harder. He'd glimpsed her once, but only from a distance. Now, as odd as it sounded, he wanted more…and was denied. As though sharing Adam's disappointment, the place's big calico cat slunk into view, stared at him through baleful eyes, then vanished. A rhythmic tapping issued from inside the cabin.

Silence fell. Mose Hawthorne moved from the desk to the cast-iron stove, fiddling with something. A few minutes later, the scent of coffee filled the air. Lulled by the peaceful tableau, Adam released a breath he hadn't been aware of holding.

Everything was fine. *She* was fine. Bedell wasn't here.

Adam tucked away his spyglass. He slung his rucksack over his shoulder, then turned. At the same instant, something came at him. Something big. Something long and rough. A tree branch.

In confusion, Adam ducked too late. The branch walloped him on the side of the head. He went down with an involuntary grunt.

The damp tang of moss and dirt filled his nostrils. Again the branch came down. It whacked the ground, collapsing his fallen hat like a squash under a cleaver. Adam shoved. His palms skidded on twigs and leaves. He forced himself upright again.

The branch caught him in the side. His breath left him.

"For the last time, stay out of my business."

Bedell. Even woozy and gasping, Adam recognized that pitiless voice. It had haunted his dreams for well over a year.

Mariana. If Bedell or his brothers had gotten to her first, she wouldn't have survived. Roughly, Adam sighted Bedell.

He honed in on his bland face with its underachieving whiskers. His fist followed his gaze. With a surprised shout, Bedell fell.

Adam seized the man's coat and hauled him upward. Without his customary hat, Bedell looked young. Too young.

Disoriented by Bedell's baby-faced appearance, Adam hesitated. It didn't feel right to hit a skinny, callow youth.

"Ah." Unmistakable cunning filled Bedell's voice, erasing all impressions of innocence. He sighted something over his shoulder, then nodded at it. "You *do* have a weakness."

Reflexively Adam twisted to look at whatever Bedell had seen. He drew his firearm, then turned back to Bedell. He fired.

At the same time, another shot rang out.

The birds fled the trees. Both men fell.

Savannah nearly walked right past the curiously squashed-up flat-brimmed hat lying on the ground outside her station.

She was so intent on retrieving her repentant fiancé's telegraph message that she glanced at the hat, did not think much of it and kept on striding toward home. Her encounter with the family at the depot platform had reinforced the dreams that had driven her west, and Savannah knew she wouldn't accomplish those dreams by dawdling. Besides, her nose fairly twitched with the seductive fragrance of coffee brewing. She wanted to get home, grab a restorative cup and check the wires with Mose.

Then she glimpsed a man's fallen body. He lay with one arm out flung, his face hidden. His knees gouged the dirt as though he'd been dropped cold while crawling toward her station. He looked like one of the lifeless "prizes" that her calico mouser, Esmeralda, sometimes left on the station's front porch.

Chilled by the realization, Savannah sank to the ground beside him. Too late, she saw that the leaves nearby were speckled with blood. Now so were her hands and her dress.

This could only be one man. One man—late but determined.

"Mose!" Savannah yelled. "Come quick!"

Her husband-to-be had arrived at last and if he died before she could marry him, they were both in big trouble.

Chapter Two

⦾⟋⟋⟍⟍⦿⟋⟋⟍⟍⦾

Several hours later, Morrow Creek's sole physician, Dr. Finney, stood in Savannah's private quarters at the station.

Near him on her rope-sprung bed, the man she and Mose had carried inside now lay insensible in the summertime heat. His clothes were mucked with sweat and dirt and blood, but Savannah had instructed Mose to give him her bed anyway. The man's face was filmed with perspiration, defying her attempts to cool him.

Lowering her improvised fan, Savannah gazed in concern at the man. Naked from the waist up—a necessity for Dr. Finney's treatment—he now lay atop the bedding, silent and pale, arms akimbo.

"It's not decent to leave him exposed this way," she said.

"It's not decent for *you* to be here at all." Dr. Finney tugged uncomfortably at his necktie. Crossly he shoved medical instruments in his bag. They clinked in place beside a tattered book on animal husbandry, two tins of curative powder and a bundle of bandages. "As soon as you're able to round up some help, I'd suggest you and Mr. Hawthorne move this man to town."

"And where shall we move him to?" Savannah asked. "The Lorndorff Hotel? The saloon? Miss Adelaide's boardinghouse?"

"Your flippancy is uncalled for." The doctor frowned, still preparing to leave. "A decent woman would not even be aware of the existence of Miss Adelaide's... establishment."

"Well, I am." Given her background, Savannah had discerned the most disreputable of Morrow Creek's businesses right away. Then she'd vowed to avoid them. "As far as we know, there's no one except me who can take care of this poor man. I can't possibly move him." *Especially if he's my secret mail-order fiancé.* "Especially while he's in this dire condition. If you would please tell me how to care for him, I'll simply—"

Dr. Finney interrupted. "I realize you are not from around these parts, so I've made certain...allowances for you." His disapproving gaze swept over her homespun gown and tightly wound blond hair. He sighed. "I know you have an unconventional occupation, working out here at the station. I understand you prefer to keep to yourself, as is your right. But none of those factors excuse you from the expectations of polite society."

"No one in polite society needs to know he's here."

"Are you asking me to lie? Because I assure you, I will—"

"I'll be here." Mose stepped forward, his expression amiable. His shoulders were wide, his manner no-nonsense, his tone gentle—as gentle as it had been when he and Savannah had first met backstage at the Orpheum Theatre almost twenty years earlier. Mose nodded at the tight-lipped doctor. "I'll serve as the lady's chaperone. I'll safeguard her reputation."

Savannah guffawed, gesturing to the bed. "The man is cataleptic! I doubt he'll threaten my virtue anytime soon."

Mose shot her a warning look. "What she means to say," he assured the doctor, "is that her character is above reproach. As a good, *respectable* woman, she only wants to do her Christian duty and care for an injured traveler. Nothing more."

"Hmm." Dr. Finney frowned. "This is very irregular."

His censorious gaze swung around to her. Pinned by his severe demeanor, Savannah sobered. Mose was right. She needed to be more careful. She and her longtime friend had traveled west to start new lives—not to repeat the mistakes of their old ones.

As a good, respectable woman...

Reminded of her goals, Savannah realized that, with a few moments' unguarded frankness, she'd nearly undone almost a year's worth of careful behavior. Since coming to live near Morrow Creek, she'd striven to present herself as the woman she wanted to be...not the woman she'd been back in New York City.

She shot a glance at her wounded visitor. For his sake and her own, she needed to make Dr. Finney accept her plan. She needed to care for her husband-to-be *here*, away from prying eyes. The faster he healed, the faster they could marry.

And the longer this took, the less likely the doctor would be to relent in his stance. If there was one thing Savannah had learned to understand in her former life, it was human nature.

"I know it's unusual for me to ask this of you, Dr. Finney. I do appreciate your help with everything. You've been positively invaluable this afternoon." Beaming, Savannah took the doctor's arm. "I'm afraid the shock of this event simply has me a little undone. I'm just not myself at the moment. I am sorry for any misunderstanding I've caused."

At her apology, the doctor brightened. "There there." Paternally he patted her hand, nestling it near his elbow. "You've been very brave through everything. I've known more than a few battlefield nurses in my time, and not one of them would—"

"Oh!" Giving a theatrical groan, Savannah swayed. "I'm sorry. I seem to be getting a bit woozy." Weakly she grappled for the bedpost. She missed. From the corner of her eye, she glimpsed Mose, his arms crossed, shaking his head. Ignoring him, she turned to Dr. Finney. "My! It's a good thing you had such a firm hold on me, Doctor. I might have fallen just now!"

"Well then. You'd better sit down." Dr. Finney helped her to a chair—obligingly kicked into place by an on-cue Mose. The doctor gave her an assessing look. "You appear quite pale."

"I feel quite pale." Savannah fanned her face. Making every effort to suppress her natural vigor, she swanned into the chair. "Yes, that's much better. Thank you so much, Doctor."

"You're welcome. I had no idea you were this delicate."

He sounded thrilled by her fragility...exactly as she'd hoped he would. Savannah hated to playact this way, but she was in a right pickle. Beggars couldn't be choosers. She had to manage with the skills she possessed...such as they were.

"Well..." Feebly Savannah fluttered her fingers. "I guess I am. And to have my moral fiber questioned in such terms… I suppose it simply took the last of my strength to withstand it."

"Oh I *do* apologize." Dr. Finney took her limp hand in his. "Truly, I didn't mean to impugn your honor. I think it would be fine for you to care for this wounded gentleman— with Mr. Hawthorne's supervision and my expert oversight, of course."

"Of course! I couldn't *possibly* manage alone."

Behind the doctor, Mose stifled a guffaw. Perhaps she was overplaying her role, Savannah realized. But it was working.

"Shall I stay a bit longer, until you're feeling restored?" Dr. Finney consulted his small, leather-bound journal. "Mrs. Marshall is expecting the arrival of a new baby today, but I—"

"Oh, no! I'll be fine. Please go help Mrs. Marshall."

The doctor peered at her. "Are you absolutely certain?"

"She's certain," Mose said. Loudly and indisputably.

It took a few more moments' performance, but eventually Dr. Finney agreed. Leaving her with medical instructions, a tincture for neuralgia and a fatherly admonishment not to "strain" herself, the doctor took himself back to Morrow Creek.

The moment the door shut, Mose turned to her, laughing. "Bravo. Your best performance yet. And the most shameless."

"The most expedient, you mean." Not the least discomfited by her own audacity, Savannah bustled to her patient's bedside. "Nothing convinces a man of a woman's fine character more than her apparent weakness. Why men expect a woman to be capable of hauling firewood, handling thirty-pound cast-iron pots, carrying babies, and hoeing knee-high weeds—all while appearing frail and helpless—is beyond me. Honestly. You're all contrarians."

"Maybe." Her longtime friend gave her a searching look—one that had nothing to do with her theories on femininity. "But at least we men take life straight out, the way it comes to us. We don't uproot ourselves, learn a new trade, finagle a wedding—"

"Stop it. We've already discussed this." Savannah knew what Mose was suggesting—that she was being foolish to force her new life into fruition. Although Mose had been loyal enough to come out west with her, he'd always been skeptical about her plan.

On the other hand, Mose hadn't been the one whose sordid personal story had been splashed across every tabloid newspaper in the States and beyond. Mose hadn't been the one who'd turned to Warren Scarne for help and comfort… only to wind up unemployed and heartbroken. Savannah had been. She'd vowed to never land herself in such a pitiable position ever again.

"Admit it. You enjoyed your show for Dr. Finney just now." Mose followed her, his expression concerned. "You haven't seemed so chirpy in months. Are you *sure* you're ready to leave your old life behind you? The stage, the lights, the applause—"

"Shh!" Worried that her patient might overhear their conversation, Savannah aimed a cautious glance at the man. Then she turned to Mose. "Of course I'm ready," she assured him. She picked up a cloth from the basin, wrung it out, then dabbed it across her patient's forehead, being careful to avoid his new bandages. She nodded at him. "*He's* the proof of it, isn't he?"

"*He* was shot in the back and left for dead."

Well, that *was* a troubling detail. Shootings weren't common in Morrow Creek. It had been all they could do to prevent Dr. Finney from calling for Sheriff Caffey and rounding up a posse. Mose—knowing that the last thing Savannah wanted was a lawman hanging about—had claimed he'd accidentally wounded the man when he'd spotted him in the trees…and that had been that. For now.

All Savannah could do now was hope that the danger was past—for all of them—and carry on with her plans as they were.

"Shot in the back," Mose reiterated. "And left for dead."

"I heard you the first time." Considering that problem, Savannah gently cleansed the man's sturdy chest and shoulders. She dipped her cloth in the basin again, turning the water pink with blood. She set back to work, washing near the bandages that crisscrossed the man's midsection. Dr. Finney had stitched up her tardy fiancé, but he still bore a gunshot wound, a couple of broken ribs, several nascent bruises and a lump on his head.

"He's a city man—a telegraph operator from Baltimore," she reminded Mose. "A pair of thieves probably followed him from the train station and robbed him. Likely he didn't know better—"

"He never arrived at the station, remember?"

"He might have taken another train. An earlier train." Disconcerted, Savannah eyed her patient. She *so* longed for him to be the answer to her dreams—the key to her future. She didn't want to admit the possibility that she might be wrong about him. "He might have arrived sometime when I wasn't at the depot."

"You've been at the depot every day. And he's armored up like a common ruffian, too." In demonstration, Mose pointed to the bedside table. On it lay the fearsome pistol they'd found on one side of the man's belt. And the gun they'd salvaged from the other side of his belt. And the knife they'd slipped from his boot. "What do you make of that miniature armory of his?"

"Like I said, he was a simple city man. He was probably worried about coming out west and armed himself for protection. You know how the penny papers like to exaggerate the dangers of life outside the States. It's a wonder anyone emigrates at all."

"Humph." Mose crossed his arms. "He looks like he could handle himself, even without all that firepower."

Speculatively Savannah bit her lip. Her fiancé *did* appear more robust than she'd expected. Even in his current condition, his torso and arms were corded over with muscle. His trouser-covered legs appeared powerful, too, right down to his big bare toes peeping out from his pants hems. Both his hands bore the scars of rough living, but they also looked elegant. She could easily imagine his fingers working the sensitive telegraphy equipment that had brought them together over the wires.

"Well, you can't reckon much by appearances. He probably has a very gentle heart, just like he told me in his letters." Savannah ignored Mose's skeptical snort. "And I'm the last person who would judge someone by what they look like—or—by what they might have done in the past. He and I are here to make a new beginning for ourselves. Together. And that's that."

"So if he's an armed and dangerous outlaw on the run, you're fine with marrying him? You're hunky-dory with that?"

At Mose's incredulous tone, Savannah smiled. She gave her friend a pat. "Of course I'm not. I *have* thought about this."

"Good." Mose appeared relieved. "I thought you had, but—"

"If he were an outlaw, he'd hardly have a respectable

name to lend me, now would he?" With all reasonableness, Savannah skipped straight to the heart of the matter. She didn't have to pussyfoot around with Mose. "You know I can't go on much longer with my own name. What happened back in Missouri proved that."

She'd first attempted to start over in Ledgerville. It hadn't worked out, to say the least. But the lessons she'd learned in Missouri had made Savannah much savvier about her next attempt to forge a new life. She longed to live in town, in homey Morrow Creek just down the mountainside, but she didn't dare approach the people there until everything was arranged just so. Until she was properly wed and respectably behaved.

Biting her lip, Savannah glanced at the *Guide to Correct Etiquette and Proper Behavior* handbook beside her telegraph. She'd studied it until the pages were nearly worn through. Now she could only hope her improvised education proved sufficient.

"Besides," she said, "all I want is a home. A *real* home. Is that so awful? For a woman to want to build a cozy home life?"

"No, but… I still don't like this." Mose shook his head, his forehead creased with concern. "We should have gone on to San Francisco. We should have found places with a theater company. We should have started over with something we know."

"You know why I don't want to do that, Mose."

He fell silent. Then said, "I know, but there are other ways—"

"You're free to go if you want to." Gently Savannah squeezed his arm. "I wouldn't like it, but I would understand."

"No." Her friend's frown deepened. "Not while *he's* here."

"I already told you, you don't have to protect me." At Mose's dubious look, she smiled. "It's all well and good that you told Dr. Finney you'd stay here, and I do appreciate your help. But I'm fully prepared to handle this myself."

To prove it, Savannah put away her cloth. Then, with careful but businesslike gestures, she set to work making her patient feel more comfortable. She pulled out the heavy quilted flannel she'd put on to protect the mattress, then straightened the bedding. As she did, she couldn't help studying her fiancé.

Not only was he bigger and stronger than she'd expected, but he was also much better looking. His face, topped by a tousled pile of dark hair, was downright handsome. He didn't show much evidence of eating too many tinned beans, either. Maybe he'd wanted to seem humble in his letters? He'd been too poor, he'd said, to afford to send a photograph, the way she had.

Savannah hadn't minded parting with one of her stage photographs—one of the final mementos of her previous life.

"He looks awfully uncomfortable." Decisively she caught hold of his leg. Using his trousers as a makeshift handle, she moved his leg sideways a few inches. She reached for the other leg, just above his ankle, then moved it, too. "That's better."

Something clattered to the floor.

"If you're intending on manhandling him like that," Mose complained, "I'd better make sure to stay here to supervise."

"Pish posh. I'm nursing him." Savannah bent to pick up the item that had fallen. Her fingers scraped the station's polished floorboards. An instant later, she straightened with a long, wicked blade in her grasp. Wide-eyed, she glanced from the knife to Mose. "And I'm *definitely* finding out more about him, too."

"I think that would be wise," Mose told her.

A search of the man's trousers and their…environs proved unproductive, much to Savannah's disappointment. She suspected that failure owed itself to Mose's lackadaisical search efforts.

"Honestly, Mose. Search harder! He might have a concealed pocket somewhere on him. Who knows what you're missing?"

"He's not a magician," Mose grumbled. Making a face, he looked up from their still-inert patient, his hands hovering in place. "I'm unlikely to pull a rabbit from his britches."

"Well, that's probably true," she agreed with reluctance. Growing up in a family of itinerant performers may have skewed her perceptions of things. Frustrated, Savannah sighed.

Finding that second hidden knife had spooked her, but good. She wanted answers about this man, and she wanted them now.

Impatiently she grabbed her supposed fiancé's shirt from the ladder-back chair Dr. Finney had flung it to. The garment possessed no pockets, secret or otherwise. Next she snatched up his suit coat, wrought of ordinary lightweight wool.

"Eureka." She felt something clump beneath her searching fingers. Trembling, she pulled out a bundle of letters. *Her letters.* She recognized the handwriting, the postmark… the sappy sentiments she'd imprudently confessed to her fiancé.

Peering over her shoulder, Mose read aloud. "'My Dearest, Kindest, Most Longed-For Mr.—'"

Flushed, Savannah folded the single letter she'd perused.

"Why, Savannah. That's very…impassioned of you."

"Hush. I'm a romantic at heart, that's all."

"So." Mose arched his brow. "Did you mean any of it?"

Hurt by his question, she gazed up at him. Her fingers tightened on the letters. She brought them to her heart, then raised the bundle to her nose. The papers and ink now smelled of fresh air and leather and damp wool. They smelled of *him*.

"I refuse to pretend for my whole life," Savannah said. "That's why we're here. To have a life that's *real*."

"And yet you're starting it with a lie."

"Finding myself a mail-order groom isn't a lie. We're both here willingly. We're both lonely, and we don't want to be."

Mose made a gruff, tentative gesture. "You're… lonely?"

His tone of sadness wrenched her. Savannah wanted to save him from it…but she couldn't. She couldn't lie about this. She swallowed past a lump in her throat. Wordlessly she nodded.

"But if all goes well, I won't be lonely for much longer. And neither will he." In dawning wonder, she and Mose stared at the man in the bed. "It's him, Mose!" She breathed in. "It's really him. My new life is finally beginning."

Chapter Three

Adam dreamed of baby-faced killers and swinging tree branches and a dark swirling pain that centered on his skull. Hot and restless, he thrashed on the fallen pine needles.

"Shh," a woman said. "It's all right. You're safe now."

But he wasn't. "Mariana!" he tried to say. "Mariana!"

His voice emerged in a croak, hurting his throat. The forest moved around him, dark and light, always changing. He needed to find his partner. He needed to find out what Bedell and his brothers had done to her. Soon it would be too late.

Something touched his head. At the contact, Adam flinched. A shameful groan burst from his chest, making the pain worse.

"Just raise your head a little," the woman urged. "Please."

Wetness touched his lips. It tasted bitter. Adam screwed up his face. If Bedell wanted to poison him, he'd have to do it without his cooperation. Swearing, he smacked away the liquid.

Something clattered to the ground. It rolled and smashed.

"He's still fitful," the woman said. "All night he's been—"

He didn't catch whatever else she said. Her voice, low and cautious, wavered in and out of his hearing. Several of her words made no sense. Adam thought he heard his gelding nearby. The horse shook its traces with equine impatience— or maybe with prescient concern. Once he'd been rifle-shot in an ambush, and his horse had carried his limp body all the way to Mariana.

Mariana. He had to rescue her. He was running out of time.

He tried to call her name again. All that emerged was another groan. Soft hands touched his face, then moved lower.

The hands patted his chest. With effort, Adam opened his eyes. The world wavered, showing him a lopsided view of a blond-haired woman. He knew her. But he didn't. He couldn't remember.

Weakly he grabbed her wrist. "Mariana?" he mumbled.

"Yes, it's me. Savannah." She slipped from his hold, then set aside his hand with a soothing pat. "Just rest now."

Adam frowned. She was treating him like a child. Annoyed and still hurting, he clenched his fingers. They encountered soft quilted fabric, a cushy mattress... Where the hell was he?

"You gave me quite a scare," she said. "But you made it here, and you're going to be fine. That's all that matters."

Savannah. *Savannah...* Drowsily Adam pondered the name.

His eyes drifted shut. Damnation. He forced them open.

Savannah's concerned face swam above him. She smiled

as she tucked a blanket snugly around him. "I'm so happy you're here."

He couldn't be happy. There was something wrong with Mariana. Something awful… But he couldn't remember what.

A heartbeat later, Adam crashed into the blackness again.

The next time Adam awakened, he opened his eyes on a cozy, dimly lit room. Frowning with concentration, he took stock of his surroundings. They were small and modest, framed by split-log walls and crammed with furnishings. A medicinal tang hung in the air, along with a flowery fragrance he couldn't place.

Beneath him was an unfamiliar bed. Nearby, an old bureau hunkered with a lighted oil lamp atop it. To his left sat an empty ladder-back chair. Rhythmic tapping came from the next room. Adam recognized the sound as a telegraph machine in use.

He was inside the telegraph station. Hazily he remembered confronting Bedell. He remembered going down, remembered hitting the man, remembered his last words: *You do have a weakness.*

They made less sense to him now than they had then, but Adam didn't have time to consider the matter further. He had to get to Mariana. He threw off the coverlet, then wrenched upward.

The motion sent searing pain through him. Gasping with it, he clutched his middle. Gingerly he spread his fingers apart.

Two bandages met his unsteady gaze. He blinked at them, then sucked in another breath. Next, he twisted to touch his back. More bandages had been wrapped near his shoulder blade. Tentatively he patted them. He was hurt. That didn't mean he could stop moving. He had to find Mariana and save her.

Another agonizing movement brought him to his feet. Adam teetered, clenching his jaw. Pain throbbed through his head, making him dizzy. His ribs hurt; so did his shoulder. His legs threatened to buckle beneath him. He grabbed the chair. A few more raspy, painful breaths fortified him enough to go on.

The tapping of the telegraphy equipment ceased. He sent a cautious glance toward the other end of the station, straining to hear. All he sensed was the occasional rustle of papers. A distant chair scraped across the floor; a shadow moved across the wall. He wasn't alone here. Propelled into motion by the realization, Adam sighted the latched door. He surged toward it.

An involuntary moan escaped him. Tightening his jaw, he made himself keep moving. His fingers scrabbled clumsily on the latch. Frustrated, he tried again. The door finally swung free, revealing the darkened woods surrounding the telegraph station.

Adam staggered outside, leaving his shirt and suit coat behind him. Warm nighttime air swirled over his exposed skin. Sweating and breathing heavily, he lurched across the station's yard, looking for his horse. He hardly felt the stones and grass beneath his bare feet. All that mattered was finding Mariana.

"Whoa there, stranger!" someone called. "Hold up."

At the sound of that deep male voice, Adam whipped his hand to his belt. His *empty* belt. His usual firepower wasn't there.

Hell. In his muzzy-headed haste to leave, he'd forgotten to arm himself, he realized. Too late. Instinctively Adam flexed his knee, but his backup knife was gone, too. He was forced to stand on weakened legs, defenseless and light-headed, as a big, dark-skinned man tromped toward him with a handheld lantern.

"Let me help you." The man put his free arm around Adam's shoulders. He looked older than he'd first appeared, but genial—and clearly determined. "I guess you're looking for the privy."

Warily Adam nodded. Deprived of his weapons, there wasn't much else he could do. Besides, he recognized Mose Hawthorne. He doubted the station's part-time helper posed a threat to him.

Together they crossed the yard, moving slowly toward the outhouse. Adam scanned the tree line as they went. If Bedell or his brothers were still out there, he needed to be aware of it.

He cleared his throat. "I'm looking for a woman. She ought to be around here someplace. Have you seen her? She's—"

"Right in there, friend." Mose nodded toward the station, interrupting before Adam could describe Mariana. He opened the outhouse door. "Savannah's been waiting on you awhile now. You have no idea what kind of hopes that woman's got pinned on you."

Having read her letters to Bedell, Adam had a fairly thorough notion of what the confidence man's mark might expect of her new beau. But that wasn't what concerned him now.

"I meant another woman. Dark hair, about this high—" Adam held his hand to chest height "—foul mouth, dirty skirts most likely, probably packing a pistol or two? She might be hurt."

"That don't sound like any woman I ever heard of." Mose frowned. "You hurt your head, though. I'm guessing you're still a little confused." He gestured. "You need help in there?"

Adam gave the outhouse a dismissive glance. "No. If you haven't seen her, then I'll have to go looking." He wavered on his unsteady legs. Mose held him up. "Did you find my horse?"

"Your horse?" This time, the station's helper cast him an even more fretful look. "You didn't have a horse. I found your rucksack over there in the bushes, but that's all. If you had yourself a horse back in Baltimore, it'll be no help to you here in the Territory. Although Savannah will be relieved to know you had that much scratch. Between you and me, I think she thought you were near destitute. She's just softhearted enough not to care." Mose nodded at the outhouse. "Go on and do your business now. I'll wait here and help you back inside when you're done."

At the man's expectant look, Adam swore. He was too dazed to follow everything Mose had said, especially all that prattle about Baltimore and Savannah Reed's softheartedness. He didn't like knowing that Bedell's mark was even more gullible than he'd thought...and so, by all accounts, was her only helper and friend. But further talking was a delay Adam couldn't afford.

His work for the agency was important; Mariana's safety was paramount. His partner mattered more to him than any mission.

He eyed Mose, wondering how to dodge the big man. If the station's helper couldn't give him answers about Mariana, he'd have to leave him behind. An upright man like Mose would expect a reason for his leaving—especially while injured. But Adam didn't have time to explain. He couldn't tell the station's helper why he'd been trailing Bedell—or why he'd been lingering outside the station. That would only lead to more questions—questions he didn't have answers for yet. He couldn't tell Mose or Savannah the truth. Not if he wanted to nab Bedell.

He did. He wanted to nab Bedell like he wanted to breathe. That meant Adam couldn't let Mose delay him any longer. He didn't know how much time had passed. Mariana needed him.

Trying to reason out what to do, Adam hesitated. His mind still felt foggy. His head throbbed. His ribs ached. His back burned with a ragged pain that experience told him was a fresh gunshot wound. Even now, a telltale wetness trickled down his shoulder blade, warning him he was bleeding.

A short ways away, the station's door banged open. Savannah Reed ran into the moonlight, a slight figure in a fancy dress.

"Mose! He's gone!" she yelled. "He's not in bed anymore."

Providentially Savannah's arrival made the decision for Adam. The station's helper turned to look at her. Seizing his best and only opportunity to get a jump on the man, Adam shoved the outhouse door at Mose. Then he took off at a hobbling run.

Dizzily he surveyed the dark hillside, trying to get his bearings. If he remembered correctly, he'd pegged his horse a half mile away. Doubtless his gelding was still waiting there for him, unnoticed by Mose in the aftermath of the shooting.

"Mose!" Savannah cried out behind him. "Look! Stop him!"

Adam heard a grunt. He glanced back. Mose stood beside the outhouse, shaking his head as though to clear it. Savannah reached him, then pointed at Adam. "Hurry up! He's injured!"

With grim resolve, Adam forced himself into the cover

of the pine boughs and scrub oak. A few seconds later, the sounds of the station helper's pursuit faded. So did Savannah's voice.

He missed it, Adam realized. Stupidly and sappily, he missed Savannah Reed's voice and her gentle touch, too. He'd scarcely gotten to know either, and yet he wanted both. Dragging in another painful breath, he put the realization behind him, then went to track down his partner—whatever it took to do it.

Struggling through the underbrush in her high-button shoes and bustle-laden calico dress, Savannah burst into a clearing at last. Mose crouched a few feet away, his back to her. He'd gotten ahead of her as they'd chased their runaway patient, but now she'd finally caught up. Breathing heavily, she stopped.

Then she realized that Mose was hunkered down in front of a fallen-down, bare-chested, dark-haired man. His prone body was just recognizable in the lantern light. *They'd found him.*

With a cry, she rushed forward. "Is he all right?"

"I guess so. Looks like he plumb keeled over." Mose glanced up at her, his face unusually pensive. In the darkened forest all around them, small creatures skittered at the edge of the circle. "He's breathing. But he's bleeding again, pretty hard."

Concerned, Savannah dropped to her knees atop the fallen pine needles. She reached out to touch her mail-order groom's heaving chest. "I'll bet he's fevered." She gazed at his face. Even in sleep, his features appeared hard edged. "For a man who looks so formidable, he sure does behave foolishly. His head injury must be worse than Dr. Finney thought." Worriedly she glanced at Mose. "Whatever would make him run like that, Mose?"

Her friend stared at the man, at first appearing not to have heard. Lost in thought, Mose frowned. Just when Savannah was on the verge of repeating her question, Mose shrugged.

"I reckon some men get antsy at the prospect of marriage."

She gave him a chastening look. "That's not funny. He *wants* to marry me, remember? He came out west specifically for me."

"Are you sure you still want him? He's a peculiar one."

"You're only saying that because he got the better of you with that outhouse door. That *must* have been an accident."

"This goose egg on my head doesn't feel like an accident."

"I'll fix up a poultice for you when we get back." Savannah stood, gesturing at her fallen groom. "Come on, let's get him back to the station and safely to bed. It's been a long night."

When Mose didn't move, she glanced at him. Her long-time friend glowered at her, his arms crossed. There was definitely something he wasn't telling her. "I say we leave him," he said.

"*Leave him?* Of course we're not leaving him." Savannah trod around the man, trying to figure out if she could possibly drag him back to the station herself. She doubted it. He was as big as Mose and even more muscular. "If you're planning on carrying a grudge just because he hit you with that door—accidentally, if I might remind you—then you'd better just stop it. He's injured! He's confused and fevered and not himself. And he's a city man, too—a telegraph clerk. I doubt he's clever enough to get the jump on a hard-as-nails, worldly stagehand like yourself. You've been around all the most dangerous people and survived."

Of course, so had she. But that was all behind her now. And if she was overstating Mose's toughness in order to spare his feelings... Well, at least it was for kindness's sake.

"I reckon..." Mose pursed his mouth. "That's likely true."

"See? Have pity on the poor man. He's liable to be in way over his head with Western life. Now he's got a passel of healing to do, to boot. We'll have to be very patient with him."

"I guess." Grudgingly but carefully, Mose lifted the man.

As her friend slung her wounded groom over his shoulder, a pitiful groan came from their patient. Heartsick at the pain-filled sound, Savannah rushed to his side. She stroked his hand.

As though he sensed her touch, his eyelids fluttered. But he didn't awaken. That worried Savannah all the more.

"*Please* let us help you," she whispered to him as they moved toward the station. "Please. And don't you run away again, either. You are my best chance at starting over—that means I'm counting on you. You can't let me down. You just *can't*. Not now." She inhaled deeply, then ladled as much fierceness as she could into her tone. "Not when I'm so close. You hear?"

He moaned but didn't speak. Savannah didn't say any more. All during the jostling trek back to the station, she watched her mail-order groom...and she thought about him, too. She might be eager, but she wasn't naive. The undeniable truth was, her injured groom's flight into the woods—like his guns and his knives—had unsettled her. Something didn't feel right here.

She might be counting on her mail-order groom but she didn't plan on trusting him. Not yet. They had a long way to go before that happened—if it happened at all. Suddenly Savannah had as many doubts as she did questions, and she needed answers.

Chapter Four

Vivid sunshine pushed open Adam's eyes at a time he judged long past sunrise. Disoriented and aching, he tried to sit up.

Raw throbbing pain cut short his motions. Gasping, he sank back again. He was in a bed. In a room. In the tiny Morrow Creek adjunct telegraph station, far from his partner and his mission.

Mariana. Last night, he'd tried to find her. He'd trudged through the wooded hillside in the dark, bleeding and hurting. After what had felt like hours, he'd found his earlier trail.

He'd located the iron post he'd used to stake out his horse. But his progress had ended there. The rope attached to the post had been hacked off, its frayed ends still in place. His horse had been gone. Stolen, if he didn't miss his mark.

Bedell and his boys had been thorough. With no horse, no sense of where the confidence man had gone or how long ago he'd left—and with a gunshot wound and other injuries to slow him down—Adam had little hope of tracking them. At least for a while.

What's more, he still had a job to do here at the station. Bedell's mark still needed him. *Savannah Reed still needed him.* If that sharper were still loitering around, waiting to make his move on an innocent woman, Adam had to be there to stop him.

Bedell didn't yet have the windfall he'd planned to steal from Savannah, Adam reminded himself. If he waited at the station, he figured Bedell would return. Doubtless, he'd do it sooner rather than later, too. Roy Bedell and his brothers had never shown any signs of being less than greedy and impatient.

And Savannah Reed had never shown any signs of being less than trusting and gullible. *You are my best chance at starting over,* he remembered her telling him last night. *That means I'm counting on you. You can't let me down. You just can't.*

Her words had been truer than she'd known. She *was* counting on him. She had to. And he, in turn, had to protect her.

Last night, all Adam had been able to think about was helping Mariana. But in the clear light of day, with a lucid mind and the force of all his hard-won experience to guide him, he thought about Savannah, too. There were so many things she didn't know about the mail-order groom she'd been waiting for.

Roy Bedell had lied to her from the start. He was a thief and a coldhearted killer. Adam had hoped to nab the knuck before it became necessary to make such revelations to Bedell's latest target. Now that plan seemed nigh impossible. But, he wondered unhappily, how did a man begin to tell a woman that she'd made arrangements to share her life with a ruthless sharper?

Adam didn't know. He'd figure out something later. Because as things stood now, he didn't have much choice. He was hurt and weak, gunshot and dizzy. Bedell and his boys were out of reach. Mariana was missing. For now, all he could do was trust that his partner had done the right thing and stayed far away, like he'd told her to do. If he were lucky, Mariana had already ridden on to Morrow Creek to wire the agency for new instructions.

And maybe for a new partner, too.

Grudgingly Adam felt heartened by the thought. Mariana was experienced. She was strong and smart and resourceful. She might not even need him to ride to her rescue, like he'd planned.

Why, Mr. Corwin! Are you still trying to protect me?

Remembering Mariana's brash, flippant words, Adam felt his heart give a sentimental squeeze. He devoutly hoped she was safe. If she wasn't, he didn't know how he'd forgive himself.

At least here at the station, though, he might still be helpful to someone else. He might still be able to warn Savannah about Bedell—to prepare her for a possible confrontation with the confidence man she'd unwittingly lured west with all her sweetly worded letters…and that pretty picture of hers, too.

Adam had spent far too much time gazing at the picture he'd pilfered. But he couldn't regret that. Not after everything that had happened. Looking at Savannah's picture had been the best part of this mission so far, he reckoned. Not that he intended to reveal as much in his mandatory report to the agency.

Reminded of that report, Adam grew newly alert. *Where was his agency journal?* He usually kept it in his saddlebags, but…

But they were lost, he remembered, along with his horse.

His journal was gone right along with them, then. So was all the proof he'd gathered over the past year of Roy Bedell's criminal nature. The official wanted poster. The newspaper clippings. The tattered correspondence from the family of the woman Bedell had murdered in Kansas City. They'd been the ones to contact the agency. They'd been the ones who'd specially requested Adam, counting on his past as a former U.S. Marshall to bring in the confidence man when others had lost his trail.

Looking into their grieving faces, Adam had sworn to bring their daughter's killer to justice. He refused to fail them now.

Maybe he could convince Savannah to let him stay at the station awhile—to lay a trap for Bedell. With her cooperation, Adam could double his chances of catching the man, and he could protect her at the same time. It was the only way to proceed.

With that decided, Adam tried moving again. Helpless against the pain in his shoulder, head and ribs, he groaned.

Instantly Savannah Reed rushed into the room. Her rustling skirts warned him of her arrival—but nothing could have prepared him for the sight of her. In the light streaming from the room's single curtained window, she appeared downright angelic. Her face was scrubbed clean, her golden hair was wound high, and her eyes were the same shade of guileless blue as the sky outside.

"You're awake! Glory be. Now don't strain yourself."

She hurried to his side. She fluttered her hands in a moment's indecision, then placed them on his arms to help him get upright. Next, she leaned to arrange the pillows behind him. The flowery smell of her skin caught Adam unawares. So did the hasty glimpse he caught of her bosom. He cursed himself for noticing it, even dazedly. Sternly he jerked his gaze upward.

That didn't help. Her face was alight with warmth, her cheeks pink and her features filled with a caring he'd scarcely seen—much less been the recipient of. He'd been a foundling child, shunted from one distant relation to another. Growing up, Adam had convinced himself he didn't *need* to be cared for. He didn't need anything. He'd always been tough, and proud of it.

But now, upon seeing Savannah gazing at him with such evident care and concern, Adam felt plumb walloped with how much he liked being looked at that way. Especially by her.

His heart opened a fraction. Sappily he smiled.

"Oh, good. You must be feeling better." Savannah beamed. "Now hold still while I give you more of Doc Finney's tincture."

Obligingly Adam opened his mouth for a spoonful of the medicine she offered. Too late, he realized he was never this trusting. But by then he'd already swallowed the foul stuff.

"That's perfect." Savannah smoothed the quilts over him. Her hands patted innocently over his chest and legs. Her face showed no signs that she realized what effect her actions might have on a man—even an injured one. "There. Is that better?"

Bedeviled by yearning, Adam pointed at his knee. "I think you missed a spot," he said in a raspy voice. "Right there."

To his mingled pleasure and chagrin, Savannah patted his knee. Her gentle touch put all manner of unchivalrous thoughts in his head. Artlessly and agreeably, she tucked in the quilts all around him. Adam fought a powerful urge to kick them loose again, just to experience the tender way she had of touching him. He felt cosseted, cared for…downright beloved.

But that was nonsensical, he told himself with a scowl. Savannah Reed didn't love him. She didn't even know him. As soon as he revealed everything about Roy Bedell, he doubted she would look at him with the same openhearted charm and forthrightness she was displaying right now. He resented having to disappoint her, especially while she seemed so out-and-out contented.

"You're a fine nursemaid," he told her, delaying that inevitable moment. "Thank you. I'm most obliged."

"It's the least I could do. Particularly after you traveled all this way just to be with me." With sudden shyness, Savannah lowered her gaze. "I'm so sorry about what… happened to you. I promise, we don't usually find such ruffians around these parts. You'll be absolutely safe here with me. I'll make sure of it."

It was preposterous—but kind—of her to suggest she could protect him. Adam didn't understand why she thought he'd come to the Territory to be with her, though. Unless she'd found his saddlebags and his journals? Unless she knew about his work for the agency? He glanced sideways. All he saw was his rucksack, full of essentials like his shaving razor and soap and extra clothes.

After you traveled all this way just to be with me.

A few seconds too late, the truth struck him. Savannah Reed, Adam realized, thought *he* was her mail-order groom!

He should have guessed as much. After all, *he* had arrived at the station just when she'd been expecting Bedell. *He* had possessed her letters and her picture amongst his things. *He* had told Mose he was looking for a woman last night.

Although Mose hadn't realized he'd been asking about Mariana, the station's helper had undoubtedly told Savannah about their conversation.

You have no idea what kind of hopes that woman's got pinned on you, Mose had said. Regrettably Adam did. Before too much longer, those hopes and dreams of hers were going to be crushed.

"Oh dear! I'm forgetting myself, aren't I?" Blushing prettily, Savannah interrupted his musings. She straightened into a formal posture, then…curtsied? Holding herself stiffly in that pose, she inclined her head. "This is a very great pleasure for me. I'm indelibly charmed to meet you, Mr. Corwin."

She sounded as though she were arriving at a highfalutin ball—one presided over by kings and queens. Her stilted manner was so at odds with her casual way of touching him that Adam almost laughed. Instead he gazed at Savannah's downcast lashes, proud nose and full lips…and something inside him gave way.

If she wanted to appear sophisticated and proper to him, he would not prevent her from it. Except in this one instance.

"Please," he said gruffly. "Call me Adam."

"Informal address already? After only one meeting? I sincerely doubt that would be—" She broke off. She gave him a tentative peek, then closed her mouth. Her chest expanded on a giddy breath. She gazed downward again. "Very well…Adam."

The breathy way she said his name made tingles race up his spine. Against all reason, he wanted to hear it again.

"Adam," she said experimentally, not knowing how handily she obliged him. Along with her tone, Savannah's posture eased. Relaxed now, she nodded. "Yes, I think *Adam* will be fine."

But all at once, *Adam* wasn't fine. Frowning with an unwanted sense of revelation, he remembered the other odious strategy Bedell had used when setting up his latest mark. When corresponding with Savannah, Bedell had used Adam's name.

It was an audacious tactic—and a taunting one, too. After all the months Adam had spent tracking Bedell, the confidence man had gotten cocky. He'd deliberately used Adam's name in his newest double-cross scheme, and that detail had truly rankled.

It had bothered him so much, Adam guessed, that he'd shoved it clean out of his mind. Mariana had given him no end of grief about Bedell's ploy, though. Every time she'd copied down one of Savannah's letters, she'd teased Adam about "his" woman, reading aloud Savannah's usual greeting in mocking, overgirlish tones.

My Dearest, Kindest, Most Longed-For Mr. Corwin....

Foolishly Adam had set aside that detail. Bedell's theft of his good name had galled him, but since he'd never expected to meet Savannah in person, he hadn't counted on its potential consequences. Now those consequences batted their eyelashes at him, creating an unexpected thrill in the pit of his belly.

Damnation. This was troublesome. His initial fascination with Savannah, kindled by her letters and her picture, was fast becoming something more. Adam didn't understand it. In all his days, he'd met saloon girls, pert prairie homesteaders, dance-hall ladies, society belles, soiled doves and down-home women who could make a man propose with a single, cinnamony forkful of their prizewinning apple pies. None of those women, however appealing, had ignited his curiosity the way Savannah Reed did.

He already knew a handful of her hopes and dreams. Now he wanted to know *her*. He wanted to call her Savannah;

wanted to have a right to do so. He wanted to make her smile at him again.

Telling her about Bedell wouldn't accomplish any of those things. But now that Adam had met Savannah, the thought of Bedell hurting her—stealing from her—troubled him all the more. He couldn't let that happen. But suddenly, he felt too woozy to reason out how he could stop Bedell from getting to her.

Doubtless that was because of the tincture she'd given him. Cursing the medicine's sedating effects, Adam nonetheless knew he needed it. His shoulder blade throbbed, his ribs ached and his head... Wincing at a fresh wave of pain, he raised his hand.

"Oh!" Savannah grew instantly alert. "Does it still hurt?"

Hazily Adam noted that her formality had dropped away. Apparently she wore her fancy comportment the way Bedell did his various—and fraudulent—accents and mannerisms...and names. Savannah's curtsies and timidity and cordiality seemed to sit outside her, somehow. They weren't nearly as much a part of her as were her golden hair and capable hands and intelligent gaze.

"It doesn't hurt so much that I've forgotten all my manners altogether," Adam gritted out. With strict determination, he lowered his hand. He smiled, the better to ease Savannah's worries about his condition. "It's *my* honor to finally meet you, Miss Reed. Until now, I'd only dreamed about this day coming."

That much was true. Fruitlessly but unstoppably, Adam had whiled away the long hours on Bedell's dusty trail by fancying *himself* as the one who'd come west to be with Savannah. He'd have sooner curried his horse with his teeth than admit it.

"And *I'm* the one who should protect *you*." Fighting

against the drowsy effects of the tincture, Adam fisted his hand in the soft bed linens. Roughly he said, "I *will* protect you, Miss Reed. I promise you right now—I swear I'll keep you safe."

He gazed straight at her, willing her to understand exactly how much he meant it. In that moment, he would have let Bedell bash him in the head with a branch twice over, just to save her.

"Oh, that *is* sweet of you, Adam. Thank you ever so much."

Clearly Savannah didn't know what he was talking about, but she smiled at him all the same. That was good. She did not, he noticed dispiritedly, suggest that he call her Savannah. That was bad. Her omission made him yearn for that privilege with an intensity Adam would have found laughable a day ago.

"But don't be silly! You don't have to protect me." Savannah curled her fingers trustingly around his. She laughed. "It seems everyone always wants to protect me! First Mose, now you. But all *you* have to do is marry me, just as we agreed."

Marry me. At those words, Adam stilled. He had to tell her about Bedell. Right now. But all at once, he felt even wearier than he had just a moment before. He cursed the medicine he'd taken. His tongue felt thick. His eyelids felt heavy. His head drooped. Dumbly he repeated her words. "Marry me?"

"Yes. I'll have some questions for you first, of course." As though she were considering quizzing him then and there, Savannah gazed directly at his face. She seemed to lose herself in his medicine-hazed eyes. Then she shook herself. "We'll get to that when you're feeling better, I reckon. And naturally we'll want to spend some more time together first, to ensure a successful partnership. You do know how I feel about compatibility, don't you?"

Adam did. He'd read her views at length in her letters to Bedell. Prompted by an absurd and inescapable desire to please her, he said, "You believe husbands and wives should be as close-knit as friends are, able to talk and laugh equally."

His reward was a beatific smile. In response, his heart skipped a beat. All his life, Adam had felt gruff, tough, ready to take on bad men of every variety and bring them to heel. But now, suddenly, all he wanted was another of Savannah's smiles.

"Why, Mr. Corwin! You *did* pay attention to my letters."

"I treasured every last one of them." Even though those words were accurate, Adam felt a fraud saying them. Further wearied by his recitation from those letters, he thumped his chest. "I carried them next to my heart the whole way here."

"Hmm. You're getting a bit tired now, aren't you?"

"Tired?" He realized he'd closed his eyes. He wrenched them open to see Savannah's amused expression. "No. Not tired. I'm never tired. I can ride for days, track a man for miles, shoot from the saddle and never miss. *You can count on me, Miss Reed.*"

His assurance sailed right on past her. She laughed and patted his hand. "I think someone's been reading too many dime novels on the train. Don't fret, though. When it comes to our marriage arrangement, I know exactly what I'm getting."

"No, you don't." Urgently, Adam caught her wrist. *Bedell might be near,* he remembered. He should warn Savannah. "Your groom is not who you thought he was! He's… he's…"

He blinked, trying to summon the appropriate words. His tongue roved around his mouth in search of them. While he struggled, Savannah slipped from his feeble grasp. She fussed over him, fixing his bandages and checking for fever.

At last, Adam found the words he wanted.

"Your groom," he announced gravely, "is a bad man."

She gazed at him. "Well. He's certainly not able to hold his medicinal tinctures for neuralgia, I can say that much for certain." A new smile quirked her mouth. "Sleep now. That's the best thing for you. I'll be back later to check on you."

Drowsiness flooded him. Adam bit the inside of his cheek, deliberately rousing himself. "Wait. You don't understand—"

"I understand all I need to." In a dreamy blur of feminine fabrics and floral fragrance, Savannah made him lie back. She stroked his arm and tucked in the quilts again, her face open and kindly. "I'd wondered how you would take to me, when we met, too. After all, we shared a great deal with each other over the wires, didn't we?"

"No. You have to listen to me now," Adam insisted, trying again to broach the topic of Roy Bedell and his scheme. "It's important. Your groom is not who you thought he was! He's—"

"He's everything I could have asked for." Savannah smiled. She brought her mouth next to his ear, letting her breath tickle his skin in a sinfully pleasurable way. "He's even better than I imagined. *You're* even better, Adam. I'm very, very pleased."

She liked him. At the realization, Adam groaned. Under the influence of that damnable tincture, he felt as clumsy as a youth, as green as a new field agent, as needful of sleep as an express rider on the last leg of a weeklong journey. But he couldn't help grinning as Savannah's approval washed over him.

"And since you likely won't remember this when you wake up…" Still hovering above him, Savannah touched his cheek. She rested her palm against his skin, then gazed unabashedly at him. "I guess I can be forthright. I think you're beyond handsome, too. So far, it's been all I could do not to swoon over you."

Adam turned his head on the pillow, bringing his gaze to hers. Plainly startled to find herself the subject of his attention—however bleary—Savannah blinked. Her cheeks pinkened.

"Now sleep," she blurted. "You're clearly hallucinating."

Then she bustled from the room and returned to her desk.

Chapter Five

Flustered and a bit overheated, Savannah headed blindly for her telegraphy equipment. On the way there, she almost collided with Mose. He stood inside the doorway as she passed through, a few steps from the desk they shared. He wore a knowing look.

She knew what that look was for. She'd gone in to check on Adam Corwin not only because it was her duty as his fiancée and provisional nurse, but also because she'd promised herself that she'd get to the bottom of the mysteries surrounding him. His well-laden gun belt. His habit of carrying contraband knives. His tendency to whack Mose and disappear into the woods for long stretches.

Instead she'd mooned over her mail-order groom like the most quixotic of heroines from an oft-told fairy tale. Bothered by the way she'd abandoned her stated goals upon her first up-close view of Adam Corwin's handsome blue eyes, rugged features, and sneak-up-on-you smile, Savannah released a pent-up sigh.

"Don't tell me, Mose. I already know." She held up her

hand to ward off her good friend's inevitable lecture. "I'll do better next time, I swear. I was unprepared, that's all."

That much was true. She'd been unprepared for the jolt of Adam's deep, masculine voice as he spoke to her. Unprepared for the impact of his protective nature. Unprepared for the way caring and honor and goodness had flowed from him to her in a perceptible wave, just like sunshine across a shadowy field.

Savannah had been truthful when she'd confessed that she'd wondered how her husband-to-be would react to her. Of course she'd been anxious. But if his forthright looks and bedazzled grins were anything to judge by, she needn't have worried.

Adam truly liked her. The proof was all over him.

And she liked him, too. Perhaps foolishly. There were so many things she didn't know about him. But she'd taken to Adam Corwin in an innate, gut-level way she couldn't deny. She didn't trust him—not yet—but she *did* trust her instincts about him.

Everything else she needed to know she would learn quickly, Savannah assured herself. Perhaps by tossing a burlap sack over Adam's head when they were together, so she could question him without being distracted by his wonderful brawny muscles and his manner of watching her with captivating, enthralled attention.

It was a good thing Doc Finney's tincture had made him so loopy, she decided. If Adam had been the least bit sensible—if there'd been any chance he would remember her hasty admission—she never would have found the courage to be so bold. As it was, she could scarcely believe she'd whispered the truth to him.

It's been all I could do not to swoon over you.

The remembrance should have been mortifying. Instead, for a lifelong romantic like Savannah, it was…thrilling.

She'd thought she'd settled for a practical, arranged union. Now she almost dared to hope she and Adam might find something more.

"I don't often lapse in my etiquette. Not these days, at least." Savannah edged past Mose, then sat at her telegraphy desk. The wires were silent, so she hugged herself, remembering. "But there's something about Adam! I plumb forgot about showing him how ladylike I could be. And when I remembered to put my good manners on display—well, I could tell he appreciated it."

He'd greeted her curtsy with something very much like hushed reverence. Savannah had savored that. And although she'd wobbled a bit while performing the maneuver, she felt proud of herself for having carried it off—just like her book instructed.

It was important to her that she erase all traces of her unconventional upbringing. She didn't want Adam to know that she'd grown up backstage at dozens of grimy theaters like the Orpheum. She didn't want him to discover that she'd learned to read by perusing playbills or to know that her mother and father had tossed her onstage like a living prop when she was scarcely more than an infant—and had gone right on doing so when her babyish antics had earned them bigger laughs and more pay.

With a significant—if stagey—cough, Mose interrupted her reminiscences...or maybe that was too grand a word to use for them, Savannah reasoned sadly. Most of her memories were disreputable, after all. Not that she'd had a choice in that. At least not until she'd grown to adulthood.

Even after that—even after she'd struck upon the notion of forming a new life for herself—she'd stayed mired in her old one for a time, Savannah recalled. It had taken her several hardworking years to save a nest egg large enough to allow her to escape the stage *and* prosper after she'd done so.

"I heard what he said." Mose crossed his arms, giving her one of his most fearsome looks. That same expression and pose had, over the years, driven away dozens of no-good backstage Jonnies. "He just told you he's a bad man, Savannah!"

She scoffed. "He didn't mean that the way it sounded. It's obvious he's gotten some wrongheaded notions about life out here in the Wild West—probably from those dime novels people read. He's worried that I want some sort of gun-slinging hero for a husband. I find his attempts to fit that mold quite endearing. He's doing it to impress me. Adam is clearly a—"

"That's another thing." Appearing further disgruntled, Mose frowned. "*Adam*. Do you really think it's smart to get so familiar with the man so soon? I thought you were all het up about behaving properly and so forth. That's what that etiquette book of yours is for, isn't it? So why in the devil would you—"

"He asked me to call him *Adam*. It's only polite to comply."

Mose gave her a chary look. Stubbornly he lifted his chin. "I notice you didn't tell *him* to call you *Savannah*."

"Well…" That was a privilege Savannah intended to save until she trusted Adam fully. But she didn't want to admit as much, especially to an already skeptical Mose. She shook her head. "Honestly. Were you eavesdropping on us the entire time?"

Her friend had the good grace to appear embarrassed. "This is a mighty small station. A man can't help but overhear."

"Well, try a little harder not to, would you, please?"

"Humph. Not while you're busy making eyes at that man,

I won't. I practically raised you. I won't shirk my duties now."

"I know. You never would." Overcome with fondness for him, Savannah smiled. She squeezed Mose's shoulder, remembering all the times he'd told her funny stories, found her places to sleep backstage, brought her hot meals when her parents forgot….

If not for Mose, she would have had a sorely neglectful childhood. Gruff as a bear and just as strong, he had made her feel protected and cherished. He'd had no patience for Ruby and Jim Reed's ambitions—or their shared fondness for liquor. These days, Mose was older and a little frailer than he'd been as a stagehand for hire, but he was still beyond lovable to her.

"That's why I'm going to ask you again." Mose leveled her with a serious expression. "Are you sure about this marriage scheme of yours? You're not hitched yet, you know. It's not too late to go on to San Francisco."

"I'm not going to San Francisco!"

"All right, all right. You don't have to get testy."

"I'm sorry, Mose. It's just that I'm done with performing. *Beyond* done with it. It was never right for me. I just didn't know any better. Being on stage was all I ever had."

"You were powerfully good at making a crowd happy."

At his loyal declaration, Savannah smiled. She *had* earned her share of applause over the years. "What I want now is to make a *husband* happy. That's all. I've been dreaming of having a regular, ordinary life for so long. I tried to grab hold of it in Ledgerville, but that didn't pan out. Now I have a new plan, and I'm certain it will work, as long as I'm patient."

Mose looked away, clearly longing to argue with her… but unwilling to do so. Savannah knew he was entertaining the same unhappy memories she was. They'd had this conversation before—before one enterprising gossip had tacked up that incriminating newspaper story for all to see. Before the rumors had flown around Ledgerville in a matter of days. Before the townspeople there had shunned her. Before the sheriff had confronted her.

Before her fair-weather friends had suggested she leave Ledgerville on the first train out and never come back.

Even Alistair Norwood, the young telegraphy operator who'd taught her all she knew about operating the equipment, had been unable to stick by her. Usually so willing to buck the system, Alistair had turned unexpectedly cold when faced with her past.

Until the scandal had turned up in Ledgerville, Savannah had actually believed that her family's story—and the notoriety it had engendered—would not follow her west. She'd truly thought that the newspaper coverage had been confined to the New York City tabloids. Those dirty papers had found the news of a husband-and-wife theatrical team who'd swindled the city's theater owners out of thousands of dollars in extortion money too outrageous *not* to print. Especially given the shocking detail that Ruby Reed had willingly seduced those theater owners herself in order to set them up for her husband's extortion demands. The fact that their daughter, dancing sensation Savannah Reed, hadn't been involved in their schemes hadn't mattered one whit. To everyone who read the papers' breathless daily reportage, Savannah was as good as guilty, too. She was a "Ruthless Reed," as the papers had deemed the family after her parents' arrest. That was all that seemed to matter to anyone.

That, and the fact that a glorified dance-hall girl couldn't possibly be considered marriageable by any decent man.

"I know you've put a pile of faith in your marriage plan," Mose said. "But do you honestly believe changing your name will be enough? You could have done that much without a husband."

"Only by lying. And I refuse to do that any more than necessity demands." Uncomfortably Savannah thought of the show of feminine frailty she'd carried out for Dr. Finney. If she were truly *that* delicate, she'd never have survived this long on her own. "Surely I'll be forgiven the occasional fib, given the circumstances. Besides, it's not as though I set out to find myself a mail-order groom on purpose, you know. The idea didn't even occur to me until I met Mr. Corwin over the wires. When we struck up our friendship, I felt truly blessed to have found a kindred spirit." She cast a wary glance at the other room, where Adam was sleeping. "The fact that our marriage will allow me to finally have a real home life is just an additional benefit. I promise I'll make him happy, too. He won't regret marrying me."

Already she could picture the scene—the two of them, hand in hand, leaving the church as husband and wife. The wives and mothers and women of Morrow Creek welcoming her, as a happily married woman, into their quilting circles and sewing bees. The men in town tipping their hats respectfully at her…instead of offering her that hungry, unsettling leer she'd grown used to back in the city. Dreamily gazing past her telegraphy equipment, Savannah imagined herself raising children, fussing over her husband, celebrating Christmases and birthdays as a family.

That was all she truly wanted—all she'd ever wanted. But she couldn't have any of that if she were still Savannah Reed, The Seductive Sensation of the New York theater circle. Yes, men had wanted The Seductive Sensation. But they hadn't wanted to marry her. They hadn't wanted to be seen with her in daylight.

Like Warren Scarne, they'd only wanted to use her.

"I have a lot of love to give!" she assured Mose. More

than anything, she hungered to love and be loved. Her heart fairly pounded with the necessity to *give* to someone special. "I know I can be a good wife to Adam. And he can be a good husband to me."

"Humph." Her friend frowned. "He'd better be good to you, or I'll know the reason why. That's for certain."

Smiling, Savannah patted his arm. "There you go protecting me again. I promise, Mose. I'm much stronger than I look."

Dubiously he raised his eyebrow.

"I am! I'm very strong. Since we came out west, I've gotten quite good at swinging an ax to split firewood. I've learned to haul heavy buckets of water, drive a wagon, fix the shutters—"

"Baltimore's not that far from New York. What if he finds out the truth about you—or knows the truth already?" Mose jabbed his chin toward the other end of the station, where Adam slept in peaceful unawareness. "What will you do then?"

"If Adam were going to recognize my name, he would have done so right away. He would have mentioned it in our correspondence. People hardly react with indifference to me, you know. The fact that Adam hasn't so much as hinted about the scandal means I'm safe for now, I'd say. And he's been nothing but respectful toward me. That bodes well, don't you think so?"

Her friend gave a noncommittal sound.

"Besides," Savannah went on, "by the time Adam gets well, gets settled in and finds out about what my parents did back in New York City, we'll be long married. He'll love me. He won't care a whit about what happened. I'm counting on it."

Even more skeptically, Mose raised his other eyebrow, too.

Uncomfortable under his scrutiny, Savannah shifted. "All right. If Adam finds out, it will break my heart. Is that what you're so keen to hear? That I'm afraid he'll leave me?"

At that, Mose's expression softened. "I'm not keen to hear anything of the kind. All I want is for you to be happy. You know that. Trouble is, I'm not sure this is the best way to go about it."

"It's not as though I plan to keep my past a secret forever!" Defensively she lifted her chin. "I'm going to tell Adam the whole story…someday. When I'm sure he loves me enough not to be scared off by knowing I have two thieves for parents."

Her friend gave a soft sound of commiseration. "It's not your fault what they did. It was *their* decision to take that money from those theater owners. You didn't even know about it."

"Even so… I'm still The Seductive Sensation." Savannah raised her worried gaze to Mose. "It doesn't show anymore, does it?" She turned in a circle. "I've been trying to erase it."

She'd traded all her spangled, satiny costume dresses for modest calico and wool. She'd restyled her hair and ditched her bosom-augmenting horsehair pads. She'd scrubbed her whole face clean and given away every ounce of powder and paint she'd ever owned. But on the inside, Savannah still felt imprinted by her life on the stage…and everything that had gone along with it.

"Well?" she pressed. "Does my stage background show?"

Wearing a smile, Mose shook his head. "All I see is a lovable lady. A lady who's trying her best to love someone."

"Good." Relieved, Savannah sighed. "Because that's exactly who I am these days—exactly who I'm going to be from now on."

A clatter arose at the telegraph, alerting them to a new message coming in. Knowing it would need to be relayed down the wire, Savannah hastily reached for her notepad.

This was the part that she already loved about her new life here in the Arizona Territory—using her expertise with the telegraphy equipment to transmit messages. Not many women were telegraph operators; most of those with an interest in working the equipment were men. Deciphering messages required a keen ear and intense concentration, especially in a crowded station like the one she'd shared with her mentor, Alistair.

He'd taught her how to decode the signals and transmit them with rapid movements on the equipment's keys. Ready to do just that, Savannah listened hard…but not quite hard enough to block out Mose's parting words as he headed outside.

"I'm just saying my prayers," he said, "that you done picked the right someone to love this time, that's all."

Bothered by his doleful tone, Savannah shook her head. Then she turned to her telegraphic apparatus and got down to work.

As the station door banged open, Linus Bedell jerked in surprise. Still lurking in the shadows of the building's narrow side, he flattened himself against the wall. He couldn't risk being seen here—especially not now. Alert with one hand on his gun belt, he listened as the door swung shut. Its hinges whined.

Footsteps crunched across the gravelly ground.

But they weren't coming in his direction. That meant he hadn't been spotted. Feeling immeasurably relieved, Linus sank against the rough split-log wall behind him. From the other side of that wall, the familiar sounds of the telegraph machine could be heard. But Linus didn't care about that.

All he cared about was that big colored fella—the one who was always hanging around the station, keepin' company with Roy's new "fiancée."

Releasing a pent-up breath, Linus shifted. He felt hot, tired and bored to tears with snooping on his brother's latest mark. He felt a mite sorry for the ladies his brother romanced and stole from. But, as Roy had explained, those women were just dumb. They went for his scams willingly. He never forced them. That's what made all the difference. At least that's what Roy said, and Roy usually knew best. That's why Linus stuck by him.

Well, that and the fact that they were brothers, of course. Brothers watched out for one another. Especially the Bedell brothers. If they'd had a motto, that surely would have been it.

Well, that, Linus considered, or else "shoot first, steal second, skedaddle third." Feeling clever for having thought up that witticism, he chuckled. But he sobered quickly. Roy was laid up. He'd been hurt bad in his tussle with that do-gooder detective who'd been trailing them. They'd all been forced to hole up in a Morrow Creek boardinghouse until he got better.

Because of that, Roy had appointed Linus as his second-in-command on this operation. That meant Linus had to buckle down. He knew his brother was depending on him. He couldn't let Roy down. Now, thanks to what he'd just overheard, he wouldn't.

That big man's footsteps grew fainter. That was a good sign. Shuffling sideways as silently as he could in his over-size stolen boots, Linus sneaked a glance around the corner of the station. The big man was all the way across the yard now, headed for the fenced corral and makeshift barn. Linus had already searched that whole area. He'd found no sign of the station lady's nest egg. Now he smelled like cow patties, to boot. That just went to show—it wasn't all wanted posters and high livin', being part of the Bedell gang, no matter what anybody thought.

Linus wished folks would recognize that. He and his brothers were just tryin' to get by as best they could. They didn't want to hurt nobody. But so long as chowderheaded ladies kept on fallin' for Roy's sweet-talkin' ways and signing up for his marriage schemes, those swindles were going to continue.

It was just like Roy had explained to him and the rest of his brothers: if they didn't fleece those ladies, someone else would come along and do it for them. Sure as shootin'. So why shouldn't the Bedell brothers reap the benefits themselves? Free enterprise was the American way, after all. Roy always said so.

Newly reminded of his reason for being at the station, Linus cocked his ear toward the window. He held his breath. But all he heard was the telegraph machine. That meant the woman was still busy. And with that big man of hers off at the barn, this might be Linus's best chance to get inside and look for the nest-egg money he was supposed to be getting.

Don't come back without the money, Roy had ordered in that stern, scare-the-pants-off-a-man voice of his. *That woman's sitting on a tidy sum, and I ain't leaving without it.*

Ordinarily Linus didn't like to disobey his brother's orders. The whole reason they'd done so well in their business endeavors was because of Roy's brainpower and good leadership skills. Until Roy had taken over, the Bedells had been truly down and out, with scarcely a sparerib to share between them.

Now each of them was doing right fine, with enough coin to spare for all five of the brothers. They had no need to work, 'cept for a bit of thievin' here and there—usually whenever something caught their fancy, like the horses and tents and bits and pieces they'd lifted off them soldiers a while back.

Roy had been plenty generous with his windfalls. It was because of him that the Bedell brothers had prospered and made a name for themselves—even if it was an infamous one. So Linus owed Roy plenty. His brothers did, too. But this time, Linus thought he might have to make a decision all on his own—because of what he'd overheard the lady and her man talking about.

I'm still The Seductive Sensation, she'd said.

Those words had made Linus's ears perk right up and have a listen. Because he knew all about The Seductive Sensation. He'd seen posters for her shows. In those posters, she'd looked all sparkly and pretty—just like she'd been wearing diamonds all over. She didn't look like that right now. But that didn't change anything. Linus wasn't as smart as Roy, but he knew what he'd heard. He wasn't fooled by The Seductive Sensation's new clothes and dowdy hair. Back when he'd seen those posters, Linus had wanted to go to her show (and maybe snatch some of those diamonds of hers, too) but Roy had put the kibosh on that.

He hadn't even listened when Linus had started in telling him about the special way The Seductive Sensation danced. Roy fundamentally hadn't wanted to hear it. He'd smacked Linus pretty hard to make sure he realized it. A few days later, they'd headed to Kansas City for their next marriage scam.

Things had really gone to blazes then. Roy's "fiancée" for that scheme had kicked up a big fuss, and Roy had had to put her down. But Linus had known better than to needle him about it. Roy was always in a sour mood whenever he had to kill someone. Linus guessed that showed his brother was still a good person on the inside, no matter what circumstances forced him to do.

This time, though, Linus figured they could get through this particular scheme and clear out of Morrow Creek afore things got bad again. That was what he wanted most. Leavin' behind dead bodies always made him worried. It made him worried for his eternal soul *and* for the eternal souls of his brothers…just in case the Almighty didn't understand how tough things were, now that it wasn't biblical times with milk and honey anymore.

That's why Linus had volunteered to go look at the telegraph station himself for the nest-egg money they were after. His other brothers weren't nearly so squeamish about what happened to the ladies in Roy's schemes. They'd as soon shoot up the place, tear it up to get the money, then bolt for the Mexican border. They were within a few days' ride— close enough to Mexico to get off scot-free with whatever they did.

That nearness made the other Bedell brothers antsy. And hostile. And twice as hotheaded as usual.

But Linus considered himself a sight subtler than that. He knew if he just watched awhile, he'd learn where that money was hidden—and he wouldn't have to kill nobody for it, neither.

So far, he *had* learned a few things. The lady who ran the place—The Seductive Sensation, he remembered with a thrill—was pretty, with golden hair. She liked to sing while she milked the cow. She'd named the cow Penelope. The chickens all had names, too.

The colored man who helped her kept funny hours, too unpredictable to count on. When he was around, he scared Linus something fierce. That big man might be old, but he moved with authority. Even though he was armed—and a decent shot—Linus knew better than to tangle with a man like that. Not if he could help it. That was the kind of man who formed posses and went after people. Linus didn't want to wind up getting gunned down by somebody's crotchety grandpa. That would be plumb embarrassing.

He'd also learned that Adam Corwin was alive. He'd been surprised by that. That surly, relentless damned detective was shot up something fierce, and he was bandaged up tighter than a schoolmarm's corset, too. He'd done a lot of groaning those first couple days. But he was alive and kicking. Under the station lady's tender, lovin' care, he appeared to be healin' fast, too.

Knowing those facts wouldn't exactly thrill Roy, Linus had kept them strictly to himself so far. He hadn't yet gone back to Morrow Creek to report in. He didn't want to get smacked again. Or hear Roy's mean-as-a-cuss voice. But *this* news—the news about The Seductive Sensation—well, this news just might be vital.

If Roy's mark was really The Seductive Sensation, that meant she was rich. Richer than they'd imagined! Likely she'd be worth as much as four or five other marks all put together.

And *he* could collect her gargantuan nest egg. *He* could bring it to Roy himself. *He* could be the hero, for once.

The idea had powerful appeal. Still lurking in the station building's shadows, Linus pictured himself showing up at the Morrow Creek boardinghouse with huge moneybags in both hands. The image made him smile like a cowboy in a whorehouse. His brothers would be damned impressed; that was for certain.

He'd have to make his move pretty quick though, afore the detective got all the way recovered. Linus *definitely* didn't want to cross Adam Corwin. That detective was one tough cuss. He was impossible to bribe (that was the first thing Roy had tried) and impossible to shake off (they'd learned that through three states and two territories so far). If Corwin got better afore Linus found The Seductive Sensation's bonanza nest-egg money…

Well, that eventuality didn't bear thinking about. Not if a man wanted to keep his wits about him. Using those wits of his to form a new plan now, Linus raised himself up. He peeked in the window. The lady had finished at her telegraphing machine. Now she just sat there with her chin in her hand, gazing into thin air like it was the most fascinating thing she'd ever seen.

Linus didn't know what she was thinking about. But whatever it was, it made her appear almost as sparkly and beautiful as she had in her show poster. For a minute, Linus almost sighed. He wished he had a reason to look all dreamy-eyed and happy.

Then he snapped himself to attention. Once he got all that nest-egg money, he *would* be happy. Hell, he'd be overjoyed!

That thought just about clinched it. He had to get that money. Unfortunately Linus couldn't risk sneaking in now. If The Seductive Sensation or her man saw him, they might run off for good—and take all their money with them, too. This time Linus had to be smart. He had to be cautious. He had to be sneaky.

Sidling through the shadows, he made his escape. He headed for his stolen horse—the horse that had once belonged to Adam Corwin, that cuss—his mind busy with formulating a new plan to steal that money and maybe make The Seductive Sensation dance for him while he was at it. That sounded mighty good.

Chapter Six

By the time another two days had gone by, Savannah had established a routine for herself and her husband-to-be. She arose near dawn, washed and dressed, checked the wires, took care of her chickens and lone dairy cow, then started breakfast.

Ordinarily she viewed cooking and baking as dreary necessities—partly because she was still so inexperienced at both. Growing up on the other side of the New York City theater footlights hadn't exactly given her authoritative skills with a frying pan. She relied heavily on advice from Mrs. Beeton's receipt book. She and Mose had endured some very poor meals, too. But these days, with her fiancé to care for, Savannah found new enthusiasm for the tasks of frying eggs and baking bread.

With Adam's smile as her reward for her efforts, Savannah almost couldn't wait to start cooking every morning.

Smiling now as she finished making breakfast, she set out a covered plate for Mose, the way she usually did. Her friend would be arriving soon. His hours were still erratic,

but he'd definitely spent more time at the station of late—
and not because he'd promised Dr. Finney he would serve
as her (unneeded) "chaperone," either.

The truth was, Mose still had a few doubts about Adam—
and her impending marriage to him, too. Mose's continuing
grumbles and sidelong looks made that plain. Savannah
couldn't reason out why he felt that way. Of course, she
didn't yet trust Adam herself. Not entirely. But as far as
she could discern, her mail-order groom could not have
appeared more commendable if he'd earned a medal from
President Arthur himself.

Humming a tune, she took a hasty bite of buttered toast
for herself, then put the finishing touches on a tray of food
for Adam. She arranged the plate, napkin and cutlery just
so, then added a sprig of mountain laurel to the tray. She
couldn't help smiling as she anticipated Adam's reaction to
her efforts.

He always said something nice about her cooking—and
not in that polite but obligatory way Mose sometimes did,
either…right before he fed his scraps to the station's cat,
Esmeralda. Unlike Mose, Adam seemed to truly appreciate
all the pains she went to.

It was almost as though the man had never experienced
down-home cooking, cheerful company, and a fond con-
sideration for his health and well-being, all in a snug home
that would soon be his very own. But of course that couldn't
be true.

Surely his family in Baltimore had cared for him.

Hadn't they?

Stuck on the troubling thought that perhaps they hadn't—
which would go far to explain Adam's excessive gratitude—
Savannah hesitated at the far end of the station's meager
kitchen with her tray in hand. She'd always assumed Adam
had been happy in Baltimore. But if that were true, why had

he agreed to come west? Had the notion of being with her been that much of a lure?

She liked to think she was attractive and kind, of course. But what woman was alluring enough to draw a man away from the life he knew and had made for himself?

In his letters, Adam hadn't confided much about his past. In fact, he'd been largely silent on the subject, it occurred to her. At the time, his omissions hadn't bothered Savannah. She hadn't wanted to bring up the subject and risk having him ask about *her* history. But now she wondered anew. What if Adam were hiding something—something dire? She ought to find out about it.

Feeling increasingly curious about him, Savannah hefted her tray. She shouldered open the kitchen door, then marched to the center of the station building. The place had been erected in haphazard fashion, with the office for the telegraphy equipment arising first, the sitting room and bedroom next, then the ramshackle kitchen tacked on last, after a need had developed for a full-time telegraph operator to live there.

The crowded arrangement had caused some awkward moments early on. She'd been forced to maneuver past a slumbering Adam to brew a cup of tea or put on a pot to boil in the kitchen—or simply to take herself to bed at the end of a long day. But Mose had solved that problem handily by stringing up fabric partitions between Adam's bed and Savannah's makeshift cot on the other side of the room. Now, as close as their quarters were, they had some necessary privacy—and some propriety, too.

Above all, preserving that sense of decorum mattered to Savannah. She couldn't become the woman she wanted to be without making sure her behavior was as near to perfect as it could be.

Striving for that same propriety now, she directed her

gaze away from the nearest of those partitions as she entered the room. She didn't want to seem too forward—or to catch Adam in an unguarded, potentially awkward moment. All the same, she truly savored this part of her day. Her heart picked up pace as she stepped forward, ready to deliver another breakfast to Adam.

She took a modest peek at the partition. To her surprise, Savannah saw that the fabric had already been drawn back. Beyond it, the bed was empty of everything except rumpled sheets, an indented feather pillow and a tossed-away quilt.

Had her mail-order groom run away…again?

Heart pounding, she set her breakfast tray on the bureau. Where could she go? What could she do? Mose wasn't even here yet. They shared ownership of a horse and wagon, but Mose used both to travel between his cabin and the station. On foot, she'd be unlikely to catch up with Adam before he got away. Or got lost. Or got into town and revealed their plans to be wed. She hadn't exactly stressed the need for circumspection with him. She'd feared any such warning would arouse undue suspicion.

And bring up questions she didn't want to answer yet.

Cursing her own lack of foresight now, Savannah hesitated. If Adam let slip her unmarried name too freely, Morrow Creek could become her next Ledgerville. Her past could follow her here, too, bringing scandal and whispers and accusations that she was a "Ruthless Reed"—someone to be wary and suspicious of.

She liked Morrow Creek. She didn't want to leave the cozy little town! She didn't want to be forced to start over someplace new. She didn't know if she could stand that. Breaking the news to Mose, packing up their belongings, striking out…

Just when she'd reached the verge of panic, Savannah

heard footsteps on the floorboards behind her. Then Adam's voice.

"Good morning," he said.

Surprised, she swiveled to see Adam crossing the room. His movements seemed surer than they had been for days. Scarcely noticing the muted clunk of the station's door shutting, she stared as Adam dropped his rucksack near the bureau.

Magnificently bare-chested, he gave her a cheerful nod. He used one of her embroidered towels to dab at his face, making that simple amalgamation of cotton and needlework appear far more interesting than it ever had when she'd used it to towel off after one of her own baths. In Adam's hearty grasp, her ordinary towel seemed absurdly delicate. Set against his sun-browned skin, its snowy-whiteness seemed blinding.

She glanced down at her own hand, then at her forearm. Her bare skin was only partly visible below her lacy sleeve, but even that tiny sample was enough to inform Savannah that she and Adam were very different when it came to skin color. She was fashionably pale. He was nearly the color of toffee. Against all reason, she found the difference between them arresting. What would it look like, she wondered, if their hands came together?

"Sorry if I startled you." Adam stopped at the ladder-back chair. He gave his face a final rubdown, then seemed at a loss as to what to do with his towel. He settled on holding it as he lifted his gaze to hers. "I woke up feeling like a grizzly bear after a long winter. It was high time for a shave, I decided."

He grinned. The effect that good humor had on his face was striking. His smile eased all the angles there, from his hard jawline to his jutting cheekbones to his strong brows. Now, without several days' worth of beard growth to obscure his features, he appeared even more attractive than he had before.

As though demonstrating his former need for a shave to her, Adam rubbed his palm over his jawline. Savannah gawked at him, instantly struck by a wild desire to do the same. She wanted to feel his bare skin under her fingertips. She wanted to know the flex and play of the muscles that formed his singular smile. She wanted to know *him*, pure and simple.

Of course she'd touched him already, she reminded herself staunchly. She'd cared for him, nursed him, watched over him. During the course of his recuperation, Savannah had become quite comfortable with the new man in her home. She'd grown accustomed to the sight of Adam's naked, hair-sprinkled chest as she'd changed his bandages. She'd gotten familiar with the feel of his strong arm muscles and taut abdomen as she'd helped him take slow, painful walks around the station as a necessary part of building up his strength. But those things…

Well. Those things, quite simply, didn't compare with *this*.

This Adam Corwin was a different man altogether. *This* Adam Corwin appeared alert and vital. *This* Adam Corwin gazed at her with directness and sharp wit, his striking blue eyes not the least bit clouded by Doc Finney's tincture. He'd been strong and considerate and grateful while he'd been injured. But now that he was on the mend, Adam was… downright fascinating.

His new vigor was a bit intimidating. Whereas before Savannah had felt fairly comfortable with fussing over him, now she felt embarrassed at the thought of the liberties she'd taken with his privacy and his person. Truly she'd manhandled him almost as much as Mose had accused her of doing, cavalierly grabbing Adam's trouser legs or his arms to maneuver him more comfortably in bed. Flushed at the memory, she averted her gaze.

Then she swerved it straight back to Adam again. Frankly the sight of him was too wonderful not to linger over.

"I'm happy to see all you were doing was getting cleaned up," she confessed. "I was worried you'd run away again."

"Never." With a grave expression, Adam came near enough to touch. "I won't leave you, Savannah. Not unless you ask me to."

"Well. *That's* unlikely to happen, isn't it? Especially now that you're so…" *Lively. Handsome. Downright captivating.*

No. She could hardly say any of those things. "So much improved," she settled for. Discomfited all over again—and likely still blushing—she dropped her gaze to the towel in his hands. "Here. Let me take care of that for you."

Savannah reached for it. At the same time, Adam murmured a word of thanks, then tried to hand the towel to her.

Their fingers brushed. Jolted by the contact, Savannah inhaled. Mesmerized, she stared at their almost-joined hands.

Together, they appeared every bit as enthralling as she'd imagined they might. Where their fingers touched, warmth surged between them. A funny tingle traveled all the way up her arm. Somehow it managed to make itself felt clear down to her toes.

Feeling unsettled, she lifted her gaze to Adam's. Like her, he stared at their hands. Then he shifted his gaze to her face. The moment he did so, something…*powerful* moved between them.

Savannah caught her breath. She would have sworn that Adam was staring at her mouth. But that was crazy, wasn't it?

She wasn't saying anything, wasn't smiling just then, wasn't doing a single, solitary thing with her mouth that would have warranted such intense interest.

And yet… She felt an equally intense interest in him. And his mouth. Which appeared full. And masculine. But soft. With her mind awhirl, Savannah tried to decide what to do about that. This situation had *not* been discussed in her etiquette book.

She settled on her failsafe maneuver as described in the *Guide to Correct Etiquette and Proper Behavior*: a curtsy. Using Adam's hand for balance, Savannah arranged herself in her most ladylike pose. To her relief, she scarcely even wobbled.

Adam fell silent. She hoped that meant he was impressed. She could not look up at him without a lapse in deportment.

Then he said, "Savannah, stand up. You needn't curtsy to me. Not ever again. Please." Sounding aggrieved, Adam raised her up with a gentle tug. "Believe me, I'm anything but your superior. I don't deserve that kind of treatment from you."

"Of course you do!" Relieved of the need to be formal, Savannah took Adam's towel from him. She tossed it on the chair. In all honesty, curtsying made her knees ache. She would not be sorry if the need for it arose less frequently. "You're a fine, upstanding man. You deserve all the best from me."

"I doubt you could give anything less than the best, just by being you." His mouth quirked on a charming smile. "But the plain fact is, I'm a 'fine, upstanding man' who's been thinking about kissing you ever since you came close enough for me to count your freckles this morning. So I'd guess that pretty much wrecks your theory about what I deserve and don't deserve."

"I don't have freckles!" Perish the thought. She'd tried every possible remedy for those blasted spots, including fresh buttermilk compresses and lumpy concoctions of dandelion greens mixed with lemon and— Abruptly Savannah stopped. "Kissing me?"

The notion bloomed in her head, bright and potent and impossible to stop thinking about. She'd been kissed before, of course. But only a few times. Sloppily and without finesse. But given the way all the other stage girls went on about kissing, Savannah knew there must be something more to the process. Something she'd never experienced… but would very much like to.

With his gaze still fixed on her, Adam nodded. "Yes."

He wanted to kiss her! He wanted, wanted, wanted….

Savannah wanted his kiss, too. Sadly she could not allow herself that.

"I'd planned," she confessed demurely, "to save our first kiss for our wedding day. So that it would feel truly special."

"Yes. Our wedding." Adam's face fell. He looked away. "About that—there's something you should know. Something—"

"But I just changed my mind," Savannah blurted.

Then she raised herself on her tiptoes and pressed her mouth eagerly to his.

Adam had known he was in trouble the moment Savannah's gaze turned wistful. When her mouth softened, turning twice as luscious as usual, he'd realized the situation was even more dire than he'd thought. By the time her bosom expanded on a hasty indrawn breath, momentarily diverting his attention, he'd understood that he was in over his head for certain.

He'd known full well he should put a stop to what was

happening between them. But a heartbeat later, Savannah had lurched upward, sparking his sense of anticipation and desire to a fever pitch. Then his whole mind had gone blank…with pain.

Damnation. Giving a strangled cry, Adam stepped backward. He put his arms on Savannah's shoulders to wrench her away.

"What's wrong?" Worriedly she fluttered her hands in an effort to help him. "Did I hurt you?"

"My ribs. You pushed—" he panted "—right on my broken ribs."

"Oh! I'm so sorry. I didn't mean to. I got…carried away."

"It's all right." He'd gotten carried away, too. Adam clenched his teeth in an approximation of a smile, not wanting Savannah to feel bad—especially for a rascally act of his own. He never should have confessed his desire to kiss her. "I've been needing to toughen up anyway. Getting out of bed to shave today was only the first step. Tomorrow I plan to start in on breaking wild horses, as usual. The day after that, I'll lay a railroad line from your front door all the way south to Tucson."

He grinned to show he was joking. But Savannah greeted his jest with pure earnestness. Wearing a concerned frown, she put her hands on her hips. Her lush, calico-covered, womanly—

"I told you, you don't have to impress me with Wild West heroics. When I invited you here, I knew what I was getting: a plain, commonsense man. If you hadn't been attacked and robbed and left for dead outside the station, we'd already be married by now. That was our plan when we agreed to this, remember?"

Adam did remember. He remembered that detail from her letters to Roy Bedell. He had to tell her the truth. Soon.

But the way she looked at him—as though he really *were* capable of Wild West heroics and fearlessness in general— somehow took all his good intentions and popped them like soap bubbles.

Mutely Adam nodded. In response, Savannah smiled broadly at him. It pleased him to see her smile. He felt like a damned hero all over again, just for agreeing with her views.

Most of the time, Savannah appeared happy, he'd noticed. Yet she had a face that looked as though it had seen its share of tears, too. The past few days, he'd wondered about that. He didn't like the thought of her being unhappy. Not ever. If he could have, Adam would have shouldered all her burdens himself.

Maybe he still could, if she would let him. Starting with the problem of Roy Bedell…and ending with whatever had made her so all-fired eager to get herself hitched to man she didn't know. Maybe if Adam could figure out that much, he could devise the best way to tell her the truth without hurting her.

"Just as soon as you're feeling up to it, I think we ought to get on with planning our wedding." Savannah fussed with the tray of breakfast victuals she'd brought him. "A private ceremony in Avalanche would be awfully nice. That would be my suggestion, but of course I'd love to hear whatever you think about the issue. Here. Go ahead and have a seat now, won't you?"

She gestured for him to sit at the small round table near the window. With his mind spinning from her sudden chatter, Adam obliged her. Savannah followed him with her tray. She exhaled, then set the food before him. Without meeting his gaze, she arranged his breakfast just so, then hurriedly went on talking.

"Avalanche is about a half-day's trip from here, partway

up the mountain. There's no rail line there, so we'll have to take the wagon. I'll drive us, since you're still recovering—"

"I'll drive," Adam objected. "I'm strong enough for that."

Savannah looked at him askance.

And no wonder, Adam realized as his own hasty words sank in. He wouldn't be driving them anywhere. He had to stop this.

It was bad enough that Savannah's long-distance beau was really a lying, thieving, no-good killer. But Adam had added to that problem by deceiving her about himself. At first that had been an accident; he'd been too insensible to assert his true identity or explain why he was at the station. But now, three days later, he knew damn well he wasn't Savannah's genuine mail-order groom. As soon as he told her the truth about that, she would boot him out the door lickety-split. Deservedly so.

Maybe that was why Adam decided not to confess everything. Not just then. Instead he nodded and smiled at her.

It was a cowardly move, but he couldn't help it. All he wanted was a little more time with Savannah—a little more time to let her feel happy. If that meant he waited an extra day or two to explain about Roy Bedell…well, that would ensure he could keep on protecting her, Adam reasoned. If Savannah tossed him out, he would not be able to keep sufficient watch over her.

"Well… I'm not entirely sure you're ready to *drive* us on the journey, but you do appear almost well enough to travel. I certainly thought you were well enough to go on foot to Morrow Creek this morning!" Wearing a faint frown, Savannah gazed at him. Whatever she saw appeared to satisfy her. "I'd hate to push you overmuch, but time *is* of the essence with our wedding."

Automatically Adam nodded. The rich aromas of fried eggs and fresh toasted bread wafted up to him. Belatedly realizing he was ravenous, he tucked into the breakfast she'd prepared.

Apparently gratified by his appetite, Savannah moved around him, making sure he had sugar for his coffee, butter for his bread, and a proper view of the flower she'd put on his tray.

Humbled by her generous efforts to please him, Adam felt a fresh pang of regret. He wished Savannah really *were* his. She was kind and gentle and determined. She was *good*. She deserved good things. It was as simple—and as complicated—as that.

He'd never met a woman so determined to make a man happy at home. Savannah's efforts to nurse him, care for him and just plain *welcome* him had been remarkable. As a traveling man at heart, Adam had never experienced anything like the hominess he felt when he was with Savannah. He knew that gave him all the more reason to be honest with her. But he hated the thought of disappointing her—and so far, she'd been powerfully tickled about having her long-awaited "fiancé" under her roof.

"'Time is of the essence'?" Remembering her words, Adam hesitated with a forkful of eggs. "What's the hurry?"

Savannah stilled. Then she snatched up a linen napkin and shook it out with a businesslike snap. "Oh, you know. I simply don't want to wait any longer than necessary to get married, that's all. We've both waited so long already, haven't we?"

She was hiding something. He could tell. After his many years as a detective, Adam hadn't acquired much faith in his fellow man—but he *had* acquired the ability to detect deception. And Savannah, he realized, was trying to deceive him right now.

Not that he could reason out why. Surprised and newly alert, Adam watched Savannah. With her gaze downcast, she spread the napkin over his lap. With her cheeks pink, she patted it thoroughly into place. Her actions were clearly an attempt to distract him from discussing their hasty upcoming wedding.

They worked. Adam shifted in his seat, his body reacting to her touch. Obliviously Savannah went on patting the napkin, seeming not to notice exactly how aggressively she did so.

Swallowing hard, Adam closed his hand over hers. "If you guard me any more diligently against crumbs," he said in a rough voice, "I might find it difficult to remain gentlemanly."

Her startled gaze flew to his. She glanced at his lap.

He could tell the exact moment Savannah realized what she'd done—and what's more, how brazenly she'd done it. She clenched her fingers beneath his hand. Then, with a maneuver he'd learned was typically paradoxical of her, she inclined her head in a stiff little bow.

"I'm terribly sorry. That was awfully rude of me, wasn't it?" She gave an awkward titter. "I promise, I'll never, *ever* touch you that way again. No matter what else happens between—"

"No." Briefly he closed his eyes. "*Don't* promise that."

At the thought of her touching him again—without the barrier of clothing and an unknown deception between them—Adam nearly lost control. With Savannah so near, and seemingly so willing, his ability to resist her felt downright paltry.

But then he'd known that from the start, hadn't he?

She inhaled, then charged onward. "I will certainly

do my best to respect your personhood and privacy, Mr. Corwin. I—"

"Adam. You promised to call me *Adam*." Despite his best intentions, Adam found it difficult to remain suspicious of her—partly because her hand felt so good held in his. He'd never touched her so boldly before. He should not have done so now. But Savannah had nearly made herself an *intimate* acquaintance of his just a second ago. He'd had to intervene.

He *hadn't* had to continue to cradle her hand beneath his. That, he simply liked.

"Adam. I don't know what's gotten into me. I'm so sorry."

Against all reason, he found Savannah's elaborate civility endearing. It stood at odds with her natural warmth and charm, but, strangely enough, it emphasized both those qualities, too.

"No more apologies. I forgive you." *But I still wonder what you're hiding.* Setting aside that question for now, Adam stroked his thumb over her hand. "Mmm. Your skin feels nice."

"Oh. Thank you! I use a special soap."

"Very soft and smooth. Not like my rugged hands."

"On the contrary," Savannah said courteously. "Your hands are actually quite—" she sneaked a peek, then frowned "—they *are* very rugged looking, as a matter of fact. How can that be, when you spend most of your days working the telegraph apparatus?"

Caught, Adam went still. Then, truthfully, he said, "I've had several occupations over my lifetime. I guess they've all left their marks on me, one way or the other."

He hated himself for the prevarication—and Savannah seemed to notice it, too. She gazed closely at him, frowning again.

"If you don't mind my asking," she said in a quiet, careful tone, "exactly what occupations were those?"

Blast. "They're not important now." With a dismissive wave, Adam went back to his breakfast. "Mmm. These eggs are delicious. I don't know why Mose is always badmouthing your cooking."

"Feel free to enumerate those occupations. In order," Savannah urged, not the least deterred by his attempt at misdirection. "You can't possibly give me too much detail."

He glanced up. "In your letters, you always said a person's plans for the future mattered more than their past."

She shrugged. "I guess my philosophy is changing. I want to know *all* about you. I couldn't be more curious." With an unexpectedly alert expression, she dragged a chair in place right beside him. She sat in it, then put her chin in her hands. "So tell me: what have you done *besides* telegraphing?"

That one, at least, was easy. He could answer honestly.

"I've worked as a ranch hand and as a drummer. I've helped out on a printing press. I used to be a United States Marshall—"

"A Marshall? That sounds fascinating." She looked at him with new admiration. "How long did you work for the government?"

Just long enough to realize that working for the detective agency would bring more bad men like Roy Bedell to justice.

No. He could not tell her that. His disillusionment with the Marshall's office wasn't at issue here. Uncomfortable with the necessity of another lie, Adam pushed aside his breakfast.

Savannah noticed. "What's the matter? Don't you like it?"

"I like it very much. But I find myself distracted."

"Oh?" She looked around as though expecting to find a tap-dancing mouse under his chair. "By what?"

"By you," Adam said. "You're *powerfully* distracting."

No longer able to resist her, he put his hand under her chin. Gently he urged her closer, his heart pounding with eagerness. He'd kissed a few women in his time. That was true. But none of those women had ever made him feel as needful as he did right now. He could scarcely remember them. His fingers shook as he drew Savannah nearer, then lowered his head.

The first touch of her lips was pure bliss. At the feel of her mouth beneath his, Adam felt nearly as swoony as he had under the influence of Doc Finney's tincture. He moaned and held on to her, daring to deepen his kiss…and Savannah welcomed him. Her hands came to his shoulders as she clung to him, sweet and soft. Their mouths met again. It was good. *So good…*

A short distance away, something banged. Loudly.

It was probably his heart, Adam reasoned as he tightened his grasp on Savannah's hand. He kissed her again, gladly. His heart was unschooled in these romantic matters. It likely didn't know what to make of the giddy pleasure he felt right now.

"Good gracious!" came a shrieking female voice from behind him. "*What* in heaven's name is going on here?"

Jolted by that shrill sound, Adam and Savannah jerked apart. An unfamiliar woman wearing a starched dress stood there, staring down at them both with an air of distinct disapproval.

"*I* am Mrs. Finney. My husband led me to believe you might require some assistance with your wounded traveler, here at the station." Her gimlet gaze traveled from Adam's unclothed, bandaged chest to Savannah's face. "But all *you* seem to require, miss, is a dose of commonsense morals!"

"No! Mrs. Finney, you don't understand. I have plenty of commonsense morals! I've worked very hard on acquiring them." Wearing a look of panic-stricken apology, Savannah bolted to her feet. She gestured wildly, her eyes wide. "I'm so sorry. What you just saw was merely a—a—"

She faltered, glancing at Adam for support.

He opened his mouth to help, but Mrs. Finney cut him short.

"I know *exactly* what I just saw." The doctor's wife lifted her chin. Her aged neck appeared strangled by her stiff, lacy dress collar. "And it is nothing with which I wish to be associated! You should be ashamed, young lady. *Ashamed.*" She aimed a censorious sniff in Adam's direction, but didn't seem to expect the same high morals from him. She gathered her ramrod posture. "And *I* should be leaving. Good day to you both!"

Before Savannah or Adam could speak, the woman marched out of the station, headed in the direction of Morrow Creek—and traveling at twice the speed, Adam reckoned, that she needed to go in order to reach the place in time for a gossipy teatime.

Chapter Seven

With her heart in her throat, Savannah picked up her skirts. She raced outside in pursuit of Mrs. Finney.

There was no time to lose. The woman's steely-eyed gaze had left little doubt of her opinion of Savannah's behavior. By noontime, every gossip in Morrow Creek would know that the local adjunct telegraph-station operator had been caught canoodling with a stranger—a stranger who was only half dressed! By sundown, Savannah expected, the sheriff would come calling with an all-too-familiar request for her to pack up and move on.

This is a good town. We don't need your kind around here.

That was what the Ledgerville sheriff had said, after word had spread about her scandalous past. Standing beneath his contemptuous gaze, Savannah had felt like the worst sort of person imaginable. None of her efforts to change had mattered at all. In the end, all that had mattered was her name.

Her unfairly sullied, notoriously recognizable name.

Blast whoever had attacked poor Adam! Not only had they hurt him, but they'd delivered a cruel setback to her plans, too. If not for Adam's attacker, she and her fiancé would have already been wed—and Mrs. Finney would not have barged in on what must have appeared to be an utterly disreputable dalliance.

As a point in fact, Savannah realized dazedly, it *had* been a disreputable dalliance. But it had felt…*wonderful*.

Shoving aside the memory of Adam's kiss for now, Savannah kept moving. Partway across the yard, she glimpsed Mrs. Finney. To her relief, the doctor's wife hadn't yet left for town. She stood beside an elaborate rig with a single spirited horse at its head, staring at Mose—who held the traces—with a mulish expression. What could they possibly be discussing?

Savannah couldn't wait to find out. She charged in that direction, but Mose spotted her—and held up his hand in a clear sign to keep her distance. Perplexed, Savannah hesitated.

As she did, Adam arrived at her side. He'd pulled on a shirt. He buttoned it—crookedly—with impatient movements.

"This is my fault." He nodded at Mrs. Finney, his jaw tight. "I'll talk to her. I know how to smooth things over."

"No. Wait." Savannah held him with a hand on his muscular, shirtsleeve-covered forearm. "Mose is handling it."

"Your hired man? What could he do about it?"

"I don't know. But he signaled me to keep my distance, and that's what I'm going to do. I trust him."

Adam squinted at her friend. Then at Mrs. Finney. "Are you sure? If Mose somehow makes things worse for you—"

"He won't." Savannah bit her lip, waiting for that distant

conversation to come to its conclusion. "I can count on him."

A few minutes later, her faith in Mose was rewarded. Her friend nodded at Mrs. Finney, then the two parted. The doctor's wife cast a speculative glance at Savannah and Adam. Behind the woman, Mose pantomimed a stage direction—a signal to take a bow.

Instantly understanding what he meant, Savannah grabbed Adam's hand. He tried to pull away—undoubtedly thinking that any physical intimacy would worsen their predicament—but Savannah held firm. She plastered a big smile on her face, then nudged Adam with her shoulder. "Just smile and wave," she told him in a taut undertone. "Everything is going to be fine now."

At her suggestion, Adam's tall body fairly vibrated with resistance. She felt a tremor pass between them. She didn't dare look at him for fear of ruining her—*their*—performance. All she could do now was pray he would trust her enough to go along.

He did. He laced his fingers in hers, then raised his arm in a salute to Mrs. Finney. At his friendly gesture, that gray-haired lady visibly eased her posture. She smiled, then waved to them. With Mose at hand to help her, she alighted her fancy carriage. Then she took up the reins and clucked to her horse.

The rig's wheels creaked. To Savannah's relief, Mrs. Finney headed away from the station, traveling at a cautious pace down the bumpy, mountainous road. The moment the doctor's wife passed out of sight, Mose crossed the station yard with hasty steps.

"You can thank me later," he said. "Right now, you two better get going. I'll keep watch over things around here."

Savannah nodded. "Thank you, Mose." She squeezed him close in a hug. Her grateful gaze met his. "I've decided

Avalanche would be best for the ceremony. That means we're going to need the horse and wagon. Will you be all right without them?"

"I'll make do." He frowned. "Go on now. No time to waste."

She picked up her skirts again, preparing to go inside and pack a few things. She'd need a picnic lunch for the journey, her best dress, the licensing paperwork she'd arranged for—

"Get going where?" Adam turned to Mose, his face set in a doubtful scowl. "What did you tell Mrs. Finney? She ran out of the station like a wildcat, but she left like a kitten."

"That's a very colorful turn of phrase," Savannah assured him. "But we don't have time to discuss it right now."

She turned away again. Adam grabbed her arm to stop her.

His determined gaze met hers. His rigid stance brooked no further misdirection. "I reckon you'd better make time."

Uh-oh. She hadn't anticipated this hard-edged aspect of his. For lack of a better strategy, Savannah batted her eyelashes at him. It was a maneuver that typically never failed. "Why, Mr. Corwin! Not even a please or thank you to go with that request? I'm awfully surprised at you. Usually you're so—"

"I guess Mrs. Finney might be more obliging about answering my questions." Adam turned, his manner purposeful as he made ready to cross the yard in pursuit. "I can still catch up with her, if I hurry."

"Don't be silly." Running after him, Savannah gave a panicky laugh. Adam could *not* confront Mrs. Finney himself. He would ruin everything! She grabbed him again to make him stop. "A man in your situation shouldn't overexert himself."

"A woman in your situation shouldn't hide things from her fiancé."

He was right—even if he hadn't appeared to want to remind her of it. Adam really was too kind. She didn't want to deceive him. Fretfully Savannah glanced at Mose. He gave her a nod.

Then he spoke up. Rubbing the top of his head in obvious discomfort, Mose said, "When I met Mrs. Finney in the station yard, I told her you two were already married."

His words were nothing less than Savannah had expected to hear. During those long days of waiting for her mail-order groom to arrive, she and Mose had discussed this eventuality at length. Adam had not been privy to their plans, however. Upon hearing them now, he seemed plainly disbelieving.

"I told her you hadn't seen each other for a while," Mose elaborated, doubtless reading the incredulity on Adam's face. "I told her that, owing to the trauma of the moment, Savannah didn't recognize you right away when she found you outside the station. I told her that's why she didn't tell Doc Finney straightaway that her husband had finally joined her out west."

"So Mrs. Finney believes we're already married," Savannah clarified—partly for Adam's sake and partly for her own. Mose nodded in confirmation. Marveling at him, she shook her head. "That was *very* fast thinking, Mose! I'll admit, I hadn't considered Doc Finney's part in all this. It was a good thing you caught all the angles—and so quickly, too. I should have expected as much from you, though."

In his heyday, Mose had been one of the most imposing and well-known stagehands working in some of the most disorderly parts of New York City's theater district. He owed his survival to staying two steps ahead of everyone else.

Modestly her friend shrugged. "You two did help sell

the notion of being hitched, what with your hand-holding, and all."

"Yes, that's true." Savannah glanced at Adam, who gave her a newly enlightened frown—clearly just then understanding their playacting. "I imagine we presented quite the picture of connubial bliss. It's a good thing you signaled me, Mose."

The two of them exchanged coconspirators' glances. Sometimes their long-term friendship came in quite handy.

Adam stared. "And you think Mrs. Finney *believed* all that?"

"Well…" Mose put his hands to his suspenders, giving a humble shrug. "I can be powerfully convincing when I want to be. And like I said, the two of you make a pretty picture together."

Savannah smiled. "Thank you, Mose. That's very kind."

Adam only squinted at them both. His half-buttoned shirt flapped its tails in the breeze, lending him a rakish air. He seemed at a loss for words. That was probably just as well, given the situation they were in. She needed his cooperation. She didn't need his understanding. Not just yet, anyway.

"Once I saw Mrs. Finney charging out of the station with her hair afire, I knew the trouble could only be one thing." Looking at them, Mose compressed his lips with evident disapproval. "I would have expected you to behave with more decorum."

"I was trying to!" Savannah felt her cheeks heat. "I simply got carried away. You know how difficult it is for me to—"

"He means me," Adam interrupted. He straightened to meet Mose's censure, then looked toward the station.

"You're right. I took advantage of an unguarded moment. I'm sorry."

Stiffly Mose nodded. "I accept."

Adam scowled. "*You* weren't the one I was apologizing to."

"Or," Savannah piped up, "the one he was kissing!"

They both ignored her, stuck in their mulish poses.

"I reckon he oughtn't be kissing anybody just yet." Mose fisted his hands at his sides. "Which reminds me. I've been meaning to warn you about taking unwanted liberties with—"

"With whom?" Adam demanded, not the least intimidated by Mose's size and strength. "Go ahead. Say it. I dare you."

Savannah couldn't stand it. Feeling like a referee at a dogfight, she stepped between both men with her arms outstretched. "Who said they were *unwanted* liberties?" she demanded.

Mose and Adam stared at her, openmouthed.

"They…weren't?" they asked in unison.

Mose appeared disgruntled by the notion.

Adam appeared jubilant. His happiness pleased her.

"I want you two to get along," Savannah told them. "Please try. For my sake. Won't you? It would mean a lot to me."

At first, her request seemed unlikely to be met. Like chastened little boys, Adam and Mose stared at their feet. Adam's were clad in dusty boots that made him seem like the Wild West adventurer he wanted to be. Mose's were outfitted with sensible brogues that spoke to his penchant for order and tradition. Between them, not much was similar— except her.

"I'll take your lack of argument as a 'yes,'" Savannah

said. "I'll expect to see a corresponding level of friendship arise between you boys before much longer, too."

Mose grunted. Adam squinted at the ponderosa pines.

Satisfied, Savannah nodded. She picked up her skirts again. "Now I'm off to pack up a few things. We'll leave in an hour."

Wearing a contemplative frown, Adam watched as Savannah sashayed off toward the station building. It was a good thing he was no longer taking Doc Finney's tincture. He had the feeling he would need all his wits to keep up with his supposed bride.

At the thought of the wedding she expected from him today, Adam blanched. He couldn't possibly go through with marrying her. Doing so would be the worst kind of lie…wouldn't it?

Although he'd known people who'd wed under similarly unusual circumstances, a part of him whispered. Trappers who married native women. Settlers who married reformed dance-hall girls. Miners and railroad workers who wrote away for genuine mail-order brides, then married them the first chance they got.

Sometimes those arrangements prospered. Sometimes all that was needed was a beginning, then the rest took care of itself.

Could he be as lucky? Adam wondered. Or was he only deceiving himself…as much as he was deceiving Savannah?

He truly did care about her. He had when he'd arrived, and he did twice as much now. But would that be enough? Still frowning, Adam watched as she disappeared inside the station.

Then, with a sigh, he transferred his gaze to…Mose.

The station's part-time helper glowered at him. Keeping

his arms crossed over his chest in a belligerent pose, he jerked his chin at Adam. "If you so much as disappoint her," Mose warned, "I swear I'll make you regret it. What happened when you were attacked will seem like a minor kerfuffle compared with what I'll do to you if you upset Savannah. I promise you that."

"I'm not here to upset her," Adam assured him, holding up his palms. "I don't intend to do anything except—"

Watch over her. Protect her. Make sure Bedell doesn't hurt her, he meant to say. But Mose was having none of it. The hired man cut him off, scrutinizing him through suspicious eyes.

"I don't care what your intentions are. All I care about is what you *do,* same as Savannah. And I'm here to tell you, the last thing she needs is more trouble. So don't you dare—"

"'More trouble'?" Adam repeated, growing instantly alert. "What kind of trouble has Savannah had already?"

Mose's mouth tightened. "Nothing you need to know about."

"I need to know about everything." His body tense, Adam stepped closer. "Has someone been coming around here?" *Bedell. His brothers.* "Have you seen someone? Did someone threaten her?"

"It's none of your business. All I'm saying is—"

"It damn well is my business. I'm about to marry her." *No he wasn't!* the sensible part of him shouted. But Adam ignored it. Prodded by concern—and outraged at the thought that Savannah might already have been endangered in ways he hadn't known about—he stood toe-to-toe with Mose. "I'm about to give Savannah my name. I'd say that makes her troubles my own."

Grudgingly Mose examined him. "That's what she said

about you, when she took you in. That your troubles were hers now."

"She was right," Adam confirmed. "I'm here for the long haul." *He was?* He couldn't be. But the statement *felt* true. Adam stood his ground. "So rather than waste your time warning me, why don't you tell me what's going on? Maybe I can help."

Maybe I can find my way out of this lie, while I'm at it.

"Maybe you could help," Mose said. "If I trusted you. But I don't."

The man's stubbornness aggravated him. "In time, you will."

"Can't think how."

"Savannah trusts me," Adam pointed out.

At his mention of her, Mose's doubtful gaze shifted from Adam's face to the station building. Inside, Savannah could be heard cheerfully humming as, presumably, she gathered materials for their nuptial trip. *We'll leave in an hour.*

"She don't trust you as much as you think," Mose disagreed.

Adam recalled the way he'd longed for Savannah to let him call her by her given name. She hadn't. He knew that meant Mose was right. But what mattered most was Savannah's safety.

"I need to know what's been going on. I can help."

"The only way you can help is by getting on down the road." Mose gazed at the pathway as it wound between the scrub oak and pines, headed up the mountainside. "And by making Savannah your wife in truth, 'stead of a lie. I don't like letting you leave with her. But it's what she wants, and it's a foolish man who denies Savannah her wishes. You'll find out that soon enough."

"If I forget," Adam said, "just give me a stage signal."

Startled, Mose stared at him.

Adam gazed back with equanimity. One of the occupations he *hadn't* claimed during his discussion with Savannah had been working backstage at a vaudeville house. But he'd done it.

During that time, he'd learned a few things about stage directions. He hadn't expected to encounter them again at a backwater telegraph station in the middle of nowhere.

"Why do you reckon," he asked Mose, "a telegraph operator like Savannah understands professional stage signals?"

"You must have misunderstood." Gruffly Mose shouldered past him. "I'd better go man the wires. Have a safe journey."

Without further discussion, the station helper strode off. The ramshackle door slammed behind him. Through the window, Adam spied Mose again, this time with his head bent next to Savannah's. She started, then looked up through the window.

Her worried gaze met Adam's. She bit her lip.

Her gesture was all the confirmation he needed. Savannah Reed was definitely hiding something—something he should have unearthed while preparing his case against Roy Bedell, but hadn't. After almost a year of tracking the man alongside Mariana, Adam had been too concerned with stopping the bastard to give much thought to the background of his latest victim.

He'd known Savannah Reed had had a sizable nest egg, Adam reflected as he considered his "fiancée's" distant conversation with her hired man. He'd known she was new to the Arizona Territory. He'd known she was vulnerable and in danger. Those had been all the details Adam had needed to ride to her rescue.

By the time he'd reached her, he'd known he was smitten with her, too. That only complicated matters all the more.

He'd thought Savannah Reed was an innocent. Now it seemed that, maybe, she wasn't. That complicated matters, too.

But it didn't change them. For a long time now, Adam had carried a grainy, creased and folded photograph next to his heart—and he'd vowed to protect the woman pictured in it. Watching that woman now, he knew he would keep the vow he'd made. No matter what he'd have to risk to do so.

Savannah prepared for their journey with astonishing speed. Bustling to and fro from the station building to the rickety waiting wagon, she carried out bundles and blankets. With her golden hair escaping from its knot in curly tendrils, she labored to pack wax paper-wrapped sandwiches, a canteen of water, small green apples and a burlap sack of oats.

"For Chester," she explained as she tossed the sack onto the wagon's bench seat, then checked the brake. "The horse."

"Ah." Watching her with a smile he felt scarcely able to hide, Adam made himself offer a somber nod. "Of course."

"He deserves a special treat." Savannah didn't look at him as she pinned on a wide-brimmed hat with a pretty ribbon trim. "I'm afraid it's a bit of a pull to Avalanche."

"Why not just go to Morrow Creek?" Adam gestured down the mountain. "It's a sight closer, and probably not so steep."

"I've already made arrangements with the minister in Avalanche." Glowing with exertion, Savannah pitched herself onto the seat beside him. She squeezed his hand. "He's expecting us."

That was probably true, Adam realized as he examined her bright profile. But she was still hiding something from him. Every instinct he had told him she was deceiving him.

Had she had an encounter with the Bedells, he wondered as he recalled his conversation with Mose, and wanted to hide it? Or was the trouble that Savannah faced something else entirely?

As though summoned by Adam's thoughts, Mose appeared beside the wagon, his expression grave. He handed Savannah a package.

"Don't open this until afterward," the big man warned. His gaze shifted ominously to Adam, then returned to Savannah. Mose smiled as he patted the package's brown paper wrapping. "I'll know if you tear into this, so no cheating now, you hear?"

"Mose!" Savannah marveled at him. "What's this?"

"Just a tiny wedding gift. Practically useless, so don't go getting your hopes up. I'm an old man without much money, so—"

"Oh! This is so sweet of you." Lunging sideways, Savannah wrapped her arms around his neck. She sniffled. After a moment, she leaned back again, gazing into Mose's face. "Thank you. I wish you were coming with us. It won't be the same without you."

"I know." Mose looked up at Savannah, his face swamped with unabashed affection. To Adam's gaze, the man appeared downright fatherly…and choked up near to the point of tears, too.

Feeling like an intruder, Adam stared pointedly in the other direction. But he felt happy, all of a sudden, that Savannah had someone in her life who truly did love and care about her. Someone who was not deceiving her in any way.

"But I'll be there in spirit," Mose said gruffly. "And I'll be waiting right here when you get back. So don't dawdle."

"We won't," Savannah promised with another hug. Keeping her arms around Mose's thick neck, she spoke in his ear. "Try not to look so worried. This is what I want most, remember?"

Her words weren't meant for Adam, but he heard them— and they jabbed at his heart, all the same. If Savannah wanted love, he had that to spare—if she would take it from a traveling man like him…a man who had experienced exactly three days' worth of down-home living in all his adult life, and those at Savannah's caring hands. But right now, he did not have the truth to give her, and he didn't know when he would. That still bothered him.

Maybe on the journey, Adam thought, he would find a way to explain about Bedell. Maybe he would finally set things right.

Mose jerked his head in a brusque nod. "I know it is."

"All right then." Savannah sniffled again, then gave an awkward laugh. She picked up the leather traces in her gloved hands, seeming surprisingly at ease with the task. "I guess we're off."

At her direction, the horse set in motion. Adam swayed and braced himself on the bench seat, uncomfortably aware of Savannah's wobbling chin and the tears brimming in her eyes.

"Mose will be all right without you," he assured her in his gentlest tone. "We won't be gone long. He'll get by."

"I know." Savannah nodded. "He'll be fine."

But an instant later, it appeared they were both wrong. Mose jogged along behind the wagon. He shouted something.

Savannah jerked the reins, and Mose caught up.

"There's one more thing I forgot to tell you." Panting, he placed his hand over his heart. Then he gestured in the other direction, toward Morrow Creek. "Don't stay more than overnight in Avalanche. Mrs. Finney is expecting you in town on Friday."

"Mrs. Finney is expecting me?" Savannah asked.

They were staying overnight? Adam swallowed hard. He had to admit the truth to Savannah, else ruin her reputation for good.

But his imagination offered up a contrary vision—a vision involving Savannah and himself, newly married and eager to celebrate their union. If only that could be real. Adam knew he could make her happy. He could make her sigh with pleasure, too. He could begin with another kiss, move on to a slow caress….

Caught up in the notion, Adam gazed at the smooth skin at the back of Savannah's neck. If he kissed her there, then undid that row of tiny buttons along the back of her dress, he could make both of them feel happy about their marriage… however false it might be. He could make it *feel* real to both of them.

He'd never in his life wanted anything more.

Oblivious to his reverie, Mose nodded. "She wants to give you and Mr. Corwin a tea party to welcome you to Morrow Creek."

"A *tea party?*" Savannah sounded aghast. "For us?"

"That's right." Mose nodded. "To welcome you to town. When Mrs. Finney left, she told me she was going to alert the entire Ladies Auxiliary Club so they could turn out to the party."

"But I've been living nearby for months!" Savannah stared in displeasure at Chester's twitching, horsey ears.

"Nobody cared to give me a tea party in all that time, now did they?"

"Well, you *were* trying to pass by mostly unnoticed."

"Yes," Savannah mused. "I suppose that's true."

That piqued Adam's interest. "Mostly unnoticed? Why?"

Savannah and Mose stared at him. Then they looked at each other. "'Nuff chitchat. Have a safe journey!" Mose shouted.

Then he smacked their horse on its rump and sent the wagon jostling down the open road, away from the station…and away from whatever certainty Adam had that he was doing the right thing by coming to Savannah Reed's rescue.

And especially by lying to her to do it.

Still, one niggling thought remained as Adam bounced along beside Savannah, headed toward a wedding he'd never expected to find himself involved in, in a town he'd never been to.

Exactly *why* had Savannah been trying to pass by mostly unnoticed in Morrow Creek? And why did marrying *him* somehow set it right?

Chapter Eight

The only thing more awkward than marrying a man she'd only just met, Savannah realized as she guided Chester uphill during the first hour of her nuptial journey to Avalanche, was making the trip to the wedding itself. She and Adam had scarcely said a word since they'd left the telegraph station. That had been some distance ago. Now the silence was beginning to concern her.

If this was the manner in which they communicated now, before they'd even exchanged vows, what would their lives be like a few weeks or months or years hence? The question set her jaw in motion, even before she could remember to be cautious.

"It's a fine day, isn't it?" she ventured.

In demonstration, she gestured with her gloved hand. The sunshine fell through the trees as they passed, lighting the area with a cheery glow. Birds twittered in the underbrush. Flies pestered Chester, who flicked them with his tail. The wagon swayed and creaked, continuing on its path to her future.

Her future as Mrs. Adam Corwin, never again to be referred to or thought of or pitied or scorned as a "Ruthless Reed."

"Yes," Adam offered tightly. "A fine day."

As he had for the past several hills and valleys, he sat beside her with his long, powerful legs braced on the wagon. He gazed at the area beyond the roadside, clearly preoccupied.

"What are you thinking about?" Savannah asked.

"Nothing."

She laughed. "Of course you're thinking about *something*."

In reply, he compressed his mouth but remained silent. The taut lines of his upper body bespoke alertness. His shoulders appeared as tight as the bandages she'd secured before starting out on their trip. His arms were held braced at his sides.

Even Mose never appeared *this* watchful when they were out.

But then the truth occurred to Savannah. She nearly sighed with relief. "You're looking out for desperados, aren't you?"

Adam blinked, clearly surprised. "Have you seen someone?" His gaze looked intent. "Has someone threatened you?"

She laughed again. "Of course not! I've been telling you the truth—those Wild West tales are exaggerations. You don't have to protect me from any desperados, real or imaginary."

"They're real, all right." Adam gritted his teeth. He swayed on the wagon seat beside her with surprising balance and agility. Apparently he was stronger and more on the mend than she'd thought. "But if they come after you, they'll be sorry."

His words were little more than a muttered threat. They sounded sincere, though, and his protectiveness—however unneeded—made her smile. She was fortunate that Adam Corwin was a brave and kind man. Although he *did* deserve better than to be misled into marrying The Seductive Sensation without knowing it.

Guiltily Savannah bit her lip. It hadn't occurred to her how unfair she was being. Adam deserved to know the truth about her past—to know, without a doubt, what he was getting into. Maybe he would even accept her as she was—her life on the stage, her ne'er-do-well parents, and her dancing included. That was what she would have loved most of all. In a little while, it would be too late to have an honest beginning between them.

Thinking of that, she cast a nervous glance at him. "You know, it's fortunate we have this time together," she began, searching for a way to broach her past. "There are probably a great many things you'd like to know about me. For instance—"

"Stop here."

"What?" Confused, Savannah frowned at him. "Why?"

"Someone is following us."

She tried to turn around. Adam pushed his shoulder near hers to prevent her from doing so, then took control of the reins. With his free hand, he flipped back his suit coat—freshly laundered and newly mended at her own hands—then settled his palm over something. Something on his hip. Something blunt and steely, holstered in battered leather and ready for firing.

"You're wearing your gun belt!" she blurted, gawking at how oddly appropriate it seemed on his person. "And your gun!"

"Keep your voice down." Grim-faced, Adam pulled Chester to a mane-tossing halt. He gestured to Savannah.

"I want you to get down here beside me. Get yourself hidden behind the wagon seat as much as you can. Cover your head." His gaze fixed itself on something in the trees behind them. "Now."

Spooked by the raw urgency in his voice, Savannah felt gooseflesh prickle over her arms. The day, formerly so sunny and bright, suddenly felt chilly and unreal.

But surely Adam was only being his usual cautious self. Surely nothing was really wrong…was it?

"Don't be silly!" she said. "I realize that being attacked and robbed on your first day here might have left you a little wary, but I promise you, I've traveled all over this road and—"

"Down." With his hand firm on her hat, Adam lowered her to her knees. He moved near her, shielding her with his body. Attentiveness emanated from him. "Stay quiet."

Affronted and baffled by his behavior, Savannah opened her mouth to protest. Then she heard it—the faint *clip-clop* of hooves against packed earth, then the jingling of tack and spurs. Someone *was* behind them. Warily she hunched against the wagon, trying to make herself disappear behind the bench seat.

Unconcerned by their plight, birds twittered nearby. A fly buzzed past Savannah's ear. Her skin dampened with sweat, making her dress stick uncomfortably to her back. From her position, all she could see were a slice of blue sky and Adam's tense frame, poised in front of her while he examined the traces.

Holding her breath, Savannah waited. The horse and rider neared their wagon, sending up dust in their wake. She smelled it in the air. Saddle leather creaked. The hoofbeats slowed.

"'Afternoon," the rider said.

Adam gave a curt nod, his hand still on his gun belt.

Savannah craned her neck. From beyond Adam's braced legs, she glimpsed a dappled mare. Its lone rider wore battered britches and an unmatched suit coat. The man spotted her. A wide, unhygienic smile split his face. He tipped his hat at her.

Startled and strangely fearful of his gesture, she looked away. Then she glanced back just as hastily, berating herself for being rude. Surely the polite thing to do would be to smile or greet him or offer an explanation for why she was crouched so peculiarly in her wagon...but then her gaze fell to Adam's calf. She recognized the faint outline of his knife.

A chill moved through her. In that moment, Savannah felt bizarrely convinced that Adam was *not* pretending to be a rough and ready Wild West adventurer. In that moment, he truly seemed to be the "bad man" he'd warned her about on the day they'd met.

His forbidding expression did nothing to diminish that impression. With his gaze pointed and his hand still ready on his gun belt, Adam examined the wooded hillside surrounding them. The rider passed by them without incident, but clearly Adam had expected...something more to happen. His whole body radiated guardedness.

Whatever he was looking for, he didn't find it. After a few long seconds, he gestured for her to get up.

Awkwardly Savannah did. She brushed off her skirts, noticing as she did that the lone rider was still visible, far ahead of them now and showing no signs of slowing down.

"See? There's no need to be alarmed." She pointed to him. "He's just another traveler. I didn't even recognize him."

To her surprise, Adam did. "It's Curtis Bedell."

"A friend of yours? All the way out here?" She laughed.

Adam remained sober. He gazed at her intently, too.

Savannah didn't know what he was looking for. But then she realized that Adam couldn't possibly be serious. "Curtis Bedell" probably didn't even exist. Adam must have invented the name in an attempt to justify their situation. Undoubtedly he felt embarrassed to have been so overzealous about protecting her—from a harmless, if untidy, passerby, at that.

"Hmm. Seeing someone you're acquainted with all the way out here? I guess that must truly be serendipity in action."

"Yes." A pause. Adam frowned. "Something like that."

Gazing at his taut face, Savannah yearned to ease his discomfort. She knew what it felt like to be on the outside of a situation—to be guilty of trying too hard to fit in someplace new. She knew that her Baltimore-based, telegraph operator husband-to-be must feel out of place here in the Territory.

"Well then. Serendipity or not, if you know him, maybe we should invite Mr. Bedell to the wedding," she joked.

Adam shook his head. "I'd sooner bring a rattlesnake to a christening." His gaze sharpened as it followed the man down the road. Then Adam looked at her, and his face softened. "Go on now. Take your seat." He helped her into his former position on the wagon bench, then assumed her place at the reins. "You don't mean to keep a man waiting all day for his own wedding, do you?"

He smiled at her then, but something about Adam's demeanor bothered her. Trying to figure it out, Savannah hesitated. She had the oddest feeling that something important had just taken place…but she'd be jiggered if she could guess what it was.

Surely Adam didn't *truly* know Curtis Bedell?

If he did, she reckoned as she glanced sideways and caught Adam peering down the road after that lone rider again, he did not like the man. Not even the tiniest bit.

Despite Adam's peculiar behavior, though, Savannah had to keep her priorities in mind. Getting herself properly wed to her mail-order groom lay at the top of the list. "Absolutely not!" she assured him. "There'll be no delays from me. The sooner we're married, the better."

Given his unusual behavior, Savannah decided, maybe she should wait just a *little* while longer to explain about being The Seductive Sensation. Just to be properly circumspect….

Standing inside the minister's small house, Adam paced as he waited for the wedding ceremony to begin. The minister's wife had gone to secure two witnesses, leaving him alone with his impatience—and his reluctance to leave Savannah unguarded.

Casting a careful glance outside the sitting-room window, Adam caught a crooked-looking glimpse of the town outside. To his relief, nothing seemed amiss. Wherever Curtis Bedell had gone to, he wasn't in sight any longer. All Adam saw out the window was the small mining town of Avalanche, perched on the rocky hillside and hugging the mountain like a stout billy goat. Some of the houses and businesses bore stilts to help them balance against the rocks; others simply stood akilter. In the distance, the tall shaft of the Daisy mine stood visible along the skyline, cutting into the jagged blue sky with impunity.

Despite Adam's expectations, no lone riders waited along that skyline. No Bedell brothers lurked at the edge of the tumbled boulders or sighted their rifles at the minister's modest house. But that didn't mean Adam could let down his guard. Seeing Curtis Bedell on their trail had spooked him considerably. For the first time since he'd awakened at the telegraph station, he agreed wholeheartedly with Savannah.

The sooner they were married, the better.

He couldn't reason out why Curtis Bedell had simply been following them, though. Especially alone. The Bedells usually traveled in a pack, with Roy at its mangy head.

The fact that Curtis was on his own left Adam feeling uneasy. Clearly the gang hadn't yet given up on stealing Savannah's nest egg for themselves. But their usual manner of operation—with Roy Bedell calling the shots and his brothers dropping predictably in line behind him—appeared to have fallen by the wayside. Now there was no telling how far the brothers would go to get the money they wanted. If Adam hadn't been there when Curtis had intersected Savannah's path to Avalanche…

Shuddering, Adam shut his mind to the thought. He *had* been there. That was all that mattered. That, and keeping her safe.

To that end, Adam strode to the single door punctuating the sitting room wall. He hesitated, then rapped firmly on it.

"Savannah? Are you all right in there?"

"I'm fine!" Savannah yelled. "Don't come in!"

"Are you sure?"

"I'm positive. For the fourth time—I'm *still* just fine."

She sounded amused and a little exasperated, but Adam couldn't take any chances. He leaned his head nearer, straining to hear. He imagined the Bedells sneaking into the room where Savannah had gone to change into her best dress, holding her at gunpoint, stealing her away from him. Beset with worry, he made a grim face. He shook his head. "Stand back. I'm coming in."

"Oh, no, you're not!" The door rattled, undoubtedly because Savannah smacked both hands on it to hold it shut. That's what she'd done the other three times he'd inquired after her. "Stay put! It's bad luck for a groom to see his bride."

Adam placed his hands on the door, too. Despite her objections, he seriously considered shoving it open. Seeing Curtis Bedell this morning had removed his doubts about the rightness of marrying Savannah, but it had not allayed his fears that she would somehow learn the truth and make him leave before he could protect her. He couldn't let that happen. He *had* to stay beside her.

But he didn't have to upset her. That's what barging in while she changed would do. Relenting for the moment, Adam spread his fingers, imagining that his palms touched the door in the same places that Savannah's did. He leaned his cheek against the door, feeling sappy as hell for doing so…but wholly unable to quit. He sighed. "All right. But I'm here if you need me."

A moment passed. Then she said, "I know. Thank you, Adam. I'm more grateful than you can imagine, for everything you've done."

Wistfully Adam closed his eyes. He'd never expected to find himself here. He knew he could love Savannah the way she deserved. But he didn't know if she could love him… afterward.

Soon enough, the truth would come out. She would likely feel betrayed. He was a crackerjack with words, able when he wanted to charm and cajole almost as thoroughly as Mariana could in her heyday. But when tender feelings were involved, Adam got muddled. He didn't like to talk about how he felt about things.

But he did like to *feel*. He hadn't known that about himself until he'd met Savannah. He hadn't known he had such a capacity to feel warmth and caring and protectiveness. Grateful for that—grateful for *her* most of all—Adam stroked the door.

"Aww. Isn't that darling?" The minister's wife bustled into the sitting room, spying Adam's pose with a knowing look. "You can't bear to be separated for a single moment. So romantic."

Caught, Adam jerked backward. "Are we ready to start?"

"Soon. Soon." Wearing a pleased little smile, the woman came closer. She lifted something in her hand. A nosegay of wildflowers. "First, you hold still while I gussy you up."

Impatiently Adam glanced at the doorway she'd entered through. "Where are the witnesses? You went to get witnesses."

"They're waiting in the anteroom. Hold still."

She came at him with the flowers. They'd been fashioned into a boutonniere, Adam saw. "I don't need those," he said. "Miss Reed likes me as I am. Let's just get started."

She gave him a peculiar look. "We will. We have the minister, the witnesses, the marriage license and—" she tilted her head toward the next room "—the bride. All we're waiting on is for *you* to be properly dandified for your own wedding."

Clearly the woman would not take *no* for an answer. Obediently Adam struck his chest forward. He held still.

"There." The minister's wife fussed with a few pins, her wrinkled hands busy at his suit coat lapel. "Fine. You look—"

"Perfect," Savannah breathed from the doorway.

Adam glanced up at her. In that moment, he was lost.

There was nothing he wouldn't have done to make her his. Her eyes were bright, her face was beyond pretty and her dress fit her as though it had been sewn by angels. But those things weren't what made him feel that he would have moved heaven and earth to make her happy. What made him feel that way…was *her*.

Savannah gazed up at him in wonder, and Adam wanted to live up to the magic she saw in him. She stepped quickly toward him, and he wanted to be worthy of her eagerness. She pronounced him perfect, and he longed to justify her good opinion. He wanted to be *better*, for her. He swore in that moment he would be.

Feeling his chest tighten with emotion, Adam inhaled a fortifying breath. "I… You look… The witnesses are—"

Wholly unable to make sense of himself, he gestured toward the anteroom. His first attempt at being *better* had not been a success. Evidently, Adam realized with a despairing heart, he was not yet ready to be a better man—even for Savannah's sake.

But somehow, she understood him. She stepped closer and took his hand, then gazed up into his face with such warmth and caring that Adam felt entirely undone by it.

"I…" she said. "That is… Your suit is so—"

Savannah's eyes widened. Her cheeks colored as she realized that what had emerged from her mouth was at least as garbled as what had come from his. Embarrassed, she glanced away, causing him to fear she might be on the verge of a full-blown curtsy.

Adam squeezed her hand. He urged her to look at him again. He swallowed past his curiously tight throat. "At least we're a matching pair," he said. "We fit together, the two of us."

She laughed then, loudly, and he knew everything would be all right. In her eyes, his jest had made him a hero again.

Filled with pride, trailed by the minister's sentimental wife, Adam led his bride to the sitting-room door. Stopping on the threshold, insensible to any curious onlookers, he gazed down at Savannah. "Are you ready, Miss Reed?"

"As long as you're beside me," she told him as she lifted her head high, "I'm ready for anything, Mr. Corwin."

They clasped hands more tightly and headed for the place where the minister waited—ready to tell lies that, if they were very lucky, might eventually come true for them both.

Eyeing his brother with trepidation, Linus Bedell shifted nervously from foot to foot. His damned stolen boots rubbed on his big toes, making his movements hurt. But his toes didn't hurt as much as the rest of him would hurt if things went bad. Ever since riding up to Linus's secret hiding place, Curtis had been getting himself ornerier and ornerier. If Linus knew his brother, that meant somebody was getting smacked pretty soon.

"I *knew* you was holding out on us!" Curtis said as he paced beside his picketed horse. "I *knew* you was up to no good."

"I wasn't. I swear! It ain't like that." Linus waggled his head from side to side as vehemently as he could without shaking it clean off. "All I was doing was watching the telegraph station, waitin' for a chance to sneak in and get that money."

"Yeah. And ride off with it all to your own self, I bet." Curtis's eyes narrowed. "Good thing Roy sent me out here to keep a watch on you." That was how Curtis had happened to spy the lady and the detective leaving the station this morning—and how he'd come to follow them partway on their journey, besides. "Likely *Roy* was suspicious of you, too. He's smart as a whip. He prob'ly knows you're a no-good, selfish liar, clean through."

"Hey. There's no call for gettin' nasty," Linus complained.

"Why not? You done let that telegraph lady 'most heal up that cuss Corwin, nearly all the way! Would it have killed you to creep down there one night and smother him in his sleep or somethin'?" Curtis frowned. "I swear, you're plumb useless."

"I am not. I just don't like the idea of killin', is all."

"Even a baby could smother somebody, Linus." His brother appeared disgusted. "I don't know why Roy puts up with you."

"Probably 'cause *I'm* going to be the one to bring in all that gal's nest-egg money." Driven to the boast by Curtis's insufferable behavior, Linus pointed to the distant station. It hunkered in the valley below the bluff they were on, peaceful and snug. "I've been waitin' on my chance, and now here it is."

"Well, the place is deserted by now for sure, I'd say. Corwin and that woman rode almost all the way into Avalanche. I saw 'em afore I turned around and came back here. They'll be gone awhile—leaving all the more time for us to git our share of that money *and* whatever else we can find, besides."

"The place ain't all the way deserted," Linus pointed out. He nibbled his lip, thinking of that big station helper who scared him. The only reason Linus hadn't yet investigated the station was that that man was still there. "There's a—"

"I wouldn't have minded if that woman *was* here, though. She's a right fine-looking piece of ladyhood." Clearly ignoring Linus in favor of his latest reverie, Curtis gazed into the distance with a hungry expression. "I sure could use me a woman like that sometime. She would treat me real nice, I bet."

Linus couldn't stand it. "She would not. She's fancy. She wouldn't even like you. She's way too good for someone—"

Like you, he meant to say, but Curtis hauled off and smacked him—as usual—cutting off the rest of his words.

Seeing stars, Linus clapped his hand to his stinging jaw. He let loose a yowl of pain, then kicked his brother. His stolen boot made a satisfying clunk as it connected with Curtis's shin.

Curtis hollered. A second later, the two of them were in the dirt, rolling and punching. Linus opened his mouth to swear at his brother. He tasted gritty Arizona Territory dust instead. Worse, he got a big lungful of Curtis's unwashed stink.

"Tarnation, Curtis! Can't you take a bath sometime?"

Another punch. "You shut your mouth, halfwit."

Linus rolled and kicked. "You try and make me."

"I will." Another hard blow to the head. "There."

"Didn't hurt a bit." Dizzily Linus panted. "See?"

He rolled over to his hands and knees, preparing to get to his feet and show Curtis exactly how wimpy his punches were. But an instant later, a big booted foot caught him in the ribs.

Linus collapsed with a helpless *oof* sound. Beside him, Curtis grunted and did the same. That was strange. That was…

A shadow fell over them both. Newly alert, Linus looked up.

His brother Edward stood there with his legs spread apart. Like usual, he appeared ill tempered, mean and tidily dressed.

"Edward." With his eyes wide, Curtis scrambled himself out of boot-kicking range. "How'd you get here so fast?"

"Shut up. You're both pathetic."

Curtis nodded dumbly. Linus only gaped in hushed reverence, afeared to move in case he called unwanted attention to himself. Everybody knew better than to cross Edward Bedell. He was almost as smart as Roy, and he was twice as ruthless, to boot.

Linus's ploy didn't work. Edward kicked him anyway.

"That's for not hearing me ride up here."

"S-sorry, Edward!" Linus cowered. "We was busy."

Curtis got a kick, too. He bared his teeth like a dog.

"There. Now you're both even. And I hear we got ourselves a party in the making." Appearing cheered by the whaling he'd given them, Edward rubbed his palms together. He nodded toward the telegraph station. "I'd say it's about time we got started."

Behind him, the final Bedell brother dismounted from his horse—the one they'd filched from that detective, Corwin. Wynn Bedell moseyed over to stand beside Edward. He spat a brownish stream of tobacco juice in the dirt, rousing a buzzing fly.

Linus couldn't imagine how he'd ignored the sounds of his other brothers approaching. That was just plain idiotic of him. He knew better. Aggravated to have his sweet setup ruined—and seeing his hopes of impressing Roy with getting that nest-egg money fadin' fast—he cast a sour look at Curtis.

"You went all the way to town and told *them*?" he asked.

Curtis shrugged. "I had time. 'Specially riding that fast horse I pinched. 'Sides, I didn't like the way Corwin looked at me on the road to Avalanche, all promisin' revenge or somethin'. I figured I'd better collect me some backup, just in case."

"*I* coulda been your backup!" Wounded by Curtis's lack

of faith in him, Linus made a face. "I ain't so small that I can't git in a lick or two when it's necessary. I swear, Curtis—"

"Shut up, the both of you," Edward said. "I'm thinking."

Instantly they fell silent. Curtis offered a meek nod.

"And what I'm thinking is this: we're going to that station down there," Edward announced, "and we're going to get…whatever the hell we want." He grinned. But his was a cruel smile, too filled with malice to be likable. "Linus, you stay up here and keep watch. Signal us if anybody comes near."

"But there's still somebody down at the station." Anxiously Linus pointed. He shuffled backward, too, just in case his warning irked Edward, who was prone to getting indignant over the smallest thing—like a wrinkled shirt. "That woman's got herself a big colored man for a helper. He's in the station—"

"He'll get what's coming to him. Don't you worry about that." Unconcerned by the notion of an innocent person being present in the place he intended to loot, Edward plucked out his firearm. He checked it, then gave a contented nod and holstered it again. For now. "Nobody stands between me and what I want."

"Well, Roy kinda does," Linus pointed out. "He's the bo—"

His words ended in a wheeze as Edward cuffed him in the head. Linus clutched his skull. He gazed sullenly upward.

"Ain't nobody *my* boss," Edward told him, just like he'd been one of them gypsies reading Linus's mind. "Not even Roy."

All the brothers nodded. Wynn shifted his wad of chaw in his mouth, sending a contemplative look toward the telegraph station. Whenever they had a job to do, Wynn got spookily quiet.

But Linus only got more morose. Especially over what had just happened between him and Curtis, who'd up and tattled on him with no warning at all. And over what had happened between him and Edward, too. His big brother might have given him a chance to help out—to share what tips he'd picked up during all his shrewd watching of the telegraph station over these past few days. That would have been the upright thing to do.

But since Edward hadn't done that, Linus vowed right then and there not to worry no more about his brothers' immortal souls. Not Edward's *or* Curtis's *or* Wynn's *or* Roy's. Instead he'd start worrying about his own soul. Exclusively from now on.

Well, maybe he'd think about Roy's soul, too, Linus amended, feeling guilty about throwing Roy to the devil like that. But only because Roy had been kindest of all to him. And that was it. He was done with watching over the rest of them.

As his three brothers saddled up, Linus made himself think cannily. He watched the others without moving, then waved them off toward the station—just like he would've done if he'd been going to do what Edward asked. Then, the minute that Edward, Curtis, and Wynn rode out of sight, Linus left his watch post.

Defiantly he scurried through the trees and down the hillside, set to warn that big colored man by whatever means his poor bruised noggin could think up. Hopefully by the time he got down to the station he'd be a few steps ahead of his eternally damned brothers and their always-ready guns, to boot.

Chapter Nine

As bad luck would have it, Savannah's wedding was delayed.

Not because someone objected to the ceremony. Not because someone turned up, as Savannah had half feared, and exposed her as a scandalous "Ruthless Reed." Not even because she or her fiancé got cold feet. The reason for the delay was simpler than that. A new member of the minister's congregation arrived on the doorstep with a shout, carrying a whiskey bottle in one hand and a bundle of mining claim paperwork in the other, and announced his intention to find "the sweet love of the Lord"—a task for which he insisted he needed the minister's help right then.

The miner, however, had the misfortune of expressing his eagerness to be saved by waving around his arms in an erratic manner. His gesture earned him a thundering tackle from—of all people—Savannah's civilized, Eastern-bred, mail-order groom.

Caught in a chokehold beneath Adam's elbow, the man

yelped. Confused and surprised, he dropped his whiskey bottle.

It shattered on the anteroom floor, sending liquor fumes into the air. The minister and his wife, their two witnesses, and Savannah all stepped backward, staring in surprise. Savannah blinked, scarcely able to fathom how Adam had moved so quickly.

For a deskbound telegraph operator, he was surprisingly light on his feet—akin to the dancers she'd met and watched perform during her days onstage in New York City…only more dangerous seeming. Roughly, Adam hauled the man to his feet.

"I'm sorry! I surrender!" The miner's bewildered gaze swung around to the minister. He held up his arms in surrender. "I swear, Padre. I didn't know the Almighty was so hard up for followers that He was getting 'em like this! I was comin' here of my own free will, to thank Him for my new mining strike."

"Who sent you?" Adam demanded.

"Nobody!" the man said. "Nobody sent me."

Adam gave the miner a hard jerk. "Try again."

"Well, maybe my lady friend, Lucille, sent me, in a way, I mean," the man blubbered. "She always was on me to mend my ways, God rest her." With panicky eyes, he gazed around the anteroom. His attention lit on the minister with his bible, the pair of wide-eyed witnesses, the minister's wife and then Savannah—with her modest bouquet of wildflowers and fancy dress—in turn. "Oh. I'm sorry, Padre. I seem to be interruptin' something here."

His manner turned unexpectedly contrite, which baffled their entire sextet. Everyone remained silent, unsure what to do in this unusual situation. Adam still appeared fairly murderous, Savannah observed, like he had on the road when meeting the erstwhile Curtis Bedell. She wasn't at all certain what to do, either. She settled on behaving in a way that best befit a reader of the *Guide to Correct Etiquette and Proper Behavior* handbook. Civilly she inclined her head to greet the man.

"That's quite all right," she said. "We hadn't even started yet. Please don't trouble yourself any further, Mr....?"

As a hint, she raised her eyebrows, the way Mose did when reminding her to mend some lapse in propriety. Adam, evidently curious about the man's name as well, gave him another jerk.

"The lady wants an answer," he said.

"H-Haywood." Casting a sidelong glance at Adam, the miner nervously bobbed his head. "It's Mr. Jedediah Haywood, ma'am."

"Well. I'm very pleased to meet you, Mr. Haywood." Savannah gave Adam what she hoped was a subtle hint to release the man. Adam merely frowned at her. "Would you like to attend our wedding? We have plenty of room for one more, I assure you."

Over the man's head, Adam gave a dark scowl. She'd swear his arm tightened against the miner's dirt-smudged neck, too.

"I—I don't think so!" Mr. Haywood said.

Adam nudged him in the ribs. Quickly the miner amended his refusal. "But thank you very kindly all the same, ma'am."

Appearing satisfied by his deferential tone, Adam nodded.

Exasperated, Savannah approached the pair of them. Gently she took hold of Adam's burly arm, then pried it forcibly away.

"I'm so sorry," she told to Mr. Haywood. "My fiancé is a bit riled up today, on account of our impending marriage."

As though in proof of that, Adam scowled more deeply. But he allowed the miner to step free from his grasp— with one further provision. He nodded. "Show me your papers."

With shaky hands, Mr. Haywood held out his papers.

Squinting, Adam examined them. No one else moved. Likely, Savannah reasoned, they feared being assaulted as well. She smiled pointedly at the minister's wife, hoping to convey the message that Adam wasn't usually violent... merely overcautious.

"Fine." With a suspicious glare, Adam gestured for the man to put away his claim forms. "You can stay until we're finished, Mr. Haywood. We won't be long. Just keep away from the lady."

What lady? Savannah expected Mr. Haywood to ask. After all, there were three women present, including herself. But the look that Adam threw her just then—protective, concerned and utterly besotted—drove the query straight out of her mind. Did Adam, she wondered in surprise, actually *love her* already?

He might, she mused. That would certainly explain his peculiar behavior. In her experience, men weren't always the handiest with tender emotions. In general, they were more likely to express themselves awkwardly. Even Mose, the kindest man she knew, was gruff sometimes. Considering Adam with newfound insight, Savannah watched as her fiancé jerkily straightened Mr. Haywood's waistcoat. With a mumbled apology, Adam brushed off his jacket, too, clearly making amends for his brutish behavior.

Savannah smiled at him in approval. Adam brightened.

Sometimes when she looked at him, Savannah reflected, she had the sense that he would have done anything for her. But just then, for the first time, she felt a glimmer of a similar emotion herself. Over the past few days, she'd come to know and understand Adam, in person, and she liked what she'd learned. She admired his bravery and fortitude, and she stood in awe of his willingness to take whatever actions were needed in a given situation...regardless of how foolish they might make him seem.

She did feel protected in his presence. And almost beloved, too. Over time, she knew, Adam would settle in and relax.

Uncomfortably aware of the chary looks the others in their nuptial party gave him, Savannah stepped closer to him. "Well. I feel quite confident that no one else will dare to interrupt us now." Cheerfully she took his arm. "Shall we continue?"

"Woowee!" yelled the miner. "Let's get a wedding on!"

Adam agreed. "My thoughts exactly," he said with a smile.

He looked gratefully to her for standing by him, and his hand, when it clasped hers, seemed to communicate a powerful sense of solidarity between them, too. This was how it would be, it occurred to Savannah. She and Adam, together against the world, united in love and bonded by the camaraderie they'd begun over the wires and through the mail...then enriched over eggs and toast and innumerable walks together around the station.

She was truly blessed, she reckoned. As soon as she had a good opportunity, she intended to acknowledge that blessing by telling Adam the truth about her past. It was the right thing to do. And yet...Savannah still felt reluctant to risk doing so.

What she needed, she decided, was a dose of Adam's courage. By following his good example, she could avoid becoming further enmeshed in the lie she was accidentally creating.

The minister cleared his throat, then opened his bible. "My friends and neighbors," he began. "We are gathered here today to celebrate the union of Savannah Reed and Adam Corwin."

"Yeehaw!" Mr. Haywood hollered, waving his hat.

A few minutes later, Savannah's wedding was well underway—rowdy evangelical miner included. And while it was true that the whole place smelled strongly of whiskey, and there were two near strangers present as well, none of those things mattered as much to Savannah as did the fond way her handsome groom clasped her hand. Or the way he gazed at her as he promised to love and cherish her. Or the way he stood tall beside her, alert and proud and heartwarmingly attentive to the proceedings.

Savannah stood beside Adam with equal attentiveness, savoring every word and detail as she was saved from her past and properly prepared for her future. She did her utmost to remember everything; that was the only way she could properly relay the story to Mose later. And the moment those crucial words were said—*I now pronounce you man and wife*—Savannah felt as though an enormous weight had been lifted from her shoulders.

"Come with me," she told Adam as she took his hand, just moments after they'd settled things with the minister and thanked everyone. "I have the perfect idea for celebrating."

To Adam's chagrin, Savannah's notion of celebrating meant parading through the streets of Avalanche and informing as many passersby as possible that they were wed. Her announcements were typically greeted with polite nods or bemused smiles and no great fanfare, but Savannah didn't appear to expect anything more. To the contrary, she seemed downright giddy with the joy of marriage alone. Nothing could dampen her spirits. Even as they continued down Main Street, past the livery where they'd stabled Chester for the night, she didn't tire.

"Hello!" she called out. "We're Mr. and Mrs. Corwin."

"Howdy." Her sixteenth target tipped his hat, then scurried away, his boot heels ringing against the raised boardwalk.

"Hello!" Savannah said again. "We're Mr. and Mrs. Corwin."

"Hello." The next person smiled. "Welcome to Avalanche."

"Did you hear that?" After the man had passed, Savannah turned her cheery face to Adam. "Did you hear him say 'Welcome to Avalanche'? Isn't that *nice?* That must be the tenth—"

"Or seventeenth," Adam observed more accurately.

"—person we've encountered so far, and not a single one of them has looked askance at us. Not even a little bit." She sighed, then hugged his arm. "I could do this all day long!"

Adam would rather have shoveled horse patties than continue to confront strangers with their marital status. But Savannah appeared to be enjoying herself. For her sake, he stayed where he was. He even nodded in greeting at her next victim.

"Why would anyone look askance at us?" he asked.

Savannah froze. Then shrugged. "They just…might. Because we're strangers here. You know how people can be sometimes."

"No." He guided her onward. "How can they be?"

Adam knew full well. People could be merciless, selfish and devious. His work as a U.S. Marshall and a detective had taught him that—and more. But Savannah appeared uncomfortable with his question for an entirely different reason than the foibles of human nature. It did not require the best of his investigative prowess to deduce that her slip of the tongue had something to do with the secret she was keeping.

"Tell me," he urged. "Whatever it is, you can trust me."

For an instant, Savannah seemed on the verge of doing exactly that. Then she jutted her chin upward. "Unkind, that's how people can be. At least in my experience. But I don't want to talk about it, especially on such a fine day."

With a determination that bordered on doggedness, she fixed her gaze on the next person who headed toward them. "Hello! We're Mr. and Mrs. Corwin." Then she spotted someone else and inclined her head. "Hello! We're Mr. and Mrs. Corwin."

"Pleased to meet you," said a tiny elderly woman.

They were up past twenty exchanges now, but still the woman's response made Savannah beam. It was as though she could not get enough of being greeted and accepted by the townspeople. She hugged Adam's arm, clearly tickled by the proceedings.

"I reckon we could meet 'most everyone in town," Adam said in a dry tone as they walked past a millinery shop, "if we made a couple more circuits up and down Main Street."

"Oh! Do you really think so?"

He'd been joking, but Savannah seemed beyond thrilled. He didn't have the heart to disappoint her. He nodded.

"Excellent." She smiled, then walked onward with new vigor.

"Hello!" she said to the next Avalanche resident they met as they approached a newly erected mercantile. "We're Mr.

and Mrs. Corwin. We're visiting town today from Morrow Creek."

The shopkeeper looked up from his broom, which he'd been using to sweep up sawdust—likely a remnant of his shop's recent construction. "Nice place, Morrow Creek. My sister lives there."

At that, Savannah stopped to chat and would not be budged.

Beside her, Adam did his best to keep up with the conversation. Mostly, though, he kept up a lookout for the Bedell brothers, the same way he'd done since he and Savannah had set out on their wedding trip. At any moment, one of those thieving killers could emerge from behind a saloon or thunder down the dusty street on horseback and turn Savannah's day of celebration into a tragedy. More than most people, Adam knew what the Bedells were capable of…and none of it was good.

Not for the first time, he hoped Mariana was safe. He hoped she was working a case far from the Arizona Territory, with a new partner to watch over her. Maybe when Adam was in town with Savannah for Mrs. Finney's tea party, he considered, he could make inquiries about Mariana. Or even wire the agency himself.

He hadn't done so until now, for fear of alerting Savannah or Mose to his true identity. There'd simply been no way to send a message without revealing who he was and why he was there. But if he found himself in town, he could probably do more.

Like track the Bedells and finally bring them to justice.

Newly galvanized by the thought, Adam sent his gaze along the mountainous ridges that made up Avalanche. There were rocky gullies and hiding places everywhere here. Boulders provided good cover for gunfights. Twisting uphill roads offered perfect ambush spots. Improvidentially, Savannah had chosen one of the worst possible places for their wedding. It would be all too easy for Bedell and his brothers to get to them here.

Adam wished he'd been equipped to take Curtis Bedell into custody when he'd met him on the road. But with Savannah beside him, he hadn't dared risk it. If she'd been hurt in a showdown with Curtis, Adam wouldn't have been able to forgive himself. Just the thought of explaining to that gentle giant, Mose, how he'd allowed Savannah to be injured gave Adam chills.

So did the thought of Curtis Bedell forcing a confrontation between them. The eventuality felt all too likely. None of the Bedell brothers were known for being patient.

"I think we'd better get along." Gently, Adam touched Savannah's arm, drawing her from her conversation with the friendly shopkeeper. "You must be hungry by now."

"Oh, no, I'm fine." She smiled. "Mr. Yee was just saying—"

"I'm feeling a bit peckish, myself," Adam pretended to confess. A glimmer of light and motion caught his eye at the looming rock face to his left. He watched it with one hand on his gun—but it was only an Avalanche resident, hanging laundry on a makeshift line. "We had those sandwiches a while ago."

"You're absolutely right." Hastily Savannah made her apologies to Mr. Yee. "Why don't we go on to the hotel? I'm given to understand they have a wonderful dining room there."

Just as he'd expected, what Savannah would not do for herself, she would do for someone else…chiefly, him. She was, he'd learned during his time with her, generous to a fault.

Feeling sorry for having misled her—but not sorry for

doing what he had to do to get her safely indoors—Adam took special care in escorting her. They chatted amiably as they proceeded to the nearby Beadle Hotel. The place catered mostly to visiting mining magnates, he learned from an overheard conversation as they approached, and had the gaudy decor to match.

Surprisingly Savannah adored it.

"Look!" She clutched his arm as they stepped into the lobby, her entire face glowing and awestruck. "It's beautiful!"

He vowed on the spot to get them a room there.

Savannah smiled. "I feel *so* at home here, for some reason."

Even as he wondered why a rural telegraph operator would feel most comfortable amongst gilt and velvet and imported statuary, Adam decided he should probably book *two* rooms. He still had an adequate bankroll hidden in the hollow cache in his boot—a precaution he'd taken since his days as a Marshall. If the lobby made Savannah this pleased, then sleeping under the ornate ceilings, fine mill-work and fancy bedsteads the hotel undoubtedly sported upstairs would send her clear over the moon.

"It's almost like one of those fancy theaters," she said. "Only from the *front* of the house, where everything is lovely."

Adam's days of working in vaudeville jabbed at him. *Front of the house* was a term used by show folk. "You like it?"

Savannah turned in place, marveling. "Oh, very much so!"

"Then we'll have to stay here tonight."

"Here?" She stared at him. "But I only came here to dine. I'd expected to sleep in the wagon. That's why I brought so many blankets. I thought if we were feeling *very* extravagant," she admitted with an adorable wrinkle of her nose, "we might find a room in one of the boardinghouses nearby. Avalanche abounds with them, you know, because of the large population of bachelors."

"I'll have no wife of mine staying in a place that caters to riffraff like bachelors," Adam teased. "We'll stay here."

For the first time, his joke drew no laughter.

"Hmm." Savannah mused. "I *do* like the sound of that…"

"What, staying near riffraff? That's a predilection you should have shared with me before we were married," Adam said, still teasing her. "If I'd known you craved the company of bachelors, I would have—"

"No. *Wife*," she breathed. "*Your* wife. I like that."

In that moment, time seemed to stand still between them. There with Savannah beneath the lobby's crystal chandelier, Adam realized to his surprise that *he* liked that, too.

He'd actually done it, he realized with a sense of awe.

He'd gotten married.

Of course their marriage wasn't official yet, he amended to himself with a frown. If he had his way, it never would be. Adam did not intend to consummate their union—nor did he intend to deliver the signed marriage license that the minister had entrusted him with to the proper authorities for certification.

That way, their marriage would never be registered or valid. It was the only means he'd struck upon to protect Savannah from the fraudulent partnership they'd entered into. So long as Adam kept from making their marriage official, Savannah would be free to walk away from it later… unblemished and, he hoped, forgiving of everything that had happened between them.

It wasn't the most brilliant solution, but it was the best he'd come up with. It would have to do.

"I did allocate a small amount of money from my nest egg toward buying us a nice wedding-day meal." Beside him, Savannah lifted her reticule in demonstration. "So I hope you're hungry!"

"I could eat a horse, tail and all."

A smile. "Then we must get started. Shall we?"

With no hesitation or awkwardness at all, Savannah sashayed toward the hotel's fine dining room. As she passed by the lobby desk and its attendant snobbish clerk, her assured movements left Adam wondering all over again. Why was a small-town woman like Savannah so comfortable with the fanciness of the Beadle Hotel? Why had she bandied about a show term like *front of the house?* And why, even more curiously, had she seemed to expect the people of Avalanche to shun her today?

Unkind, that's how people can be, she'd said, appearing indescribably sad. *At least in my experience.*

More curious than ever to know what she was hiding, Adam stayed beside Savannah as they entered the dining room. He kept his hand protectively on her waist, guiding her with care and interest. If anyone could unearth her secrets, he reckoned it was him. But would he have enough time to do so?

More than anything, Adam yearned to believe the ruse they were presenting. He yearned to introduce Savannah as his wife and know it was true. He wanted to hold her hand and care for her and prove that he'd *meant* the vows he'd taken today. He did intend to love and cherish her. Promising that had been easy.

Savannah made it easy. She was lovable and kind, funny and capable and self-sufficient. If Adam had been the sort of man to daydream himself a perfect wife, Savannah would have fit the ideal he'd imagined. Even more so, had she known the truth about him. Adam had the sense that

Savannah admired his work for the Marshall's office and understood his other varied jobs as well. Savannah would have probably approved of his detective work, too. She might even, with her inherent love of adventure, have been interested in hearing about the cases he'd worked on.

He'd only ever shared those stories with Mariana—and she'd been a less-than-avid listener, owing to her own involvement in several of those cases. But his platonic work-aday friendship with Mariana was nothing like the growing affection that had arisen between him and Savannah. Adam felt drawn to Savannah in a way he'd never experienced before and likely, he realized as the maître d' approached them, would never experience again.

Determined to soak up as much of this day as he could, he smiled. "I'm looking forward to this meal. I don't often dine in restaurants—mostly beside campfires and the like."

"Campfires?" Wrinkling her brow, Savannah gazed up at him. "But in your letters, you told me you were a connoisseur of the restaurants in Baltimore. You mentioned several by name."

Blast. Adam opened his mouth, hastily searching his mind for an excuse. He was adequate enough at concocting a cover story—something that was a necessity in his line of work—but here, with Savannah, he found himself slipping up far too often.

It was almost as though he *wanted* to be found out in the accidental lie he'd engaged in. But more than that, Adam figured, he was simply suffering from a lack of information. And it was costing him now. Although he and Mariana had had access to Savannah's letters to her romantic "pen pal," they had not been able to read Roy Bedell's private correspondence to her. Nor had they been privy to all the conversations that Savannah and Roy Bedell had shared over the wires these last few months.

All they knew was that Edward Bedell had taken a job as a telegraph operator in Des Moines some time ago, and that Roy had intimidated the other operators into letting him loiter about the station while his brother worked. Eventually they'd robbed the place, of course, with the help of Curtis, Wyatt and Linus. But they hadn't made away with enough money to make Roy abandon his lucrative marriage schemes. Despite Edward's efforts to move the gang into other, more easily divisible "opportunities" for thieving, Roy Bedell had targeted Savannah next…and all the way across the country, Adam had been hired to stop him.

"It's all right. There's no need to appear so worried. I won't spill your secret." Laughing, Savannah linked her arm in Adam's. She nodded to the maître d' as he led them to a fine, cloth-covered table. "I quite liked the impressed look he gave you as he approached us and overheard your Wild West tale about campfire dining. That was very inventive of you."

She thought he was embellishing his past in an effort to appear suitably rugged, as befit life in the Territory, Adam realized. Well, for now it was best to let her believe that.

"Yep," he said loudly, so the maître d' would hear him. "There's nothing like a good elk steak thrown over the fire. Especially if you wrestle the critter to the ground first."

"I hear that makes for extra-tender meat." Savannah gave a sage nod, speaking at an equally noticeable volume.

"That's right," Adam agreed. "A good sockdolager to the nose, and the elk just gives up and begs to become your dinner."

"I hope the food is just as tasty as that around here." Wearing a skeptical expression, Savannah gracefully took her seat. "Otherwise, I'll be depending on you to go elk wrestling."

"I'm hardly dressed for that, am I?" Stifling a grin, Adam pointed to his wedding-day suit as he, too, took a seat. He felt ridiculously grateful to Savannah for indulging his supposed flight of fancy. "I'd need different boots, at least."

Savannah pretended to examine him. "Yes. And maybe a hat."

United in mischief, they gazed across the table at each other. The maître d' stiffly signaled for a waiter, who scurried over and began outfitting them for their meal with napkins and cutlery and goblets of water. The waiter's and maître d's attitudes of hushed reverence only seemed to make Adam's and Savannah's shared joke even funnier.

"Is a black bowler hat good for elk wrestling?" Adam asked Savannah with his most thoughtful expression. "Or do you think a flat felt cap would be more appropriate?"

"Oh, I'm not entirely sure…" She pretended to vacillate.

Apparently seizing upon an area in which he could offer additional service, the maître d' gave a discreet cough. Adam glanced up at him. The man leaned his head nearer.

"I would suggest a Winchester rifle and a wool derby, sir."

Solemnly Adam pretended to consider it. "Very good. I'll bear that in mind." He could not look at Savannah, for fear of bursting into laughter. Straight-faced, he said, "Thank you."

"You, sir, are most welcome." The maître d' bowed.

He made ready to leave, as did the waiter. Adam waited for their departure with his breath held, knowing that the slightest movement might make him laugh. But then Savannah raised her fingertips in a genteel signal. She nodded at the maître d'.

"I will require my meal to be freshly wrestled, just as my husband would obtain it," she specified in an amicable tone. "I trust that will be possible in your establishment?"

Another, somewhat stilted, bow. "I will make inquiries."

"Very good. Once a lady is accustomed to life with a hard-driving, *truly W*estern man, it's extremely difficult to settle for less," Savannah said, chin high. "I'm sure you understand."

"Indeed, madam." The maître d' nodded. "I certainly do."

Both men left—and just in time, too. Marveling at Savannah's audacity, Adam took her hand across the table. He couldn't help laughing. "Thank you for playing along. That clinched it—if I didn't love you already, I would definitely love you now."

The words slipped easily from his mouth, surprising even him. But the sentiment he'd accidentally confessed was no less true, Adam realized. In so many ways, Savannah was the ideal partner for him—compassionate, clever *and* playful.

The fact of the matter was, he'd become jaded in his line of work. He'd dealt with bad people for so long that he'd started believing they made up the whole world. With her good example, Savannah had restored his faith in the goodness of people—no small feat, given the depth of his cynicism.

"Right now," Adam continued with complete honesty as he tightened his grasp on her hand, then lifted his gaze to hers, "I feel very, very lucky to be here with you."

"And I feel lucky to be here with you," Savannah

said—exactly as coolly as she might have confirmed a shared affection for green beans. She picked up her menu, then raised her eyebrows at him. "Now then. What shall we eat?"

Chapter Ten

By the time the night grew late enough for Savannah to accompany Adam upstairs to the pair of rooms he'd booked them for the night, she'd forgotten most of the details about the delicious food and drink she'd shared with him...but she hadn't forgotten what Adam had said just before they'd had dinner.

If I didn't love you already, I would definitely love you now.

Savannah still could not believe she'd actually replied to that statement by asking Adam what he wanted for dinner! His had been such a momentous declaration...and she had answered it by inquiring about the state of his appetite. For the tenth time that evening, Savannah wanted to kick herself. She'd *longed* for someone to care about her. And now that someone did...

Well, to put it frankly, she feared she'd ruined it. The plain fact was, Adam had caught her unprepared. She'd been so busy poking fun at the notion of hand-wrestled elk steaks that she hadn't been thinking about the wedding day they'd shared or the importance her mail-order groom might have attached to it.

If I didn't love you already, I would definitely love you now.

Thrilled by the memory of his gruff assertion all the same, Savannah smiled at Adam. But her new husband merely cast her a vaguely morose look—the same look he'd worn for at least five minutes now, ever since they'd left the dining room, crossed the lobby and started ascending the stairs to their private rooms.

Worried, Savannah bit her lip. The fancy staircase underfoot might have disappeared, for as much notice as she paid it. The richly colored carpet runner, shimmering chandeliers, dark paneled walls and all the rest... Everything faded from view as Savannah took stock of her new husband's tight jaw, grim eyes and squared-off shoulders. He appeared so resigned and miserable, he might as well have been going to the gallows.

Clearly she'd hurt his feelings, Savannah thought. The realization made her heart ache as well. Adam had been so good and fine and upstanding today. He'd come all the way west to marry her and start a new life together. And how had she repaid him? By opening a menu and offering a silly query about food!

Well, she would simply have to make it up to him, she vowed as they rounded the landing and ascended the staircase leading to their second-floor accommodations. She would have to cheer him up first, and then she would have to make amends somehow.

The first part would be easy. The second... Well, the second she'd deal with when the time arose.

After all, it was of paramount importance that she and Adam not be at odds with each other, especially tonight of all nights. She knew from gossiping with the other dancers and stage performers in New York City that a wedding night positively foretold *everything* about a marriage—its compatibility, potential happiness and longevity…even its fruitfulness.

Savannah wanted her marriage to be fruitful. She knew that *fruitful* meant children, and she hoped that she and Adam were blessed with many. But if her friends from her old life had been correct in their whispered confidences, if she did not begin her marriage happily, she and Adam would be doomed for certain.

Another glance at his glum expression settled the matter once and for all. She couldn't allow this to continue. Even if it *weren't* proven bad luck to begin a marriage discontentedly, she would have wanted Adam to be as joyful about their union as she was. To that end, when they reached the door to their room, Savannah turned to Adam. With a nonchalant, wifely gesture, she straightened his suit coat lapels, then let her hands linger.

"*That* was a most delicious meal, wasn't it?" Coquettishly she fluttered her eyelashes—the better to hide the sleight of hand she performed—then gave his suit coat another pat. She glanced up with elaborate innocence. "Do you have the key?"

Adam patted his coat pocket. "Yes, I do. It's right—"

"Yes?" She raised her eyebrows in overt innocence.

A frown. "It was right here a minute ago. I'd swear I—"

"Maybe you didn't put it in your pocket. Maybe it's somewhere else. In your boot, perhaps?"

He automatically bent to look, just as she'd known he would, giving her the chance to execute the second part of her secret maneuver. Deftly she palmed the key, which she'd plucked from him during her eyelash fluttering and coat patting.

Once upon a time, this routine had been a part of the Reed family onstage act. It, like the boot joke that went with it, had always been a crowd pleaser. But tonight, to Savannah's distress, her efforts didn't draw so much as a ghost of a smile. To the contrary, Adam appeared just as somber as ever.

"My boot? No, I'm sure I put it in my coat." He juggled the satchel he'd had retrieved from their wagon, then checked his pocket again. "Maybe it fell out on the way upstairs."

He frowned down at the carpet runner, appearing even more dismayed than he had a second ago. Savannah felt her heart turn over. It was a good thing she knew how to cheer him up.

"Oh! I think I see it." She lifted onto her tiptoes.

Adam stopped, his gaze following hers. "Where? In my hair?"

"No. In your *ear*." Savannah flexed her fingers in the same practiced move she'd used with the lost little girl on the train depot platform. Grinning, she waved the key. "Got it. See?"

Adam clapped his hand to his ear—the way everyone always did—staring at her in amazement. "How did you do that?"

"A good magician never shares her secrets."

His smile looked dazzling. "You can tell *me*."

"No, sir." Savannah took her time looking over Adam's broad-shouldered form, his capable hands, and his now-smiling face. She felt as though she'd accomplished a minor miracle by erasing his gloomy expression. That pleased her enormously. "I'm afraid I can't even tell you. But it's entirely possible that I *won't* be able to keep my secrets—" here she broke off, allowing a devilish smile to sneak onto her face "—if confronted with a little bit of…shall we say… *persuasion?*"

Adam gazed down at her, his hands on his hips. "Are you *daring* me to extract your magician's secrets from you?"

"That depends." Savannah twirled the key, a delicious sense of anticipation coming to life inside her. She didn't know where she found the gumption to be so daring…except for those words she kept remembering. *If I didn't love you already, I would definitely love you now.* Yes, those words emboldened her beyond all measure. "Are you interested in doing such a thing?"

"I hadn't planned to," Adam said. "I'd secured two rooms for us, in case you were feeling tired after the long day—"

"I am feeling," Savannah assured him, "wide-awake."

Still, Adam persisted. "If you'd rather take that key and go to bed early, you're certainly welcome to—"

"Wide," Savannah repeated, "awake."

She stepped boldly nearer, until their bodies almost touched, swaying with a mixture of eagerness and nervousness and wild bravado. Feeling more alive than she had in years, she put her hand to Adam's shirtfront, then trailed her fingers lower.

"So if *you* would rather take this key," she told him, "and hold it in your hand while you give me a proper wedding-day kiss, then you're certainly welcome to do exac—"

As she'd hoped, his kiss cut off her words. With a low moan, Adam lowered his mouth to hers, then cradled her jaw in his hand. The hotel key dropped to the floor with a muted *ping*, its descent scarcely noticed as their kiss went on and on.

Breathless and dizzy, Savannah twisted her fingers in Adam's shirtfront, then kissed him back with all her might.

The union between them felt *wonderful*. And it felt right. Arching higher, she pressed herself wholeheartedly against him, sending them both crashing against their hotel room's closed door.

The wood rattled beneath the impact, but Adam simply dropped her satchel and raised his other hand to her face, holding her still for his next slow, soft, heart-poundingly intense exploration of her mouth.

Savannah's lips tingled. Her breath escaped her in a surprised flutter. Adam angled his head to the side and kissed her again. Still holding her in his arms, he smiled.

"Open your mouth a little." He nudged her lower lip with his thumb, coaxing her. "That's it. That's...perfect."

Obliging him, Savannah felt as though she'd achieved an astounding feat. An instant later, Adam pulled her close once more, lowered his head, then swept his tongue inside her mouth.

Startled, she jerked backward. *This* was not something the ladies backstage had warned her about. Still reeling from the surprise of it, Savannah put her hand to her lips.

She gazed at Adam. He appeared concerned.

"I'm sorry," he said. "I should have held myself in check."

He turned away from her, then retrieved the room key and thrust it in the lock with a savage jab. He turned the knob.

The door swung wide, revealing a dim hotel room lighted by the glow of the hallway's chandelier and wall sconces. He gestured for her to precede him inside—probably for the night.

Feeling disappointed, Savannah held her ground. "No, you were wonderful! This is my fault. I don't like surprises," she explained hastily. "Just ask Mose! I do whatever I can to plan for every possible eventuality. But that kiss—"

"Was not what you wanted. I understand." Adam took out the key to their second room, then fisted it. "I'll be right next door. Don't hesitate to call on me if you need *anything*."

He didn't understand. She hadn't *disliked* that kiss. She simply hadn't been ready for it. She knew she could do better, now that she'd been forewarned and knew what to expect.

Dismayed, Savannah watched as Adam opened the adjacent hotel room door. He set her satchel inside, then paused in the doorway. Clearly he had no intention of reentering the room he'd designated as hers. He tipped his hat. "Good night."

Again he gestured for her to take her place in her own room. Not sure what else to do, she did. She spent a few minutes fiddling with the oil lamp on the bureau, listening to the sounds of Adam settling into his own room. Something clanked. The bedsprings creaked. She imagined him sitting on the bed, all alone, while his new wife paced at a loose end next door.

Well. That was plumb ridiculous. They shouldn't be apart!

An instant later, Savannah marched purposefully to Adam's room. She gave a sharp rap. He opened the door immediately. His hair stood partway on end, as though he'd been tugging on it.

At the sight of his familiar face and rumpled locks, Savannah felt something inside her give way. Her whole heart seemed to expand in that moment, enlarging to make room for her newfound feelings. She smiled then, and Adam's expression eased.

"I find I *do* need something," she said firmly.

"What do you need?" He grasped the doorjamb, leaning partly outside—the better to scour the hallway with an intent look. "What's the matter? Did you see someone? Is your room not—"

"I need *you*," Savannah said, "and I won't settle for less."

With all the determination and unshakable assurance she usually displayed, Savannah strolled into Adam's room as though she owned the place. Swearing under his breath, Adam watched her. He'd thought he was free for the night. He'd thought he'd gotten Savannah safely stowed next door. But now she was *here*, tempting him again, and her unexpected arrival left him feeling nearly at the limits of his resistance.

He'd tried his best to keep a safe and platonic distance between them tonight. He'd done all he could to keep his vow not to make their marriage real—for her sake. Even on the way upstairs, he'd forced himself to take every step with a strict reminder that he could *not* take liberties with Savannah. Doing so would not be fair to her.

The effort required to do so had taxed him. So had the apologetic, worried looks that Savannah had kept casting him. He'd known he was disappointing her, so he'd tried to brighten his mood…but that had only led to kissing her. Kissing her and holding her and, ultimately, pushing her too far.

Remembering the startled way she'd pulled back from him was an effective damper now, even as Adam lifted his gaze from the seductive side-to-side swoosh her skirts made as she moved.

"You need me?" he repeated, deliberately misunderstanding her. There was always a chance she'd meant her remark to be innocuous. *I need you, and I won't settle for less.*

"Well, we're married now," Adam went on, "so you've

got me." He smiled. "Forever. Or at least as long as you want me."

"Those are the same things. I'll *always* want you."

So she said now, Adam reminded himself amid a surge of regret…when she didn't yet know the truth.

Uncomfortably he edged toward the room's bureau, looking for some busywork to occupy himself with. He needed something more innocent than contemplating how lovely Savannah looked in her best dress, how appealing she seemed as she stood there puckishly watching him, and how much he wanted to pull her in his arms again and kiss her into downright insensibility.

Deliberately he crossed his arms and examined the hotel room. The place was about as ornately decorated as he'd expected. His room boasted flocked wallpaper, an elaborate four-poster mahogany bedstead and velvet curtains to grace the single window overlooking the starlit hills and valleys of the small town below. His gaze lit on the filled water carafe.

He lifted it. "Would you like a glass of water?"

Appearing lost in thought, Savannah shook her head. "No."

Hastily Adam thought harder. "A chair? You don't have to stroll around in here." *Especially given the graceful, alluring way you're doing so.* "I'm sure the settee is very comfortable."

Mentioning it was a mistake, though. Suddenly all he could think about was lowering Savannah onto that settee and kissing her. Unfastening her gown's tiny buttons, revealing her smooth skin, making himself better acquainted with all her tantalizing curves.

Oblivious to his imaginings—and still seeming lost in thought—Savannah spared the cushioned seat a glance. "No."

"A blanket, then? A wrap? Are you cold?"

"No." Shaking her head, Savannah moved to the bedstead. She trailed her fingertips over its fancy quilted coverlet, then sat on the plump mattress. She gave an experimental bounce.

A delighted smile crossed her face.

Adam nearly groaned aloud. Savannah could not possibly know the kinds of notions such a move put in a man's head. She was an innocent—no matter what secrets she might be hiding. Still, her energetic bouncing called to mind something entirely *wicked* to him. He felt hard-pressed to stop staring as she bounced a little more vigorously, making her bosom jiggle enticingly.

Somehow, he made himself look away. "I'm sorry I don't have more entertainment to offer," he said awkwardly. "If I could offer you a book to read, or some other diversion, I would—"

"That won't be necessary." Savannah slid off the bed, the whisper of her skirts against the coverlet sounding loud in the stillness. She fixed him with an alluring, boldly challenging gaze. "As I said, all I need is you. Especially tonight."

Her words were as close to an outright invitation as any decent man could expect to receive from a respectable woman. If Adam had entertained any doubts about her intentions, the look she cast him next would have laid them to rest for certain.

Savannah wanted to be with him, Adam realized with a fresh jolt of eagerness. She wanted him. But *he* would have to resist her. It was the only responsible thing to do.

Desperately he gestured at the window, still hoping to find a suitable diversion. He felt, somehow, that he should have earned a medal for being capable of rational thought at all, given how preoccupied he was with Savannah's nearness. Her softness. Her warmth and charm and overall allure.

"The view is nice," he managed to say.

"Indeed, it is," Savannah said. "I heartily approve."

But she wasn't looking outside at the nighttime view of Avalanche, Adam noticed. She was looking, instead, directly at *him*. She was looking at him, in fact, the same way a hungry kitten might have viewed a bowl of cream. Intently. Curiously. And with a clear sense of anticipation.

Adam didn't know where that anticipation came from, since he was sure Savannah was inexperienced in carnal matters. Only *he* truly understood the togetherness he wanted them to share. But he also understood desire when he saw it…and seeing it reflected in Savannah's gaze made him quiver in his boots.

"I'll get you a glass of water," he blurted.

But Savannah stopped him before he'd so much as lifted the carafe. "Thank you, but I'd rather…try kissing again."

Adam frowned, knowing he must have misheard her.

"Especially that *other* kind of kissing," she specified.

She sounded breathless. Adam felt that way—deprived of breath and sensible thought alike. How had he gotten in this fix? "You should go back to your room," he said roughly.

Otherwise, I might find myself unable to resist you at all.

"Kissing *you* again," she specified, as though his frown owed itself to some romantic confusion—and as though he hadn't just mentioned her leaving. "Kissing you in that special way."

That special way. Kissing Savannah *had* been special. Adam remembered the breathy sound she'd made when he'd pulled her nearer. He recalled the inexpert but endearing way she'd returned his kisses. He thought about those few moments of intimate contact as she'd opened her mouth beneath his and allowed him entry.

"I'd like that, too," he said in a husky tone. Frowning, he cleared his throat. "But the night is getting late."

It required all the discipline he possessed to put his hand to Savannah's back and usher her to the hotel room door.

Her perplexed expression didn't help matters. Neither did the stubborn way she slapped her palm on the door, then confronted him with a wide-eyed look. "But… Don't you *want* to kiss me again? Was I so terrible at it that you—"

"No." Anguished, Adam closed his eyes. "Don't say that."

"—didn't enjoy it? Because with practice, I'm sure I can improve." Savannah set her chin, giving him a direct look. "I can be very diligent when I set my mind to something."

Something like…driving you witless with desire, Adam heard—but only in his own mind. Because that's exactly what Savannah seemed to have set her mind to accomplishing tonight. This wedding night was going to be the death of him. He would expire, surely as sunrise, from unmet desire.

"I have *no* doubt you can be diligent." He opened his eyes on an unforgettable view of Savannah's vivacious face, golden hair and downturned mouth. He longed to curve her lips in a smile…to hear her sigh in his arms again. "I'm trying to do the right thing. I promise I am. But I'm only a man. I can't—"

"Of course you can." Unexpectedly Savannah smiled. "If you're concerned about your injuries… Well, I'm sure that whatever you can manage in your condition will be just fine. The important thing is that we begin our marriage correctly. And passionately." Her cheeks colored pink. "You're well enough for that, aren't you? You've seemed quite strong all day today."

She thought he was hesitant to kiss her because of his hurt ribs, sore head and gunshot wound? But Adam had been healing quickly. Besides, over the years he'd been involved in many confrontations like the one with Roy Bedell—usually with more providential results, but all the same… He felt fine now.

If being tortured by wanting Savannah—and not having her—could be counted as *fine*.

"I'm very strong," he said. "That's not the problem."

"Then what is?" Savannah wrinkled her nose. The lamplight danced across her features, making her appear both impish and alluring. "Is it the way I pulled away from you before? Because when things don't go exactly right the first time, that's just another reason to try again, isn't it? Here. Hold still."

Daringly she raised herself and pressed her mouth to his. Caught by surprise, Adam stood as immobile as a board while the flowery fragrance of her soap washed over him. Helplessly he savored the soft flutter of her hands against his chest. He imagined all the other places that Savannah might touch him—with that same gentleness and care with which she did everything.

At the thought of it alone, Adam groaned.

"Oh! I've done it again. I've hurt you, haven't I?" Looking aggrieved, Savannah put her hands to the sides of his face. Keenly she examined him. "I'm terribly sorry. I don't know how I keep making a hash of things this way, but I apologize immensely. Honestly, I do. I hope you'll forgive me. Please."

Paradoxically it was her use of such politeness that finally broke him. Savannah's overt civility was so like *her*, such a part of every good thing he associated with her, that Adam couldn't bear it any longer. He had to give in.

"You could only hurt me by staying away." He raised his

hand to hers, then clasped her fingers in his. Surrendering at last, he gazed into her eyes—undoubtedly wearing an expression as sappy as his feelings. "All *I* want is *you*, Mrs. Corwin. Now and forever."

And even though that couldn't be—even though they could never have *now and forever* between them—it pleased him to admit the truth to her. He'd think about the rest later.

"Oh." She blushed prettily. "That's very romantic. Thank you very, very much. But now that we're married, you simply *must* call me—"

"Yes?" Breath held in anticipation, Adam waited. Would this be the moment that Savannah trusted him completely?

"—Savannah. Please call me Savannah."

It was. Humbled and awed, Adam felt his fingers shake as he went on holding her hand. To cover his lapse in self-control, he squeezed her hand more assuredly. "I will. Thank you."

"But you look so solemn!" She laughed, then nudged him in his flat midsection. "Go on. Let me hear you say it."

Despite her laughter and her urgings, Savannah appeared almost as grave as he felt. She *was* trusting him, Adam realized. She was trusting him absolutely, with her well-being and her heart alike. That made his situation all the more precarious…*and* all the more irresistible.

Buoyed by her trust, he smiled. "Very well… Savannah."

She gave a girlish squeal of approval. "Well done!"

"Savannah," Adam repeated in a hoarse tone. Her mouth tempted him, so he simply gave in and kissed her. "Savannah."

She sighed with satisfaction, so he kissed her again.

"Savannah," he said, enjoying the sound and intimacy of her name on his lips. "Savannah, Savannah, Savannah…"

Before he fully realized it, Adam had drawn her into his arms again. He punctuated each breathy repetition of her name with another kiss, feeling his whole body lean toward hers with increasing urgency. He wanted her, now more than ever.

But he had to resist. He had to resist…for a reason he couldn't quite recall. Not while he had Savannah in his arms, warm and curvy and smiling up at him with an adorably contented expression. She had no idea, it occurred to him with roguish insight, exactly how contented she *might* be feeling, very soon…if he had his way. He knew he could make her feel good.

"Just to be clear." She blinked up at him as though to reorder her thoughts, then glanced away with a demure expression. "Now that we're finally married, I—" She broke off, fiddling with his coat buttons with trembling fingers. "I want you to know, I'm fully prepared for whatever happens between us tonight."

"You are?" Lightly he stroked her cheek. "Are you sure?"

She nodded, sending his imagination spiraling. There were all sorts of *happenings* they might share, both on the big four-poster bed behind them and beyond. Adam's body tautened with anticipation. His muscles flexed in readiness. He would be gentle with her. Very gentle. And considerate and passionate…

"I promise I won't get skittish again, like I did before," Savannah vowed, her gaze earnest on his. "I assure you that I'm more than ready to accept whatever you have to offer me."

He had everything to offer her. *Everything.* If only he

could allow her to take it. If only doing so wouldn't be a violation of the same trust she'd just given him. If only...

If only her sincere admission hadn't touched him in a way he'd thought he'd become fully hardened against. But it had. He *needed* her faith in him, Adam found, almost as much as he needed her. Savannah had become as essential to him as water or air.

With a fond smile, he drew back—the better to drink in the sight of her...and remember her. For later. "All I have to offer is myself," he confessed. Then something else occurred to him. He gestured around the room. "Well, that, plus a glass of water, a seat on the settee, a view of the town outside our window—"

"Why, Adam!" Smiling just as fondly, Savannah shook her head. "Don't you know? This situation *definitely* doesn't call for such formality between us. If you're going to be a real Wild West hero, you simply *must* learn what's appropriate."

"Ah." At her joke, his heart lightened. He arched his brow. "And what is appropriate in this situation, then?"

"For me to tell you that *I* only have love to offer you," she said. "Well, that, and my nest egg of savings to share."

At her mention of it, Adam sharpened his gaze. Until today, outside the hotel dining room, she'd never confirmed the money she supposedly had secreted away. Of course Savannah had mentioned that money in her letters to Roy Bedell, he knew, but only in passing—only enough to spark Roy's thieving interest.

Reminded of the Bedell brothers and all the trouble Savannah was in, Adam frowned anew. With Curtis Bedell so clearly on their trail, time might be running out for them.

Already the gang had been more patient than any thinking person had cause to expect, given the Bedells' notorious history. Surely they wouldn't wait much longer to make their move.

But now, tonight, there was nothing Adam could do about that. Nothing except wait and wonder…and try to keep watch over Savannah. Deliberately, he shoved away his worries, then smiled as Savannah kept talking.

"And that if that's enough for you," she went on, "then I'd say the two of us are luckier than most people ever get to be."

"Well, now that's true." He held her in his arms again "Love is more than enough for me." *If only I could keep it…*

Savannah nestled comfortably against him. "Excellent."

At the emphatic way she said it, Adam smiled more broadly. The vigor with which Savannah approached life never failed to astonish him. Neither did her openness and enthusiasm for the physical aspects of marriage. He hadn't expected that, but he felt delighted by it, all the same.

"Are you sure about more kissing?" he asked her.

A nod. "Yes. But we might have to take things slowly."

"I promise we will," Adam assured her. "But first, now that we've settled that, I find myself wanting to know." He lifted his head to give her a rakish, unswerving look, akin to the one she'd offered earlier in the hallway. "Are you finally ready to reveal your secret?"

Chapter Eleven

"My secret?" Feeling her heartbeat quicken, Savannah gaped up at Adam. He didn't mean—*he couldn't mean*—her past. Could he?

"Yes. Your magician's secret. From earlier tonight." Adam mimicked the showy maneuver she'd used to pluck the key from his ear. "Remember? You said you might be persuaded to share it."

She nearly sagged with relief. "Oh! *That* secret."

His expression appeared quizzical. And handsome. And altogether irresistible. No wonder she'd allowed herself to be caught off guard by his inquiry. She hadn't been thinking straight since their rendezvous in the hall. Perhaps earlier.

"What other secret are you keeping?" Adam asked.

I have a disgraceful past and a disreputable name, Savannah thought. But she couldn't tell him that. Now was not the right time. Not when they'd been getting on so well. Not when they'd been on the brink of some wonderful discoveries together.

"Why don't you come closer and find out?" With her

most flirtatious look, Savannah beckoned him nearer. "After all, it's our wedding night. I have a feeling we'll be learning all sorts of secrets about each other soon."

Adam blanched. His odd reaction stopped her where she stood. Curiously Savannah scrutinized him. Were there things *Adam* didn't want to share with her? Did he have secrets, too?

She wondered what they could be. Wondered who or what they might involve. Wondered if Adam's secrets were as scandalous as her secrets, or if they were more innocuous in nature.

But a second later, just as she became truly inquisitive, Adam stripped away his suit coat, revealing his fine white shirt and the strapping muscles beneath it, and Savannah forgot all about her musings. In his shirtsleeves now, Adam appeared much too appealing for her to continue thinking complicated thoughts. She simply wasn't capable of it. Openmouthed, Savannah stared at him, wondering how she'd been fortunate enough to find a man like Adam Corwin to love her and protect her and stay with her.

And initiate her, she thought with a private thrill, into the intimate ways of married life. Whatever they entailed...

"Learning about each other sounds good," he told her. "I want to know *everything* about you." Before she could panic over that statement, Adam distracted her by tossing his coat on the settee. He loosened his necktie and the top button of his shirt, sparking her curiosity to new heights. "I want to learn about you, Savannah, starting with the top of your head," he promised, "and working all the way down to your toes."

"All the way down to my toes?" Savannah could scarcely imagine such a thing. It sounded downright sinful. But before she could launch into an intriguing attempt to envision it, Adam provided the very experience he'd described.

Just as he'd vowed, he began by kissing her on the top of her head.

The gesture should have been brotherly...but it wasn't. In Adam's capable hands, even a relatively innocent kiss felt wicked. He tightened his hand on her jaw, holding her still as he kissed her forehead next. Then her right temple. Then her left temple. Savannah's knees buckled, but Adam only held her more securely, then went on keeping his promise. His breath feathered subtly across her cheek as he kissed her there, too.

"You," she managed to say, "are being very conscientious about your promise."

"Yes." He kissed her jawline, inciting a shiver. "I am."

"That's—" she swayed "—very well done of you."

"I hope so." Expertly he kissed her neck. "Let me know if there's anything else you'd like. I'm here to please you."

Another kiss. A cascade of goose bumps prickled from the side of her neck all the way down Savannah's body. Gasping, she clutched Adam's shirtfront to keep her balance. "Oh! I'd like more of *that* please. Who could have known that would feel so—"

"Good?" Adam whispered in her ear. "I hope it feels good."

Dumbly she nodded, afraid to move out of his reach and end this tantalizing contact between them...but too preoccupied with the novel sensation of feeling his tongue swirl gently along her earlobe to muster a coherent sentence. Naughtily Adam bit down.

Savannah shivered anew. "I'm happy I wore my hair up!"

"I am, too. At least for now." As though reminded of that fact, Adam slipped out one of her hairpins. Then another. She couldn't possibly have refused him a third or fourth hairpin—or anything else he desired in that moment. "You looked beautiful today," he said. "You always look beautiful to me, Savannah."

Savannah. She loved the sound of her name on his lips. She could have listened to Adam whisper it all day. She couldn't imagine why she'd waited so long to grant him permission to use her Christian name so familiarly. Now that she had, she wanted to hear Adam say it again and again.

But first, she realized, she needed to offer a reply. Adam was still speaking with her, and all she'd done for the past few heart-pounding moments was nod and quiver. It would only be correct and proper to further their dialogue, she realized, even while she wriggled and gasped beneath his continuing kisses.

"You looked very handsome, also!" Savannah divulged in a breathless tone. There. She'd done it. She'd conversed with him, and in a complimentary fashion, too. But her well-cultivated manners were fading fast. The authors of the *Guide to Correct Etiquette and Proper Behavior* handbook would have been appalled. Feeling muddled, she searched for more polite conversation. "Also, you're very good at this head-to-toe kissing," she struggled to say. "I find that I quite like it."

"I love it." His smile charmed her. Uninhibited and freely given, Adam's smile lighted the room like a beacon of good humor and enjoyment. "I love kissing you. Just like I knew I would," he said, "from the moment I first imagined it."

"You imagined kissing me?" The notion seemed astonishing.

His masculine laughter rang out. "Endlessly."

Pleased at that, Savannah preened. Certainly she'd made men want her as The Seductive Sensation. But they hadn't really wanted *her*. They'd wanted the illusion she presented.

"I could go on this way," Adam said, pressing another kiss to the side of her neck, "all night long."

As though in evidence of that, more hairpins fell away, coaxed free by his talented hands. Soon her hair fell past her shoulders in silky, unbound waves. She'd worn her hair loose while onstage sometimes, of course, but it felt different to let down her hair with Adam. It felt personal, like a gift. A gift to him. Adam seemed to recognize that fact, too.

Reverently he gazed at her. "You're so pretty, Savannah."

Shyly she ducked her head. Surely this was pushing the boundaries of good fortune, to have a husband who complimented her so freely. "You mustn't get carried away," she warned him, staring in abrupt fascination at the tanned triangle of skin exposed by his open shirt collar. "After all, we have a whole life together to look forward to. Perhaps you should save some of your sweet talk for later, so you don't run out."

"And miss telling you how much I enjoy the curve of your mouth? The feel of your lips? Never." Adam demonstrated his affection with a kiss. He cradled her cheek in his hand, then smiled at her. "Besides, I make it a policy not to count on later. Not when there's so much to be savored now. Like this."

His mouth came down on hers, showing her all there was to appreciate in this moment, magically enticing her lips to open. This time, tutored in this style of kissing, Savannah participated enthusiastically. She clutched Adam's shirt and levered herself upward on her tiptoes.

At her eagerness, Adam raised his head briefly, then chuckled. But he approved, she could tell. Because he kissed her again, deeply and thoroughly and with spine-tingling intensity.

Lost in the miraculous slide of their lips and tongues,

the gentle warmth of their mingled breath, the seductive moan that Adam made as she kissed him back, Savannah felt positively giddy. Surely this clever variety of kiss was like a drug, encouraging innocent people to partake again and again.

"There." Finished, she leaned back. "Was that better?"

A nod. "You're a natural talent. Soon you'll be instructing me." Adam's hooded gaze lowered to her lips. "But we'd better make sure of that. We wouldn't want to get lackadaisical."

"I'm nothing if not thorough," Savannah agreed.

He kissed her again. She wriggled with delight, making her skirts swoosh sideways. Beneath those layers of worsted wool and lacy petticoats, her loins felt heavy, her bosom full and tingling. All over, she felt warm—but not in the ordinary way she did while cooking or riding to town in the sunshine. This warmth felt far more pleasurable than that. It felt...*essential* somehow. Craving more of it, Savannah crowded closer to Adam, daring to splay her hands over his broad shoulders and chest.

Carefully she stroked him. He murmured his approval, so she did it again. He felt hard and solid beneath her palms. Warm, too. She wondered if he experienced the same warmth she did.

"Is this...enjoyable for you?" she asked solicitously. "Or would you rather be doing something else? I'm not quite sure what to expect with regard to our wedding night, so—"

"All I want is to be with you." Adam cradled her face again, leaving her feeling as though his thoughts were only for *her.* "But if this is happening too quickly for you—"

"Oh, no! No." Vehemently Savannah shook her head. "In fact, I'm very much enjoying myself. You're an excellent... partner."

She bit her lip, distressed that she didn't know how to properly address him under these circumstances. Adam only smiled. "That's very generous of you," he told her with heartwarming courtesy...and adorable roguish pride. "Thank you."

"You're certainly welcome." She gasped as he kissed her neck again. Momentarily her thoughts fled. Savannah tried mightily to muster up more conversation. "It's only the truth."

She tried to keep talking, but her words stuttered to a stop as Adam slowly, methodically, undid the buttons on her dress, kissing her all the while. Cool air touched her skin as he spread apart her dress. Carefully he scooped her hair over her shoulder, stroking her heavy locks as he did. But then he dipped his head to kiss the back of her neck, and she forgot about being chilled altogether. All she could think about were the soft impact of his lips, the subtle rasp of his beard stubble, the ticklish teasing of his tongue and teeth.

"You know," he mused as he dragged his mouth pleasurably and slowly along her bare shoulder, "you don't have to keep talking. You're allowed to simply feel. *Feel this,* for example."

His hands followed his words, sliding down her back in a warm, gentle caress. With surprise, Savannah realized that Adam had bared her entire back. She hadn't even noticed. Even as she marveled at the sleight of hand *he* had exhibited, she was startled to feel her very best dress fall in a puddle at her feet. With a chivalrous gesture, Adam helped her step out of it.

Suddenly Savannah felt exposed. She felt, despite her chemise and drawers and layers of petticoats, almost naked.

But Adam had the cure for those feelings. His eyes shone with affection as he gazed at her. His attention lingered complimentarily over all her barest, most tender places. And his hands, when he came nearer again, touched her with something very much like fascination. Caught up in his reverence, Savannah felt cherished…and downright beloved.

Raptly Adam stroked her shoulder, then her arm. His heated gaze dropped to her bosom. To her astonishment, Savannah yearned for his hands to follow that same path. She wanted to feel his hands all over her, to allow him to touch her even more boldly.

As though he'd somehow guessed her thoughts, Adam murmured something, then cupped her breasts in his hands. Carefully he stroked her. In response, her nipples budded. The heat between her thighs increased. The pace of her breathing quickened, just as though she'd run a mile. Even more than those things, a sharp yearning came to life deep inside her, urgent and undeniable. Savannah had no idea how to satisfy it, but she hoped Adam did.

Helplessly she closed her eyes. This was beyond wonderful. This was…*sublime*. Surely a woman could not be expected to withstand much more pleasure. She must have reached some sort of apex of sensation—from here she would simply return to living her everyday, normal life in her everyday, ordinary body. But as Adam went on caressing her, Savannah discovered she was wrong.

She was very wrong. Because in Adam's hands, her body felt anything but ordinary. And there was definitely more pleasure to be found in his continuing caresses—in letting him untie her chemise and bare her breasts to the quiet, lamplit night. There was infinitely, spectacularly more pleasure to be taken, Savannah realized next, in watching him lower his head, draw in a fervent breath, then kiss her in a place that until now no one had even seen, much less touched with such remarkable effect.

Shocked but needful of more, Savannah arched her back beneath him. She closed her eyes again, caught up in the good feelings of Adam's tongue swirling over her nipple, of his palms cradling her, of his lips kissing and kissing and kissing...

"I...feel a bit faint," she said in a husky voice hardly recognizable as her own. Feeling her knees tremble, Savannah gazed hazily at Adam. "I don't know how much more of this I can stand."

He smiled again. "That means we're doing this correctly."

"Surely not! How can we be expected to—" Abruptly Savannah stopped, belatedly becoming aware of a change in her husband. Whereas before Adam had been busy kissing her, which had provided a magnificent distraction, now he was only holding her...and all at once, she discerned a hard, hot, overwhelming *firmness* pressing against her belly. It felt urgent and large. Very, very large. Wide-eyed, she stared up at him. "Are you all right?" she asked.

Unable to resist, she glanced down. Adam's trousers were distended to an impressive degree. Even in the lamplight, she could tell that such a reaction could not be comfortable.

"You should take off your clothes," she decided. "Mine are already gone, mostly. And yours look...restrictive. Please."

"I will. But first..." With a brush of his fingers, Adam lowered her chemise strap from her shoulder. Then he closed the short distance between them. "You should be properly undressed."

"Properly?" Drat. Another thing she didn't know about this marriage business. "Meaning...what, exactly?"

"Meaning undressed by me," Adam specified. "Meaning that I'll remove your clothing one item at a time—"

"That doesn't sound particularly proper." Still fascinated

by his masculine…*endowments*…Savannah dipped her gaze to the front of his trousers again. "But if you say so, I suppose I—"

"—and kissing every inch of you that I reveal," he finished. "Slowly, gently, and tenderly." His wolfish expression promised that he meant to keep his word as strictly and as thoroughly as possible. When she looked at him, doubtless agog at the notion, he only shrugged. "You didn't let me finish."

"But when will *you* undress? I'm worried about your—"

"Soon," he said, and began with unlacing her bustle.

As he'd promised, Adam performed his undressing duties with plenty of kisses—kisses, caresses, and more than a few murmured compliments, too…everyplace he could reach. By the time her last lace-trimmed petticoat joined the pile of cast-off clothing on the settee, Savannah felt positively weak in the knees.

Standing only in her chemise and drawers, she decided now was the time to draw the line—else lose her wifely authority altogether. "Your turn," she said as Adam faced her.

"Soon," he said. But she was unbending.

"I do know a little about what's supposed to happen between us tonight," Savannah said. "And I know we'll both need to be naked. This situation as it stands is simply inequitable. So go ahead. Take off your…" She let her gaze rove over him, taking in his tousled hair, sturdy jaw, broad chest and narrow hips. With effort, she moved her attention from the region of his trousers. "Shirt," she finished with a wave. "If you please."

To her surprise, Adam raised his arms, bent his elbows, then whipped off his white cotton shirt in a single swift motion. His disrobing revealed his brawny, hair-sprinkled chest, his assortment of enthralling muscles, and his tightly wrapped bandages. Staring at them, Savannah was reminded of what they were here to accomplish tonight: consummating their marriage.

She couldn't afford to waste any more time, lest Adam became skittish again, the way he had outside her room.

"Well done." She swirled her fingers in a signal for him to turn around. "Now if you'll just face the wall, please?"

The moment he did, Savannah efficiently shed her own remaining garments in record time. She dived for the bedstead, scrambled to overturn the coverlet, then made a mad lunge beneath the sheets. The mattress creaked beneath her weight.

Adam turned partway. "Is everything all right?"

"It's fine." Lying rigidly in place, Savannah straightened her arms alongside her body. But that didn't feel quite correct. She tried crossing her arms over her chest. But that felt even more peculiar. Oh *what* was the protocol for a situation like this one? Never had she yearned more for a sneak peek at her handbook. She could not afford for Adam to be disappointed in her or her first wifely performance. She inhaled. "I'm ready."

Eagerly Adam turned. His puzzled gaze swept over her, took in the chemise and drawers she'd dropped in her haste, then lifted to her face. His expression changed. "You look…"

Beautiful. Irresistible, Savannah imagined. "Yes?"

"…terrified."

"Oh." *Not irresistible.* She'd failed. Disappointment assailed her. "I'm so sorry. I'll try to do better."

With three big steps, Adam reached the bed. Before she could say another word, he lowered his trousers. Shockingly naked, he flipped back the coverlet, then got in bed beside her.

She only had a brief glimpse of his naked form, but based on that hasty view, Savannah found him to be…*intriguing* to look at. Squirming with a combination of nervousness and timidity, acutely aware of her own lack of expertise in this situation, she nudged herself sideways, trying to make room.

"Stop. I want you nearer, not farther. And don't be afraid." Adam smiled, then touched her hair. He curled a tendril around his finger, seeming as relaxed as a man could be. "We don't have to do anything you don't want to do, Savannah."

"I'm not worried about doing it." She swallowed hard, then shifted her gaze to him. "I'm worried about doing it properly."

After all, her entire future—the happy marriage and cozy, joyful home full of children that she dreamed of— depended on it. That potential future was so close she could feel it. But her dreams of starting over had been snatched from her grasp before. They might be again, if she didn't proceed correctly.

For a long moment, Adam only looked at her, his expression intent and kind…and uncomfortably perceptive. Then he nodded. "In my eyes, you can do nothing wrong. Not here or ever. There's nothing you could do that would upset me or drive me away—"

Guiltily she shifted, knowing full well there was at least *one* thing about her that would drive away any decent man who'd been allowed the foresight to know it: her scandalous past.

"—including," Adam promised with an unusually vulnerable expression, "whatever happens between us in this bed tonight."

"Well…" Tentatively Savannah glanced at him. "Could

it please involve some kissing? That *special* kind of kissing?"

She thought that would likely relax her. Possibly it might even ease the throbbing that had taken up residence inside her like an insistent heartbeat, demanding…something. Something she knew Adam could probably give her, if he tried.

Now, he only smiled. "You're a bossy wife, aren't you?"

On the verge of apologizing for that, Savannah made herself stop. It was, quite possibly, the only time she had allowed herself to behave naturally in the past year, without guidance from her etiquette books or help from Mose or anything else. Stripped of the security those things offered and, quite literally, bare to Adam's view, she nodded. "Yes. I guess I am."

She held her breath, waiting for him to disapprove—to glimpse in her some part of that tarnished background she so wanted to leave behind. Fearful yet defiant, Savannah stilled.

Adam laughed. "I like that about you. Be sure to keep it up," he said, "and let me know if I displease you."

But there was no need for that, Savannah discovered as her new husband rolled over and took her into his arms, as easily and freely as though he'd been doing so for years. Because as Adam showed her all the ways that she could love and be loved—as he covered her with his body and brought her to new realms of pleasure she'd never even imagined before—Savannah could find nothing at all to be bossy about. Beneath Adam's tender gaze and patient hands, she learned about a part of herself that was both generous and greedy, loving and demanding. She learned that love could be naked and serious. Or it could be lighthearted and intense. It could be everything she'd ever dreamed.

She also learned, as Adam raised himself over her, finally making their union complete with a hoarse shout of her name, that the only thing to fear about giving herself to her husband was the inevitable aftermath. Because not long after their first encounter was over, she wanted to experience even more.

Cradled in Adam's arms, feeling his heartbeat thunder beneath her cheek, Savannah dared to smile. Tonight, her heart had opened to Adam in a whole new way—and his had opened to her.

From now on, nothing would ever be the same between them.

"You know," she said as she lay her hand on his chest, entirely comfortable now with touching him, "I do believe we could get even better at these romantic endeavors."

Adam panted. "Better?" he asked, his tone disbelieving.

"With a little practice, I mean," Savannah clarified. "I realize I'm new at this. However, I've always ascribed to the view that practice makes perfect, so…"

"So you want more?"

Would that be horribly greedy? it occurred to Savannah to ask. Or *only if you do!* A polite reply would probably be appropriate, she knew. But then she remembered that she no longer needed to be on her best, most gracious behavior at all times. Not with Adam. The realization was liberating.

"Yes. I think I might want more and more and more!" Enthusiastically she wriggled her backside. The movement made Adam groan. "So prepare yourself, husband. I've already warned you that I can be *very* diligent in pursuit of a goal, so—"

But Adam cut off her words with another kiss, then slid down her body with a devilish grin. "I think I can oblige you, wife." With his hands on her hips, he lowered his head, then gave her his most scandalous kiss yet. "You'd better hold on."

Obediently Savannah put both hands on his head, then braced herself for whatever was to come. But she didn't really need to, she realized with a smile. Now that she and Adam were truly together, she was ready for anything. Anything at all.

Although she couldn't help wondering, as Adam made her giggle, then squeal with delight as he kissed her again, if she weren't tempting fate just a *little* too much these days....

Chapter Twelve

Adam realized something was amiss from the moment the telegraph station came into view the following afternoon. Even as he guided the horse and wagon down the road, he squinted through the trees, trying to pinpoint what was wrong.

An overall air of stillness lay over the station, making the place appear strangely deserted. One of the windows had a smashed pane; its shutter hung crookedly. Near the barn, a portion of the fence railing was broken; it lay on the ground. Most alarming of all, no smoke came from the station's chimney. By now, Mose should have been there, tending the wires.

Concerned, Adam urged the horse to go faster. The wagon jounced along the rutted road, its wheels and springs scarcely equipped for such speed. The trees flew past in a rush.

Beside him, Savannah grabbed her ribbon-bedecked hat. It appeared on the verge of flying away in the breeze.

"What's the matter? Are you in that much of a hurry to get home?"

Her tone was teasing, her demeanor carefree—exactly as it had been since they'd awakened in each other's arms this morning. Their wedding night had been more than Adam could have dreamed, full of laughter and passion and far too little sleep. Their togetherness had continued on into today, with a shared bath that had sloshed soapy water all over their hotel room floor. But he and Savannah hadn't cared. They'd only sank deeper into the bubbles, laughing and kissing, and decided to worry about sopping up the puddles later…much, *much* later.

But now they couldn't delay any longer. *Later* had arrived, and with it, Adam's remembrance of all he had yet to deal with. He could not regret marrying Savannah to protect her—nor even consummating their marriage afterward. Because of that, Savannah would not be able to obtain an annulment, the way he'd planned; that was true. But now Adam dared to hope she wouldn't want to.

For the first time, he dared to hope that she would want *him*…even after he told her the truth about who he really was.

But the troubles they'd left behind during their wedding trip hadn't gone away while they'd been in Avalanche—to the contrary, in fact. Judging by the wrecked appearance of the telegraph station, trouble had come looking for them.

"Someone has been here." At the farthest edge of the yard, Adam pulled the horse and wagon to a stop. He set the brake, then put his hand to his gun belt. He checked his knife, too.

Savannah noticed. "What sort of 'someone'?" She cast a nervous glance at the station. "Mrs. Finney, perhaps?"

"I doubt it." Grim-faced, Adam jumped to the ground.

Savannah did, too. "Mose?" she called. "Mose, are you here?"

She headed for the station, but Adam rounded the wagon first. He caught her arm, then shook his head. "Let me go first. As soon as I make sure everything is all right, I'll call you."

She seemed on the verge of disagreeing. Then she nodded.

"All right." Savannah squeezed his hand, her worried gaze searching his. "But this doesn't feel right. Be careful."

Adam didn't have to promise he would take care. Now more than ever, he had reason to keep himself safe—because he had someone to stay safe for. All the same, he gave a curt nod.

"Get on the other side of the wagon, away from the station. Keep the wagon between you and anyone you see come out."

"Come out? Exactly who do you think will come out?"

"Please." Adam checked his firearm. "Just do it."

Pale-faced, Savannah agreed. As he'd instructed, she scurried around to the other, safer side of the wagon.

The horse shifted at its head, undoubtedly longing to be freed of its traces, groomed and fed, as usual. The creature knew they were home and, spotting the barn, it wanted to be comfortably inside it. Savannah patted the horse's long neck, murmured something to it, then vanished on the other side of the wagon. It was just like her, Adam thought, to spare a moment to reassure the horse, even when they faced unknown troubles.

With his shoulders taut, Adam made sure Savannah was out of sight, then he advanced toward the station building. The front door hung aslant on its hinges, he noticed with deepening alarm. He could see a sliver of the station's living quarters in the gap formed between the door and the jamb. Spotting no movement inside, Adam ran stealthily around the corner of the building.

Here, there were signs of horses. At least three of them. The ground was torn up with hoofprints—and with dank tobacco-juice stains. In all the time Adam had spent at the telegraph station, he reflected, few people had visited there—only Doc Finney and his wife. As an adjunct station, the place mostly relayed messages along the wires instead of taking them down for customers. Three visitors was definitely unusual.

Frowning, Adam scanned the tree line, then the slope leading up the nearby mountain. He saw no movement amid the ponderosa pines or scrub oak. Even the birds and ground squirrels were still. The road leading to town was empty.

Proceeding as he'd been trained, he circled the building, trying to assess what had happened. On the far side of the station, another window was smashed. Now that he was close to the damage, Adam expected to see shards of glass on the ground.

He didn't. Perplexed, he nudged himself upward. He looked cautiously inside the window, keeping his head as far out of shooting range as he could. If the window had been broken from the outside, as he suspected it had been, there would have been glass on the floor inside the station. There wasn't.

Since the station appeared deserted, Adam glanced back to make sure Savannah remained safely out of sight, then headed for the barn. Savannah's individually named chickens scratched in the grassy ground nearby, chasing bugs. They clucked in annoyance as he strode between them, scattering their flock.

Holding his weapon steady, Adam nudged open the barn door with his foot. It opened with a creak that made him cringe. He paused, then ducked inside the shadowy interior. The smells of hay and aged lumber struck him first, then a faint, earthy tinge of soil and manure. Outside, the chickens clucked. Sunlight splintered between cracks in the barn walls, giving Adam just enough illumination to see that the cow's stall was empty.

The creature hadn't been in the paddock, either. Frowning anew, Adam hastily checked the rest of the barn. He glanced upward toward the loft…then froze as a voice came toward him.

It sounded low, but it was getting louder. He couldn't make out any words. Newly alert, Adam ran toward the barn door.

Now he heard footsteps, too. With his gun still raised, Adam concentrated on the sound. Only one person. He could handle one person—especially since they seemed to be headed toward the barn. Given the sunny day outside, Adam's position inside gave him an advantage. Whoever entered next would be temporarily blinded by the dimness.

More footsteps. Then a low mumble. It sounded like…

Adam stepped out, his gun raised. "Stop right there."

Mose stood silhouetted in the barn doorway. He raised both arms in surprise. The leather lead in his hand jangled. He squinted, his expression showing surprise…then annoyance.

"Humph. Fine time for you to show up, Corwin, now that all the trouble's over with." The station's helper grumbled, then lowered his arms in disgust. "Put your firearm away, why don't you, and help me put this place to rights again."

As it turned out, Adam tried to do exactly that. But first he went back to the wagon to collect Savannah and make sure she knew everything was all right. And from there, Savannah wouldn't hear of him and Mose working on the damage to the station until she'd taken a turn at fussing over her longtime helper…and peppering him with questions, too. They all settled inside the station, with Savannah busy at the stove as she talked.

"Honestly, Mose. You nearly frightened me to death!" She hurried to the station's dining table—where she'd stalwartly placed Adam and Mose—with a tinware coffeepot in hand, busily refilling their cups. As though the brew were a bona fide cure-all, Savannah nodded for her friend to have a sip. "When we got here and saw you weren't around… Well, I feared the worst. I'm *so* happy nothing truly awful happened."

"This looks pretty awful," Adam said.

He aimed his chin at the general disarray inside the station. The place appeared to have been thoroughly ransacked.

Cupboards and drawers were open, their contents spilling onto the floor. Savannah's cheval mirror was cracked. Her clothing was strewn about. Books and papers and maps lay in chaotic piles. The bedstead had been dragged out from the wall; now the mattress lay atop it at a haphazard angle, the bedding and pillows piled higgledy-piggledy on one corner of it.

Up near the business end of the station, the situation was a little improved, but only because, as Mose had explained, he'd tackled that cleanup job first. He'd also swept up all the broken window glass, explaining to Adam's satisfaction why he'd seen none of it on the ground or on the floorboards inside.

"Yes, but *Mose* is all right," Savannah said in a robust tone. "That's what truly matters." She smiled unsteadily at him, then patted his shoulder, still hovering nearby with the coffeepot. "I swear, Mose. If anything had happened to you—"

"Nothing's going to happen to me. Not this week or ever." Mose stared into his coffee cup, appearing embarrassed by all the ruckus. "I'm too crotchety to go down without a fight."

"Maybe." Savannah pursed her lips doubtfully. "But you're not bulletproof! If I'm not mistaken, those are *bullet holes* in my costume trunk." She pointed to the offending splintery spots in a nearby chest. "That could have been *you*, Mose!"

The big man only shrugged, then exchanged a long-suffering look with Adam. For the first time, Adam felt a sense of camaraderie with him. Now that they were both under Savannah's official purview, it was clear they'd have to endure a whole lot of well-meaning nurturing.

"This all happened yesterday?" Adam asked. He knew that Savannah was right in one respect: those bullet holes were troubling. Because shooting up the places the gang looted was the particular calling card of Wyatt Bedell. Adam had no doubt that he and his brothers were responsible for this. "You didn't see anyone? Hear anyone?" he asked Mose. "Are you sure?"

"I'm sure." The station helper nodded. "Like I said before, all I heard was a crazy kind of mooing coming from the cow. I could tell right away she was in trouble, so I hustled out there to see what was wrong. What I saw was that paddock fence, all busted up like you just saw it, and the cow—"

"Poor Penelope!" Savannah shook her head.

"—trotting clean up the hill like she'd been herded that way. I didn't see anybody else. But she was spooked pretty bad. The way she was running, it took me the better part of the afternoon and on into the evening to round her up and get her safely to Mr. Yarnell's place, down toward Morrow Creek."

Because of the damage to the paddock fence, Mose explained further, he'd decided against leaving Penelope in their own barn after he'd caught up with the cow and harnessed her. Instead he'd relied on the generosity of their neighbor to temporarily house Penelope until the fence could be repaired. Mose had been coming back from milking her when he'd met Adam.

"I reckon it's pretty clear that somebody wanted me out of the station," Mose went on. "I don't know what they were looking for, and I don't know if they found it. But they banged up the telegraphy apparatus pretty good while they were here."

"I'm just relieved they didn't get to you!" Savannah gave his grizzled hand a heartfelt squeeze. "If anything like this ever happens again, don't you wait for an excuse like Penelope getting out, you hear? You just run away as fast as you can."

Mose frowned. "I'm not running away from anything."

"I want you to! You don't have to be brave," Savannah insisted, pouring him more coffee. "You've already demonstrated enough bravery to last you a lifetime, Mose. You know what I'm referring to." She gave him a meaningful look. "I'd say you've earned yourself a little surefire safety by now."

Mose shifted in his seat, then gulped back more coffee. He didn't look at Savannah as he set down his cup. It seemed evident that he felt uncomfortable—and Adam knew why.

"It would put my mind at ease to know you agree," Savannah pressed, her knuckles white on the coffeepot. "That's for sure."

Mose rubbed his temple, sitting conspicuously silent.

"He's not running, Savannah," Adam said gently. "No man would. Any man worth being called a man would stay and fight, if he had the chance."

Mose nodded. He cast Adam an appreciative glance, then appeared to remember he was "crotchety" and scowled instead.

"Well, that's plumb ridiculous." With her mouth down-turned, Savannah headed back to the stove, where she'd already begun assembling a hasty meal of fried eggs, corn-meal mush and stewed, cinnamon-spiced dried apples. "If you can save yourself from something, you ought to do it. That's simple common sense. It doesn't make you less of a man to do that."

Adam and Mose shook their heads in unison. "Yes, it does."

"Especially if a man's property is threatened," Mose added.

"Or his family is in danger." Adam tightened his hold on his coffee cup, his whole body rebelling at the very thought.

If he and Savannah had been there when the Bedell brothers had arrived... He hated to think what might have happened.

No wonder they'd encountered Curtis Bedell on the road to Avalanche, he realized. Curtis had probably been scouting Adam and Savannah's location—the better to assure himself that he and his brothers would have plenty of undisturbed time to raid the telegraph station. They simply hadn't counted on Mose.

Or had they? he wondered. Mose *did* appear to have been deliberately lured away from the station, Adam considered.

But that didn't make sense at all. It certainly didn't match up with what he knew of the Bedell brothers. Most of the time, the brothers were undeviatingly ruthless.

Setting aside those questions for now, Adam glanced up at his new wife. "There's no point arguing about this. If you were a man, you would understand. A man stays to fight. A man protects what's his." Hoping to lighten the mood, he smiled. "But I'm powerfully glad you're *not* a man, because—"

"Poppycock! All that talk about staying to fight is just pure nonsense," Savannah disagreed. "I won't hear any more of it."

"It's the truth." Mose drained his coffee, then stood.

Adam did the same. "I would lay down my life for you, Savannah. There's nothing you can do to change that."

"Me, too," Mose affirmed in his thundering voice. "I reckon I already have, once or twice over the years. Can't be helped."

Savannah shook her head, stirring the contents of her cast-iron skillet with far more vigor than the food probably required. "What if I don't want you to do that?" she pressed. "Doesn't that matter at all? I don't *want* either one of you to fight for me." With her wooden-spoon-holding hand on her hip, Savannah raised her chin. "It was bad enough that Mose was in danger at all. Bad enough that my first-ever glimpse of *you* might have been my last, Adam, had you not recovered from your injuries. How in the world could I live with myself, knowing either of you put yourselves in danger for my sake?"

The room turned silent. Skewered by her fierce look, Adam and Mose exchanged shrugs. There was no sense trying to change what couldn't be changed. Men were protectors. That was all. Adam had filled that role with Mariana and with the clients who hired him, too. He prided himself on that. Any man would have.

"If I do my job right, it won't ever come down to that," he said. "Besides, I'll be fine. I always have been."

"Except when you get shot in the back and left for dead!" Inexplicably fervent, Savannah stared him down. "I will *not* have either one of you endangering yourselves for me. Do you hear?"

She shook her spoon, giving them both stern looks.

"The way I see it," Mose said in his usual practical tone, "there's not much you can do to stop us. We're grown men."

Adam agreed. "We're going to do what we have to do." He grabbed his hat, then plunked it on his head. He smiled at Savannah. "Try not to get all het up about this. When the time comes, you might like having two heroes fighting for you."

In response, Savannah only appeared exasperated. She looked away from him, then resumed stirring her cornmeal mush with jerky motions. "I just might have resources you're not aware of, Mr. Corwin. Sometimes I still get my way, by hook or by crook."

"Hmm." His smile broadened as he came nearer. "I'll just bet you do, Mrs. Corwin. You'll have to show me sometime."

He tipped up her chin, then pressed a kiss to her mouth.

At first, Savannah stiffened. But then, as Mose busied himself with tidying up the mess, Savannah kissed Adam back. Glad to have a moment's privacy, he grabbed a handful of her skirts, then hauled her closer while her thick yellow mush bubbled away on the stovetop. He didn't like being at odds with her—especially about something so vital as protecting her.

Fortunately his kiss seemed to succeed where logic had failed. When he and Savannah parted, she appeared to have forgotten all about their disagreement. Rosy-cheeked, she laughed, then swept her disheveled hair from her eyes.

"Well. I can see how *you* settle arguments!" With her free hand, Savannah gave him a teasing swat. "That's an... interesting approach, but I won't get a lick of work done while you're kissing me. Do you want me to burn all this food?"

"No, ma'am." Contritely Adam grinned. "I surely don't."

"Then skedaddle until I'm finished. I've got a lot of work to do, you know." Her gaze skittered past him, taking in the mess that Mose was diligently working on tidying. She shook her head. "It's going to take a while to clean up in here."

"Don't worry. I'll help you," Adam promised.

She burst into peals of laughter. "*You're* going to clean?"

"If that's what it takes." After all, if he'd nabbed Roy and his brothers when he'd had the chance, they would not have looted the station. "Do you think anything is missing?"

Biting her lip in thought, Savannah looked around. She shrugged, then shook her head again. "It's hard to tell. Whoever did this did a pretty thorough job of wrecking the place."

He'd have to be more direct. Tipping back his hat brim, Adam gave Savannah a straightforward look. "I'm asking about your nest-egg savings," he said. "That's probably what they were looking for. Is your money still here?"

Savannah's startled gaze met his. She frowned. "Why would anybody think to look for my savings here at the station?"

That was unexpected. "If not at the station, then where?"

He almost wished the money *had* been at the station.

Adam didn't want Savannah to lose her savings, but he knew he could provide well for her. If the Bedell brothers had gotten what they'd wanted, maybe they would have left Savannah alone for good. As it was, Adam had the unpleasant feeling the gang would be back, one way or the other—unless he confronted them first.

"How do you know about her savings in the first place?" Mose demanded, shouldering his big body nearer. His gaze shifted to Savannah, intent and concerned…and plainly unhappy. He nodded at Adam. "You told him about your savings?"

"Only since our first correspondence!" She stirred her cornmeal mush, then put a lid on the pot. "Remember? I told you that a long time ago."

Mose cast Adam a suspicious look. Then he relented. He turned to Savannah. "I thought you were going to keep that money a secret, all to yourself. You know…because of Warren."

This time, it was Savannah's turn to appear uncomfortable. She turned away to collect three speckled enamelware plates from the cupboard, her chin held high. "I changed my mind about that. Now, wasn't there something you boys were going to do, while I finish up in here? I'd say that paddock fence ought to be first to be repaired. Penelope doesn't like to be away from her own stall. She's very particular that way. Her milk will suffer."

"Who's Warren?" Adam asked.

"A crook," Mose offered in a biting tone, well before Savannah could answer. "A lowdown, no-good, lying son of a—"

"Warren was a man I was…in business with." Savannah hurried past Adam with the plates in her hands. Efficiently she set the table. "I made a mistake in trusting him, and I promised myself I wouldn't ever be so gullible again."

"Humph." Mose scoffed, drawing Savannah's reproachful gaze.

"What kind of mistake?" Adam asked, feeling mystified and increasingly concerned. *Warren* had never been mentioned in Savannah's letters to Bedell. Now, Adam wondered why. "Gullible how? If he hurt you, I can make sure he pays."

At that, Savannah smiled, probably thinking he was trying to be a Wild West hero for her sake. "I'm sure that living with his own guilt over deceiving me is recompense enough for what Warren did."

Not in Adam's view, it wasn't. But if he could find out the man's full name, learn where he lived, make use of the agency's resources to track him down... "What did he do?"

"You don't have to protect me, Adam!"

"What," Adam repeated patiently, "did he do?"

"He stole my wages and much of my savings before I realized it. He was in a position of authority. I didn't question him at first. We were engaged at the time, so I trusted him." Her gaze shifted to Adam's, gauging his reaction. "I learned my lesson quickly enough. Shortly after that, I headed west. I promise this has nothing at all to do with you. It's over with now."

Her guarded expression revealed nothing more. Nor did the glance she cast Mose, appearing to warn him to keep silent.

"Is that enough for you?" Savannah asked, stiff necked and flushed. "Or shall I dredge up a few more embarrassing details?"

Repentantly Adam touched her arm. "I don't want to embarrass you, Savannah," he said. "I only want to help you."

For a long moment, she simply gazed at him. The disarray

all around them, the pots of simmering food on the stove, even Mose all faded as Savannah appeared to consider what he'd said.

"If you truly want to help me, then believe me," she told him. "That's all I need. Whatever you hear from anyone else, *believe me* first. Can you do that?"

Puzzled, Adam nodded. "I promise I will."

"No." Her gaze sharpened. "You can't be flip about this. I mean it. I need to be able to count on you, no matter what."

"You can always count on me," Adam insisted.

"That's what Warren said," Mose piped up in a discontented tone. "But all you could count on *him* for was heartache."

"Hush, Mose," Savannah said. "That's enough."

"He broke your heart?" Adam frowned. "Savannah—"

"No. Warren did *not* break my heart." She wiped her hands on a dishcloth, her expression certain. "To do that, he would have had to have *had* my heart first, and I never gave it to him."

Mose gave an apologetic murmur. Savannah brushed it off.

"You can't keep walking on eggshells around me, Mose. I'm fine! See? I waited to give my heart to a *good* man." In obvious demonstration, she went to Adam. She wrapped her arms around his elbow in a defiant gesture. "Because of that, everything is going to be wonderful now."

Fondly she squeezed him. Guiltily held in her grasp, Adam glanced away. He would make her hopes come true, he swore to himself in that moment. For Savannah's sake, he would make sure everything truly was wonderful. Somehow, he would.

But when his gaze lifted again, colliding with Mose's doubtful one, Adam knew that he may have taken on more than he could manage. In saving Savannah, he just might have to break her heart…and he would almost certainly have to let her go.

When the time came, would he have the strength to do that?

"Now get on outside, you two." Savannah released Adam, then shooed him and Mose toward the station's yard. "Get to work, would you? I'll have the food ready soon, but until then…" Brightly she smiled. "This place won't right itself, you know!"

That was something Adam knew all too well. Glancing at Mose, he had the sense that the station helper had realized the same thing. United in a shared mission, they headed outside. For better or worse, the only way to start was to just dig in.

Chapter Thirteen

Sitting in the upstairs bedroom of a white clapboard house at the east end of Morrow Creek, Linus Bedell stared moodily at his brother Curtis. For the past hour or more, Curtis had been passed out in a chair beside the bedroom window, snoring fit to beat the band. With his feet propped up on the windowsill and his hat on crooked, his lips flapping with them snores of his, Curtis appeared to be planning to snooze for a while longer, too.

Linus felt fortunate he hadn't been paired with Wyatt for this endeavor—or, for the love of all things holy, *Edward*—but that didn't mean he liked it. He didn't like it one little bit.

He especially didn't like it because of the fact that Curtis was making him do all the work. At least now he was, now that Curtis had done his piece by sweet-talking somebody into letting the two of them "rent" the place for a month or so.

In truth, he and Curtis wouldn't be at that house for more than a few nights. Maybe less, depending on how things went off. They only needed the place in order to keep a watch on the house across the street, like Roy had ordered them to do. But that would have sounded strange to most folks—and like Curtis had explained to Linus, what the house's owners didn't know wouldn't hurt them. As far as anybody was concerned, Curtis and Linus were just another pair of prospecting brothers, doing their utmost to strike it rich in the territory's mining districts.

'Course, they hadn't bolstered up their story by carrying in any mining pans or pickaxes, the way Linus had thought would be smart when they'd taken up residence. In fact, all they'd brought was a spyglass (filched from them soldiers, like Linus's boots) and a whole caboodle of tequila and mescal. Curtis liked to have a swallow now and then, to keep up his spirits while he was watching the house across the street. Not that he'd done much looking at it so far, Linus reckoned with silent annoyance.

According to Roy, the lady who lived across the street was hostin' a party, and Savannah Reed—The Seductive Sensation—was supposed to be there. Tonight. The very idea made Linus feel all quivery and anxious. Not because he was keen to see her again, though. Because he felt powerfully guilty, even more than usual.

Squirming in his chair, Linus aimed another peek through the spyglass. The distraction was of no use, though. Linus still felt peculiar—and that was sayin' somethin' for a man who'd done some of the things he'd done. He reminded himself that he'd managed to save that big colored man a beatin'—or worse—by lettin' loose that cow and walloping the beast to make it run away. But that didn't help much. Not even the memory of the station's helper comically chasin' that cow could lighten his sprits. Linus knew, deep in his gut, that what he and his brothers had been doin' for a living just weren't right.

Take the other day, for instance. The Bedell brothers had out and out *ransacked* The Seductive Sensation's place. He knew that had been necessary, like Roy had explained, but the way it had happened still bothered him. That station had been a nice little place. They could've searched it without makin' it look like a tornado had struck it. Hell, Wyatt had even shot up some of the lady's pretty things, for no good reason at all 'cept pure orneriness. He'd made Linus take aim at a couple items, too. Linus had fired crooked and missed on purpose, but what they'd done didn't sit well with him. No sir. Not at all.

Linus didn't like to think about how Savannah Reed had felt when she'd come home and found all her things ruined like that.

It was even worse than that, though. Ever since Roy had got hurt, their plans had taken a turn for the nonsensical. That made Linus plenty worried. Bein' foolish was liable to get them all caught or killed, and he'd tried to explain as much to his brothers. He'd told them how tearin' up the telegraph station would only put that hard-nosed detective, Corwin, on the alert all over again. He'd recognize it was them, the Bedells, sure as shootin', Linus had prophesied, and come lookin' for them, same as he'd done for months now. But all Linus's explaining and bad feelings hadn't mattered to anyone. Not one little bit.

In fact, all his brothers had done was laugh at him, like usual, then tell him they'd take care of that detective if he ever showed his do-gooder face around them again—which they didn't think would happen anytime soon, on account of Corwin having filched Roy's new "fiancée" and bein' busy with her.

Linus had disagreed. But bein' laughed at by his brothers wasn't any fun. Neither was bein' made fun of for his sentimental feelings toward The Seductive Sensation. So he'd shut his mouth instead of arguin' anymore. Not long after that, Wyatt, Edward and Curtis had all but turned that telegraph station inside out and upside down.

The awfulest part was they hadn't found squat inside. No nest-egg money, no jewelry, no valuables of any ken, really. When Roy had found out that news, he'd been fit to spit nails. Just remembering the look on his brother's face made Linus feel sick inside. Roy could be fearsome when he was upset.

As it was, owing to Roy's lingering injuries from his encounter with that detective, Linus and his brothers had gotten away with nothing worse than an irate jawing and a couple of well-placed punches in places Roy could reach easily. Linus counted himself lucky for that. Still, like all Roy's tirades through the years, it wasn't very nice to think about.

To distract himself, Linus leaned his elbow on the windowsill of the upstairs bedroom window, rested his chin in his palm, then looked outside. For the past half hour, nicely dressed Morrow Creek residents had been arriving at the house across the street. The place had been lit and gussied up, and now it looked just like a little home in a doll town. All the lamps glowed brightly inside. Convivial chatter wafted outside.

The view made Linus wish he could be inside there, too. It looked nice and cozy, full of laughter like he didn't usually hear. Not around his brothers. Their laughter was mean. But Linus couldn't join the party. All he and Curtis were supposed to do was watch until The Seductive Sensation showed up. After she did, they were supposed to nab Roy's latest "fiancée" and…

Forcefully Linus quit thinking about that. He'd get Curtis to do that part, he reckoned. That was all there was to it.

Just like he'd cued it to happen, another snore rent the

air. Grumpily Linus glanced at his brother. Then he winced, making a sour face. Drinkin' mescal gave Curtis awful breath. It smelled like an unholy alliance between cow patties and pickles, with a dash of horsehair thrown in. Which reminded Linus of a joke he'd heard at Jack Murphy's saloon, when he'd been waitin' around for Roy to come up with a foolproof new plan for them.

"Hey, Curtis." He nudged him. His brother only sniffled, then snored louder. Linus grinned. "You smell so bad, the horseflies are fightin' over who gets to land on you first."

His brother opened one eye. With a sense of dread, Linus realized that Curtis hadn't been sleepin', exactly. He'd only been ignorin' him, just like a coiled-up snake. Until now.

"Shut yer face." Curtis cuffed him. Hard. "You're supposed to be lookin' out for that yellow-haired woman and her money."

"Hey! So are you!" Linus grabbed his cheek. It stung something fierce. "How come *I* have to do all the lookin'?"

"'Cause *I'm* going to have to do *all* the rest, and we both know it." Curtis pulled down his hat. Wearing a look that showed off his vinegary disposition, he crossed his arms, then glanced out the window. In the street below, more people were arriving for the party. "Wake me up when it's time to get to work."

Eyeing his brother with trepidation, Linus nodded. But a part of him hoped he wouldn't have to wake up Curtis at all tonight. A part of him hoped that Roy was wrong, and The Seductive Sensation wasn't even going to be at that party. Then she would be safe…and Linus wouldn't have to imperil his immortal soul any further by doing something bad. Again.

But the plain fact was, Roy was never wrong, Linus acknowledged with a growing feeling of doom. If he was right again tonight, that woman and her smart-alecky detective companion were going to have to pay a pretty big price for it.

Nearing the residence of Dr. and Mrs. Finney on a fine summer evening, Savannah kept one hand on her hat and the other on the jostling wagon seat. Beside her, Adam sneaked his arm sideways, then cradled her hand in his. In the fading light of the deepening sunset, he smiled at her, his appearance both dapper and reassuring.

"If you two are going to get all spoony like that," Mose grumbled with a slanting glance from the driver's seat, where he'd managed the wagon for the past few miles, "I suggest you do it someplace more private, where *I* don't have to see it."

"*You* didn't have to be here at all," Adam pointed out, not budging his hand. "You're the one who decided a trip to the saloon for a game of Faro would suit you—tonight of all nights."

Mose jerked up his chin. "Yep. Faro suits me fine."

"I wish you would come to the party with us, Mose." Savannah knew the real reason her old friend had come to town, and it wasn't to indulge his nonexistent fondness for gambling. It was to protect her. The raid on her telegraph station had spooked him. Evidently Mose still didn't trust Adam to sufficiently watch over her. "There'll be plenty of room for you. I told you that Mrs. Finney enlarged the gathering from a tea party to a full-on evening reception, didn't I?"

"Yep." Mose clucked at the horse. "You told me that."

"Then won't you come with us? Please?"

"I'll be busy." With a watchful gaze, Mose examined the street ahead of them, then the businesses to the sides. "But I'll come back to collect you whenever you want me to."

As they drove through town toward the east side, they arranged a mutually agreed-upon time. At that point, Mose would leave the saloon, collect the horse and wagon from Owen Cooper's livery stable, then drive over to the Finneys' place to pick them up. Even Adam seemed satisfied with the plan.

But Savannah still wasn't ready to quit. "If you're not there, you won't be able to see everyone's awed reaction to the wedding gift you gave me, Mose! It's positively lovely."

Her friend glanced at her, taking in the appreciative way she stroked the antique lace shawl he'd given her. It had belonged to Mother Hawthorne. Somehow Mose had managed to smuggle it all the way across the country without Savannah knowing it. He'd been planning for her new life for a long time, she'd realized when she'd unwrapped Mose's wedding gift. She hoped his faith in her ability to start over would be justified.

"It looks right at home on you, just like I knew it would." Mose nodded at her lacy shawl, then stared ahead past the horse's twitching ears. "Mama would have liked you, Savannah."

Touched by his declaration, Savannah smiled. "And Adam, too. Isn't that right, Mose? Mama Hawthorne would have loved Adam."

Mose cast a dubious glance at Adam. He gave a snort.

"Now, Mose. Don't be churlish," Savannah coaxed. "Go on."

Beside her, Adam grinned. "It's all right. I don't mind."

"You should mind," Mose said. "Mama was a fine woman and a good judge of character besides." He angled his neck in a proud pose. "I like to think I take after her in that respect."

"Well then, Mose," Savannah said with a nudge. "That means your good opinion will matter doubly to Adam, won't it?"

This time it was Adam's turn to snort.

Mose gave him an incredulous look. "Are you laughing at my mama? Because I assure you, you *will* regret laughing at my mama."

"No." Adam sobered. "I'm laughing at the notion of a man who barely converses with anyone, yet feels equipped to fairly judge people."

"Humph. Listening is more important than talking."

"Unless nobody will talk to you at all," Adam said, "because all you do is growl and glower most of the time. Then—"

Adam went on talking, and so did Mose. But all of a sudden, Savannah felt in no mood for their usual manly squabbling. Because in the next instant, the lights and gaiety of the Finney household loomed into view, and her heart seized with panic.

According to Mrs. Finney's latest message, all the most important people in Morrow Creek would be at the reception tonight. Including the mayor. What if the townspeople at large didn't like her? What if they sensed something disreputable about her? What if they simply turned their backs on her?

That had happened before, Savannah remembered with a fearful clutch of her shawl. Although she'd done all she could to make sure that wouldn't happen again, there was no way to be one hundred percent positive. If being properly married, tutored on etiquette, and trussed up in a modest gown and hairstyle weren't enough, she would have nowhere else to turn.

In a very real sense, this reception was the final test of her hopes and dreams. Would she be able to have the life she wanted, with a good husband by her side and children on the way?

Or would everything be snatched away in a single night?

"Don't worry," Adam said with a comforting squeeze of her hand. "You'll have a good time tonight. Everyone will love you. I can't see how they could do anything but that."

Startled by his insight, she glanced up at him. "How did you know I was worried about the party?"

Mose looked Adam's way, too. He raised his eyebrows.

"Because you squeezed my hand in a death grip," Adam told her, smiling. "For a minute, I thought a grizzly had climbed in the wagon beside me and wanted to 'get all spoony like that.'"

At Adam's teasing reiteration of his words, Mose scowled.

But Savannah only laughed. "I hope you have a good time tonight, too. I wish I could stay entirely by your side—"

"Me, too," Adam said, "to show you off."

"—but proper etiquette *does* demand that we circulate."

Mose cast her a proud glance, then gave her a gruff nod. His pleasure at her remembrance of that rule made Savannah wonder exactly how often Mose had been sneaking glances at her etiquette handbook. She'd only caught him at it once or twice…

"I'll try to stay within earshot," Adam assured her. "I don't intend to let you out of my sight, either."

As he said it, his arm and shoulder tensed against hers, giving Savannah reason to wonder about Adam, too. Exactly what dangers did he think she might encounter at a fancy reception?

"Don't be silly," Savannah told him. "I'll be perfectly safe. You can't spend all your time watching over me."

"Oh, yes, he can!" Mose said.

"Yes, I can." Adam said at the same time. "And I will."

But their combined insistence gave Savannah other ideas—ideas about slipping out of sight once or twice... just long enough to prove to Adam and Mose that she would be fine on her own. After all, she hadn't come all the way west to feel even *less* free than she had while working on the New York stage!

If she didn't start out her married life the same way she intended to go on, there would be trouble ahead for sure. She had to assert her independence right now, Savannah decided.

A few minutes later, they reached the party. Mose parked the wagon near the two-story clapboard house across the street from the Finneys, then issued a few admonitions of his own.

Finally, after saying their goodbyes to Mose, Savannah and Adam joined hands. They headed together inside the brightly lit reception, where Savannah would learn if their future together was a real possibility—or only a dream that she would have to abandon...all over again.

"My goodness! I didn't even know there were this many people in all of Morrow Creek," Savannah said later, fanning herself in the crush, "much less that so many of them would willingly squeeze in so tightly for a party! Can you imagine?"

"Well, it's not often that someone new takes up residence in our little town. We're all *very* curious about you." This came from Sarah McCabe, the town's friendly, bookish schoolmarm. She cast a glance at Adam, who stood a few feet away amid several other partygoers, talking with her husband, Daniel, the town blacksmith. "We're all very curious about your husband, too, of course. Tell me… How did you two meet?"

At Sarah's inquisitive expression, Savannah blanched. Foolishly she had not prepared herself for this question. Now that it had inevitably arrived, she could not have felt sorrier for her lapse. She wanted to begin her new life truthfully. But she could hardly confide that she and Adam had met over the telegraph wires, become romantic pen pals, then arranged for a long-distance wedding…could she?

Fumbling for a reply, Savannah decided to buy herself some time. Affecting a perplexed expression, she leaned forward with a hand to her ear, then gestured at the milling crowds of partygoers. "I'm sorry. It's so loud in here! What did you say?"

Sarah smiled. "I said, how did you and Mr. Corwin meet?"

"Oh! Well, we have a shared interest in telegraphy, you see," Savannah began, casting a sideways glance at Adam, "and—"

"Ooh! Do tell us all about that, please." This came from Grace Murphy, Sarah's sister and—as Savannah had learned—a staunch suffragist with interests including journalism, bicycling, hosting several women's groups, and assembling educational lectures. "I have an avid interest in all forms of machinery," Grace confided, "and the telegraphy apparatus seems especially fascinating. In fact, it would make an absorbing discussion topic for the next meeting of the Social Equality Sisterhood. Would you consider speaking to the group?"

"Of course." Surprised—and relieved to be saved for the moment from discussing the story of her courtship with Adam—Savannah nodded. "But are you sure your members would be interested? I've heard that only men have the correct aptitude for understanding things of a mechanical or technical nature."

"Nonsense!" With vigor, Grace waved away her concerns. "All women need are opportunity and education. If only we could—"

"Now you've done it." Grinning, Sarah interrupted her sister. "Please, Grace. No lectures tonight." She turned to Savannah, her expression good humored. "Next Grace will be trotting out her picket signs, ready to protest the local telegraph station for not hiring women operators."

Grace's eyes brightened. "That is an *excellent* idea!"

"But they already have hired a female operator," Savannah hastened to point out, feeling giddy to be included in so much jovial conversation. She'd been cheerfully surrounded and welcomed from the moment she'd set foot inside the Finneys' home, over an hour ago. "They hired me, didn't they?"

"Oh, but won't you be quitting soon?" This from a rosy-faced Mrs. Finney, who stood beside Sarah with a glass of spirits in her hand. "Surely you'll want to start a family?"

The other women in their group nodded. All around them, the reception carried on in full swing, lighted by expensive oil lamps, augmented with fiddle music, and embellished with the sights and smells of delicious foodstuffs from the buffet.

"She will be able to do both, if she wishes." Another Morrow Creek resident approached with a dark-haired baby on her hip. The child clutched her mother with tiny, plump hands, making Savannah suddenly yearn for a similar babyish grasp. "That's what I've done, after all, with a few fits and starts."

Sarah introduced the newcomer as her sister, Molly Copeland, "one of the town's best bakers." Although she'd had a bit of trouble keeping up with the many people she'd met so far tonight, Savannah smiled at Molly. The woman's charming face, full figure and convivial manner would be easy to remember.

"If you're going to speak at one of Grace's women's club meetings," Molly said, "as I heard you say earlier, you'll have to agree to come address one of *my* favorite groups, too."

"Of course," Savannah said. "Which group is that?"

"The cinnamon bun group." Molly offered a dimpled smile. "Or the snickerdoodle cookie group, the apple pie group—it's your choice, really. They're all available down the street at my bakery. Does your husband like sweets? Because mine are rumored to be especially...potent." Molly gave an impish look.

"Potent?" Savannah asked. "How so?"

"They make men fall head over heels in love," Sarah said with a twinkle in her eye. She smiled in the direction of her husband, who'd been joined in conversation by several other well-dressed men. Sarah nodded at Adam. "Not that you'll need any help with *that,* with such a devoted husband at your side."

"That's true," Molly mused, looking in the same direction. "Have you noticed the way Mr. Corwin keeps glancing over here? It's almost as though he can't bear to be apart from you for an instant, Savannah! That's *so* romantic."

All the women sighed, even starchy Mrs. Finney.

And even, Savannah noticed, the suffragist Grace Murphy.

"Yes. You're very lucky," Grace said. She aimed a warm-hearted, private glance at her own husband, the saloon-keeper Jack Murphy, then returned her attention to the women. "Now then. On to practical matters." With a confiding air, Grace leaned nearer. "Savannah, I simply *must* tell you about my female archery group. I think you'll be a perfect fit for our club."

"And my sewing circle!" Molly put in. "You must join us."

"And my book group," Sarah added with a quelling glance at her chattier sisters. "The two of you can't monopolize the most interesting new resident of Morrow Creek all to yourselves."

"Us?" Molly protested. "You just wait until Mama gets over here. I overheard her telling Papa how interested she was in having Savannah over for a nice Grahamite meal."

"That's right," Grace agreed. "And I heard the editor of the *Pioneer Press* wants to do a piece on Savannah's work at the adjunct telegraph station. Mr. Walsh is very choosy in his subject matter, so that is quite an honor, Savannah."

Overcome and flattered to be the subject of so much positive attention, Savannah fanned herself. It appeared that her new life *would* be possible here, she realized. If the reactions of the people she'd met tonight were indicative of Morrow Creek residents' opinions in general, she might truly be safe from revelations of her scandalous past.

Happily she glanced sideways as the chatter continued. Adam stood across the room, just as much a focus for attention as she was, laughing heartily with a group of men. He noticed her looking, smiled, then offered her a naughty wink.

She blushed and was forced to fan herself with more vigor.

"Now now now! Let's not get carried away with making all these plans, ladies!" Mrs. Finney was saying in a loud voice when Savannah looked her way again, hoping to rejoin the conversation. "Remember, we hardly know Mrs. Corwin."

Savannah went instantly still. With a sense of unreality,

she realized that this could be the moment when Mrs. Finney—who was older, wiser and undoubtedly more suspicious than everyone else—revealed some proof of Savannah's scurrilous past.

Such a turn of events suddenly felt inevitable. Bracing herself for the worst, Savannah tried to think of a possible escape. She could feign illness. She could run for the door with no explanation whatsoever. She could change the subject.

But then it was too late to do anything at all. Mrs. Finney continued stridently onward, raising her glass of spirits for emphasis. "It is entirely possible," she said, "that Mrs. Corwin would prefer *my* sociable little group of knitters for company!"

All the women laughed. Savannah felt positively faint.

"Excuse me," she said. "I—I must get some air."

She lifted her skirts and dashed through the party, intent on reaching the Finneys' gaily decorated porch before she burst into tears from the strain of it all—or worse, blabbed a confession that she'd unfairly succeeded in deceiving them all.

For the first time, it occurred to Savannah to wonder, as she slipped safely into the coolness of the night outside: was it truly an improvement to have escaped one secret past… only to pile up more secrets in the wonderful new life she'd found?

Or was there—could there be—another way?

Chapter Fourteen

Striding purposefully down a Morrow Creek back alley, Adam stripped off his necktie. Shrouded in darkness, he stuffed it in his suit coat pocket. He checked his gun belt. He hoped he wouldn't need any of his weapons tonight, but he liked knowing his firearms were holstered and his knives were at the ready.

Just in case.

The sounds of tinkling piano music and husky male laughter followed him down the alleyway, coming from the nearby saloon. Most likely, Mose was in that saloon—Mose, who would not approve of Adam leaving Savannah behind at the party while he pursued his agency mission. Bothered by that reminder of his own divided loyalties, Adam frowned. But the only way to be sure Savannah was safe was to find the Bedells—and to do that, he needed either to locate Mariana or contact the agency.

Familiar with the town from his earlier scouting forays there, Adam skirted the jail and Sheriff Caffey's office, then headed first for the telegraph station. If he were lucky, there would be a note there from his former partner. Their protocol was to use local telegraph stations—which were plentiful all over the country—to relay messages to one another. Within a few minutes, Adam would know if Mariana was safe, if she'd been reassigned and if she'd uncovered any additional information about the Bedell gang.

Adam pulled down his hat, then entered the station. The lone operator was busy at the telegraph apparatus. Listening to the sound of a message being relayed, Adam took in the place's long counter, cubbyholes of papers, twin desks and single uncurtained window. Although the station was an essential part of town life, it appeared surprisingly humble.

"Yes, sir?" The operator looked up. "What can I do for you?"

"Messages for A. Sayles, please."

"I'm not sure we have any unrelayed messages."

Adam showed his old Marshall's badge. "Check again."

"All right." A skittish glance. "A. Sayles, you say?"

Adam nodded. The name followed the format he and his fellow detectives used—the first initial of the intended recipient, followed by the last name of the sender. To his relief, the operator located a pair of messages stuffed into a corner desk.

He passed them over the counter, scratching his head. "This is beyond odd. We don't usually keep unsent messages around."

"I'm obliged to you." Adam dropped a few coins on the counter, then pocketed his messages. "Thank you for your help."

The operator watched him leave. "Don't you want to answer them messages? I can take down a reply for you, if you want."

To be honest, Adam didn't even want to open the missives in his pocket. The news might not be good. But he knew he had to.

He shook his head. "That won't be necessary. Neither will your mentioning you saw me here tonight." He tipped his hat, then gave the operator a stern look. "Understand?"

The operator nodded. "Yes, sir. I understand."

Typically folks felt cooperative once they got a look at Adam's old badge. Adam didn't like using it that way, but right now he couldn't afford to waste time. His badge was expedient.

"You're a credit to your community, son," he told the telegraph operator. Then he gave a nod and headed back into the night, ready to read Mariana's messages and formulate a plan.

Standing in the Finneys' small yard, Savannah inhaled deeply of the blooming creosote that flourished in Morrow Creek. Its tangy scent went a long way toward clearing her head.

With her heart still pounding, she glanced back at the house. The party continued in full frolic, with laughter and conversation and music spilling into the outdoors. Idly Savannah hoped that all the neighbors had been invited as well. Otherwise, they were liable to be quite annoyed at hearing so much fuss over a simple married couple come newly to town.

Here in the secluded corner she'd found, though, things were more quiet—and that was exactly what she needed to recover her equilibrium. Being accepted by everyone in local society meant a great deal to her. She could scarcely believe it had finally happened. The thought that Mrs. Finney might have wrecked it all, just as Savannah had begun to relish it, had simply been too much for her overwrought nerves to stand, she supposed.

Feeling better now, Savannah savored another deep breath. She fussed with her dress, then recalled the rascally way Adam had winked at her from across the party. Her heart warmed at the memory. He really was everything she'd ever dreamed of in a man.

Footsteps approached. In the shadows cast where the house's lights couldn't reach the yard, two male figures loomed. Savannah didn't recognize them—but then again, most of Morrow Creek had been invited to the party tonight. Almost everyone in attendance was new to her.

"Miss Reed?" one of the men asked.

"Yes?" she replied, quite automatically. "I am Miss Reed." Then she remembered and gave a small laugh. "I mean, I am Mrs. Corwin, these days, but—" She broke off, gazing curiously at the two men as they came nearer. "Do I know you? Have we met?"

"Not officially, ma'am." The man who'd already addressed her held his hat in his jittery hands. "We haven't met, but—"

"Aw, shut up, Linus. We can't take all night!" the other man complained. He strode to Savannah and examined her. He frowned. "You don't *look* like no 'Seductive Sensation' to me."

"Don't be mean, Curtis! That ain't right."

Confused and suddenly afraid, Savannah glanced at the first man—the one who had, however awkwardly, defended her. "I'm afraid you both have the wrong person. Please excuse me."

Blindly she headed for the house. She could not think about who these men were—could not fathom how they knew of her onstage persona as The Seductive Sensation.

All she knew was that she had to get away. She had to get away and get to Adam.

Behind her, the ruder of the two men swore. There was a minor scuffle. Something hard smacked Savannah in the skull.

With a surprised cry, she stumbled. The ground rushed up to meet her. She was falling. *Just like Adam*, she thought disjointedly...then she struck hard-packed earth, and everything around her went black.

"I'm telling you, sheriff," Adam said, "you're going to want a posse. If the Bedell brothers are here in Morrow Creek, they're up to no good. I can't stop them alone."

"Seems to me *you* can't stop them at all." Sheriff Caffey looked up from his desk. The lawman had remained comfortably ensconced with his feet up ever since his deputy had admitted Adam into the place. He folded his hands over his belly. "Not if you've been here all this time and haven't caught up with them."

"I told you, I was injured." He'd explained the details when he'd first come into the sheriff's office, hoping for help.

He didn't have much longer before Savannah realized he had left the party, Adam knew. When he'd slipped away, the men had been in the midst of decamping to Doc Finney's billiards room for cigars, and Savannah had been securely chatting with the women. But as the night wore on, Adam could not be assured of her safety. Even now, he worried she would set off for Mose on her own or wander imprudently outside while looking for him.

The sheriff gave him a sweeping gaze. "You look all right to me. These Bedell fellas must not be as tough as you think."

"They're worse," Adam said. "You must have heard

of them. They're wanted killers, Roy Bedell and Edward Bedell alike. I've tracked them across three states and two territories so far."

"Hmm. Is that right?" Unconcernedly Sheriff Caffey blinked up at him. He shared an amused glance with his deputy. "You carryin' any proof of these claims you're makin', *Detective?*"

Filled with frustration, Adam set his jaw. The lawman's derisive tone sounded all too familiar to him. Some peace-keepers cooperated happily with the Pinkertons and other agencies. Others felt threatened by their "competition" and got surly. Evidently Morrow Creek's sheriff belonged to the latter group.

Adam frowned. "My proof was stolen along with my horse."

"You got a stolen horse?" The sheriff perked up. "That's serious business. I might be able to help you out with that."

Fighting for patience, Adam considered the messages in his pocket. He hadn't been pleased to read either of them. First Mariana had left word that the Bedell boys had moved on to old Mexico, with her in hot pursuit of them. The second message had been more brief: *Bedells gave me the slip. Meet you in San Fran.*

At the bottom was scrawled: *Sleep tight. M.*

The moment he'd glimpsed his partner's sloppy handwritten addition to the bottom of the paper, Adam had felt his tight chest ease. Most likely, that extra personal scribble— an aberration for his usually taciturn partner—was Mariana's way of letting him know she was safe and sound. She probably didn't want him to "fret over her," the way she so often accused him of doing. As for the rest of the message, Adam was gratified to know that although Mariana had lost the Bedells' trail someplace en route to Mexico, she'd headed for the closest agency office.

Adam had already reckoned that the Bedells could not be in Mexico—since he'd seen Curtis Bedell here in the Territory again with his own two eyes—but he was relieved to know that Mariana had made it out safely before the Bedell brothers had found her—foolhardily alone—on their trail. He hoped she'd already been assigned to a new partner or a new case…or both. But that didn't mean that Adam intended to give up. Not when he knew the Bedells were close by and in reach. They had to be.

"I don't want my horse back," he said. "I want a posse. Or at least whatever men you can spare me. We've got to bring in those Bedell boys." Frowning, knowing he had to get back to the Finneys' party before Savannah missed him, Adam withdrew Mariana's messages from his pocket. Seeing no other avenue, he handed them to the sheriff. "Maybe these will convince you."

Dubiously Caffey took a look. "These messages say this gang of yours already headed off to Mexico and got away."

Adam shook his head. "They're in town. I saw one of them."

"Maybe you just thought you did." The sheriff glanced at the messages again, then passed them to his deputy. "I know what it's like not to want to give up on a chase, Mr. Corwin. Believe me, I do. I hate to see a bad man escape. But the problem here—"

"I saw Curtis Bedell." Adam clenched his hands, saw the sheriff's gaze dip to his fists, then sighed. He had to rein in his temper. He turned his gaze loose on the office in an attempt to do so, taking in the empty, iron-barred holding cell, the dirt-smudged floor and darkened window, the wall papered with tattered wanted posters, and the deputy's desk

with its untidy scattering of bullet boxes, gloves, books and old newspapers.

Ruthless Reeds Strike Again In New York City! one headline screamed.

Glancing idly at it, Adam realized that he remembered that case. He hadn't thought about it in a long time, but now he recalled the frenzy in the tabloid papers, the resulting gossip and scandal as the particulars of the audacious thieving had spread, and the unwholesome interest people had shown over the case—a few of his fellow detectives included.

To be fair though, it *had* been a scandalous crime. The Reeds, two married stage performers, had stolen thousands from New York City theater owners—gullible men who'd fallen for the duplicitous wife's charms, then found themselves the subject of extortion demands from her husband. It required a particular brand of cheek, Adam reflected wryly, to commit such daring crimes. Even the youngest Reed, a golden-haired stage performer of some renown, had been linked to her parents' schemes. For all anyone knew, deceitfulness ran in the family.

In that instance, too, Adam remembered as he scowled anew, the police had assumed control of the incipient case. Then they'd spilled details of the crimes to the city's newspapers, probably earning a handy profit for themselves in the process.

The deputy glanced up, Mariana's messages still held in his grasp. "When did you say you were attacked, Mr. Corwin?"

Adam told him. "But if you can't help me, I'll have to do what I can on my own." He put his hand forward to have Mariana's messages returned to him. "I'll be back later."

With the Bedell brothers in custody, he vowed. *And with Savannah safe at last.*

At the thought of her, something nudged at the back of his mind. Adam glanced at the newspaper again, then gave a mental shrug. He was tired and troubled and harassed. He wasn't thinking straight. After so many days of worrying about Mariana...

"Hold on just a minute." The deputy waved the first message. "The reason I'm asking is because this here note is dated the day before that. It's dated *before* you were hurt."

"That can't be." Adam strode to the deputy. He looked.

Sure enough, the conscientious telegraph clerk had noted the date and time at the top of the transmittal form—the form that would have been discarded, had the message been relayed as usual. Had Mariana known something would happen? Was this some sort of signal?

Concerned and baffled, Adam stared at the messages.

Then he had a revelation. Hurriedly Adam snatched both papers. He put on his hat. "I know where the Bedells are," he said. "And they'll never see me coming."

Chapter Fifteen

The first thing Savannah noticed when she awakened were the mingled smells of kerosene, cigar smoke and perfume. The next thing she noticed was that her skull ached something fierce.

With an unsteady gesture, she put her hand to her head. The movement made her realize that whatever she was lying on felt decidedly lumpy...and a little unsavory, too. Curiously and confusedly, Savannah thrust out her arms. Clumsily she patted.

A mattress. She was lying on a bed, she realized. Which only served to confuse her further.

Could Mrs. Finney truly be so poor a housekeeper that she *never* properly turned her mattresses? That seemed unlikely. But where else could she be, except Mrs. Finney's house?

Muzzy-headed, Savannah blinked. The room around her came into view, wrought of cheap lumber walls and sparingly decorated with two beds, including the one she occupied. She could glimpse only the foot of the other bed, so she couldn't discern if it also offered its dubious lump-filled comforts to someone else from the party. The room contained a single curtained window, offering a view of the dark night outside, and several chairs.

Six chairs, she counted. But who needed that many chairs?

Surely Mrs. Finney and Doc Finney, whose children had already grown and moved into their own households, didn't require that many chairs. Or if they did, they would have used them at the party. Wouldn't they? Except, Savannah realized, she couldn't hear the party. The music and frivolity had vanished.

Either that, or *she* had vanished from the party.

Sitting up in alarm, Savannah swayed. The movement made her head hurt worse. Somewhere not too distant, a baby started wailing in a way that Savannah wished she could mimic…but something warned her not to. With effort, she tried to pay closer attention to her surroundings. She was rewarded when other sounds gradually drifted nearer. She made out the *clip-clop* of a horse moving down the street outside. Then a burst of piano music. Judging by the bawdy tune—one she recognized from her days on the stage—the melody was coming from a saloon.

Then she glimpsed a woman in the room, crouched before a banged-up potbellied stove as she tended the fire inside. The woman was dressed in a very practical fashion—a fashion definitely not intended for the party—and Savannah surmised that she must be one of the Finneys' neighbors. Perhaps someone had found her in the yard, alone in the blackness, and had brought her inside? And this woman was here to care for her?

All at once, she remembered the two men who'd assaulted her. Their faces returned to her in a rush, along with their coarse voices…and the memory of what the second man had said.

You don't look like no "Seductive Sensation" to me.

Someone here knew who she was! Savannah realized in a panic. Those two men… What could they possibly want from her?

Her first thought was that Warren—her former fiancé *and* former stage manager—had somehow used his considerable influence to find her here in the Arizona Territory. Maybe Warren wanted to punish her for leaving, Savannah thought. She was under no illusions that he pined after her in some lovelorn fashion, but she *had* cost Warren a significant amount of money when she'd refused to perform anymore. And he *was* the vengeful type.

Still, as far as she knew, Warren did not have associates all the way out west. If he or his lackeys had ransacked her outlying telegraph station, he wouldn't have bothered hiding afterward. Above all else, Warren Scarne was a man who felt entitled to whatever he wanted. Including—at one time—*her.*

No, Savannah decided, this attack had to have been the work of someone else. But who? Searching for clues, she scrutinized her surroundings. The crude walls, the sparse decor, the close proximity to the saloon and to horse traffic… They all told her one thing, now that she was alert enough to realize it.

This was *not*, as she'd first thought, a neighborly dwelling where someone had taken her to recover from her attack outside the Finneys' party. No, this was a *secret* place—a place where no one would ever think to look for her…or find her.

She had to get out. Fearfully Savannah examined the room again. To her left stood a single door, but it was closed. Maybe even locked. Unfortunately the sleight of hand she'd honed on practicing minor magic tricks was of no use with lock picking.

If the door *were* locked, she couldn't simply run away. The window appeared latched, as well. *Where was she?*

Uncertainly Savannah looked toward the woman at the woodstove again. Maybe she had been brought here against her will, also. Maybe if they worked together, they could escape?

Then Savannah realized that the plainly dressed woman was not tending the fire, as she'd first assumed. Instead the woman had crouched in front of the stove's fiery maw in order to methodically feed in stamped and addressed letters—letters that crisped at the edges, then sent up acrid smoke as they burned.

Those letters appeared curiously familiar, Savannah thought in a distracted fashion. The envelopes and seals seemed…

She took a second startled look. Those were *her* letters, Savannah realized. They were her letters to Adam, sent during their long-distance courtship. But how in the world…?

Had someone gotten to Adam, too? Before she could consider that urgent question any further, the door opened. Clutching her lacy shawl protectively against herself, Savannah looked up.

A shabbily dressed man entered the room, taking exaggeratedly slow steps in an apparent effort to be quiet. His hair was pale and cut quite short. His face was lean, his cheeks raw with either windburn or sunburn. Overall, he gave an impression of someone who spent a great deal of time outdoors.

When he saw her watching him, he widened his eyes. "Oh! You're awake!" He hurried to straighten his suit coat and shirtfront, then offered her a nod. "How are you feeling?"

Solicitously he headed toward the bed. Savannah jerked and lunged backward in fear, scrambling across the lumpy coverlet. She wanted a weapon, but nothing came to hand—not even her reticule, which, she noticed belatedly, lay at the other woman's feet, its contents spilling carelessly onto the grungy floor.

"Aww, I won't hurt you." The man seemed dismayed. He hooked his thumb toward the open doorway, then kicked the door shut with his foot. "That was Curtis who hit you before. I'm sorry about that. I brought a rope, so we wouldn't have to do anything like that. But Curtis... He laughed outright. He said a rope was a dumb idea." Apologetically the man offered a shrug. "Curtis has different notions about things than me, that's all."

Cautiously Savannah held her position. She recognized his voice now. He was the first man who'd spoken to her in the yard. That meant he wasn't completely disdainful of her, at least. But she still didn't trust him. She didn't trust anyone here.

"Be quiet, Linus." The woman glanced over her shoulder. Her impatient gaze took in Savannah, then shifted to the man—Linus. She frowned and fed another letter into the flames. She watched it turn black and curled at the edges. "I doubt she wants to hear about your brother right now. Did Curtis head out to collect Roy and the others, like he said he was going to?"

Linus gulped, then nodded. "Yeah, he did. Like usual, I didn't get to do it," he grumbled. "It figures. The *one* time Roy's goin' to be happy about somethin', and I won't be the one what did it. Curtis will hog all the credit. I never get to take credit for nothin', not even nabbing one little lady." He ducked his head, then cast an apologetic look at Savannah.

"Sorry, ma'am. But if you knew what I went through with my brothers—"

"Hush, Linus. You're going to get yourself in trouble." The woman's gaze skated back to Savannah. "Until this matter is settled, I guess we'd both better just do what we're told."

"I always do what I'm told!" Linus blurted. "Always!"

The woman narrowed her eyes, seeming—in that moment—surprisingly astute. She paused. "'Course you do, Linus."

"That's right. I do! Don't let nobody tell you different." Linus shook his head. "If Roy ever asks you, you be sure to tell him that, all right, Mariana? He'll listen to you. He'll—"

"All right, all right." The woman, Mariana, sighed. She shuffled the letters in her hands. "Don't get all tetchy, now. I don't know how much pull I got with Roy these days, anyways."

"Oh, I think you got *plenty* of pull," Linus assured her kindly. "Plenty." Lanky and uncomfortable-looking, he ambled nearer, then gazed down at the letters in her hands. "Otherwise, Roy wouldn't have trusted you with *them*, now would he?"

His encouraging tone seemed peculiar, given the situation, but it served to put Mariana at ease. She gazed down at the letters, then shrugged and fed another of them into the fire.

"I reckon that's one take on it. Another is that Roy plain don't want no proof layin' around for later. And I'm just—"

"Proof of what?" Savannah asked. Her heart pounded.

They both looked at her as though surprised to find her capable of speech. Still clutching her shawl, Savannah raised her aching head. *In for a penny*, she decided, *in for a pound*.

"Who's Roy?" she pressed. "What do you all want with me?"

Mariana frowned. She looked away, clutching the letters.

"Those are *my* letters," Savannah went on, growing increasingly bold as she pointed to them. These two, as odd as they were, didn't seem dangerous to her. "How did you get my—"

Linus silenced her by holding up his hand. Wearing an anxious expression, he hastened to take a seat on the other bed.

"I'm sure you're plumb full up with questions right now," he said in a sympathetic voice, glancing over his shoulder at an indifferent-seeming Mariana, "but it's better for you if you just stick to givin' out answers, all right? When Roy gets here, he won't put up with no questions from the likes of you."

"Why not? Who is he? What does he want from me?"

Linus exhaled. As though she were a simpleton, he gave an elaborately tolerant head shake. "Now see there? That's what I'm talkin' about. Those are just *more* questions. You can't—"

"What if I just leave?" Nervously Savannah glanced at the door. She didn't think Linus had locked it when he'd entered. If she could get up without falling flat on her face, she might be able to get away. "You can't stop me from leaving."

"Now that's where you're wrong." Reluctantly Linus edged his hand to his gun belt. His fingernails were chewed to the quick, but they were clean, and his grasp on his gun seemed frighteningly steady. "I'm powerful glad you ain't hurt bad," he said, "but that don't mean I won't stop you from leavin'."

He shifted his gaze sideways, as though making certain that Mariana heard him make that threat. He scowled, too. Savannah hadn't noticed his gun belt before. But now that she had, she felt riveted by the sight. Carefully and slowly, she nodded.

"I'm a bad man," Linus confessed. "I done bad things, and my soul is prob'ly lost forever because of it. So don't you go testin' me none, because I *will* make sure you do what you're told to do." Still fingering his firearm, he bobbed his head again. "I'm sorry, but that's the truth, sure as shootin'."

"Oh, quit scarin' her." Mariana surprised Savannah by standing, then carelessly pocketing the last few letters that remained unburned. "You men and your blusterin'. I swear, it gets downright tiresome." With a beleaguered sigh, Mariana sat on the bed beside Linus. In a curiously straightforward, almost mannish fashion, she leaned her elbows on her knees, then fixed Savannah with a determined look. "Here's the situation: you got yourself mixed up with a real sharper, Miss Reed—"

"It's Mrs. Corwin." Wondering how these two even knew her name at all, Savannah raised her chin. "If you please."

A look of illumination crossed Mariana's careworn face. For an instant, she seemed downright pleased. Which made not a lick of sense. Especially while Linus was still sulking. Even as Savannah had the thought, he took out his shooter and examined it. The motion drew Mariana's attention— and erased her curious expression of enlightenment, too. She sobered, then went on.

"When you decided to go wandering the telegraph wires lookin' for company a while back, my man, Roy, took notice of you. He struck up a correspondence to see what he could find out. What he found out was that you was lonely for a man."

"I was *not* lonely for a man!" Affronted to be described in such disagreeable terms, Savannah protested. "Not for just *any* man, at least. Besides, during slow times, the telegraph operators often talk to one another. It's not the least bit unusual for us to strike up friendships over the wires when we—"

"'Friendships'? Is that really what you want to call 'em?"

What else would I call them? Savannah wondered hotly. She had, after all, entered into her relationship with Adam under good faith. She didn't know how Mariana knew about her activities on the wires, but the truth was, she and Adam had simply been two ordinary telegraph operators, just passing some pleasant time together between transmittals. Their friendship had blossomed from there, to be certain. But this *Roy* person...

She still didn't know how he factored in.

Apparently Linus did.

"I don't know if this is wise, tellin' her all this," he interrupted with a wary glance at the closed door. He frowned at Mariana. "I don't reckon Roy would be pleased."

"Roy ain't here," Mariana pointed out in a dismissive tone. "He won't be back from the saloon for a while yet. You know he can't be rushed when he's busy. 'Sides, don't you think makin' sure *she* cooperates is worth a little plannin' ahead?"

Mariana jabbed her chin derisively toward Savannah. Linus, compelled by her gesture, studied Savannah, too. He nodded.

"Well... I would like to make things go smooth, I guess."

"All right then." Mariana gave a brisk nod, then returned her attention to Savannah. "Like I was sayin', Roy took notice of you and decided to try a little sweet talkin' on you. And you… Well, you was ripe for the pickin', I guess. Since you promised to marry him, I reckon it worked, didn't it?"

Baffled, Savannah shook her head. Mariana's depiction of things *did* fairly describe her long-distance relationship with Adam, but as for the rest… "I don't even know anyone called Roy," she said. "This must be some kind of mistake."

Maybe they would let her go, she dared to hope. Maybe—

"It ain't a mistake." Mariana shook her head, then patted her pocket. "These letters I've got prove it. Written in your own hand, just like you said." She sighed again, appearing beleaguered. "Don't you know no better than to believe a man who promises you the moon? They don't never mean it, not ever."

Linus cast Mariana a questioning look.

"Not when they're working a scheme, especially," Mariana hastened to add. "The truth is, Roy cares about me, Mrs. Corwin, not you. All he wants from you is that nest-egg money you kept on bragging about in your letters. So my advice to you is this: When Roy and the boys come back, don't waste no time pretendin' not to have that money. You give it over. No matter what."

Her savings? They wanted her savings? *That* was what this was about? Savannah wondered. But she'd been so discreet about her nest-egg money…except when it came to Adam and Mose.

"Yep." At that, Linus gave a vigorous nod. "You don't want to make Roy irate. He ain't a nice man when he's irate."

"Just cooperate." Mariana seemed annoyed at Linus's nasty depiction of "her man." "Just do like Roy says, keep your mouth shut otherwise, and maybe you'll make it out of here alive."

But her warning was lost on Savannah. Because just then, she realized something unexpected. "*You're* the ones who wrecked my station!" She peered at Mariana and Linus in newfound enlightenment. "You *were* looking for my money. Adam was right."

"Well, I dunno about that, but *Roy* is usually right about things." Linus shifted, his expression a peculiar amalgamation of pride and discomfort. "Roy told us that money had to be there at the station someplace. He told us how you don't trust no banks with your money, on account of not being gullible."

Astonished, Savannah gaped at him. *I'm leery of entrusting my savings to any bank or institution,* she'd written at least once. *I've become cautious of late, on account of recent events.*

She'd meant her entanglement with Warren. She'd wanted to avoid giving another man easy access to her money. Yet Savannah had felt compelled to admit having it. She'd wanted, as much as possible, to conduct her long-distance friendship honestly. She'd also wanted to make it clear that she was independent—that she wouldn't be relying on her new husband to pay her way.

Remembering those words she'd written, Savannah glanced at the pocket of Mariana's workmanlike dress. How could the woman have Savannah's letters, she wondered, when she'd seen those same letters in Adam's possession on the day he'd arrived?

"Did you snatch Adam from the party, too?" Without thinking, she bounded to her feet to search. "Where are you keeping him?"

Linus blinked. "The detective? We don't have *him*."

"Detective?" Savannah frowned. These two definitely had some wrongheaded ideas about things. "What detective? Adam is my husband. We were together tonight at the Finneys' party."

Frustrated and fearful, she rounded the room. Mariana and Linus only sat there for a moment, watching her in bafflement.

"Your husband was supposed to be *Roy*," Linus said in a hard-thinking tone. "Leastwise, that was the plan for this town. But if you say your husband is named *Adam*, then I reckon—"

"She married the detective. Her name is Corwin now. She just said so, remember?" Mariana snapped. "For heaven's sake, Linus. Try to keep up, why don't you?"

Savannah wasn't sure how he could. She certainly couldn't.

"Adam," she specified, edging closer to the door, "is a telegraph operator from Baltimore. I'm telling you, you have the wrong woman. This is all some sort of terrible mistake."

Suddenly Linus laughed. "I get it!" He slapped his knee in cheerful understanding. "She thinks Corwin is *Roy*, on account of Roy stealin' Corwin's name for this scheme." He nudged Mariana. "That sure did tickle Roy, when he thought up that idea. He knew that would rankle that detective. I bet it did, too."

Upon hearing this puzzling explanation, Mariana only shrugged. She looked at Savannah. "You mean Corwin didn't tell you nothin' about *any* of this? Not even after you got hitched?"

Struck by a powerful sense that she was missing something important, Savannah paused. It was possible that she could sneak away—just open the door and run from wherever she found herself standing—but the insightful expressions on the faces of her captors made her feet stick in place.

"What *should* he have told me about?" she asked.

As Adam approached the Finneys' house, with its lights and music and laughter spilling onto the small yard outside, he closed his fingers on the two messages in his pocket. Because of Mariana's quick thinking, he knew where to find the Bedells.

Sleep tight, she'd written. *Sleep tight.*

Those weren't words that a no-nonsense female detective like Mariana used often. Or ever. His partner was sensible to a fault, never one to waste words on niceties. Adam had overlooked that phrase at first glance, but now—given what he knew about the local lawmen's reluctance to get involved in bringing in the Bedell brothers—he saw his partner's words through new eyes.

Sleep tight, Mariana had told him…because at some point, Adam reasoned, the Bedells had gotten themselves holed up in a local hotel or boardinghouse, and Mariana had seen them do it.

She was still on the case. Her message *had* been a clue—probably left as a last-ditch effort, because she'd likely met with the same indifference he had from Sheriff Caffey and his deputy. Now all Adam had to do, he told himself as he strode onward, was make sure Savannah was safely in Mose's care, then search Morrow Creek for Roy Bedell and his brothers.

As though he'd summoned the big man himself, Adam glimpsed Mose alighting from the telegraph station's wagon. Wearing his coat and a concerned expression, Mose hurried to the Finneys' house as fast as if his shoes had been on fire.

He moved easily among the partygoers who'd wandered outside for a spell.

"Mose!" Adam waved. "Wait."

Mose didn't so much as slow down. Adam ran after him.

He caught up a few steps shy of the Finneys' front porch, then reached out to touch the station helper's arm. "Mose, I need you to stay with Savannah. I've got to do something—"

"Corwin." Turning, Mose narrowed his eyes. "What are you doing out here? You're *already* supposed to be with Savannah."

"I had business to take care of. All you need to know is—"

"I *knew* I should have watched her myself!" Looking besieged, Mose jerked out of Adam's grasp. The regret in his face was evident. "Get out of my way."

Surprised, Adam stepped back. Then he followed Mose.

They entered the house, both of them shouldering aside gregarious Morrow Creek residents who tried to engage them in conversation. They passed the parlor, the sitting room… Their mutual haste would have been comical, had their cause not been so urgent. Craning his neck to search for Savannah, Adam felt increasingly concerned as they passed more partygoers with no sign of her. He cupped his hands around his mouth. "Savannah!"

Mose did the same, his voice thundering through the house.

Grim-faced and tense, Adam doubled back. Maybe he'd missed her during his first pass. Maybe she was outside. Maybe…

Swearing, Adam cut off those hopeful thoughts. All that

was left to do was find her. Just find her, hold her and love her.

"Mr. Corwin?" came a tentative female voice.

Someone touched him with a light hand. He turned to see Molly Copeland, the town baker, standing there beside her sister, Sarah, the schoolteacher. Worriedly Molly twisted her hands, heedless of the partygoers drifting toward them.

"Have you seen Savannah?" Molly asked. "I heard you calling for her. You see, she left to get a breath of fresh air quite a while ago, and we're wondering… Is everything all right?"

She bit her lip, gazing earnestly up at him. Behind her, the crowd of partygoers seemed to grow. Hazily Adam recognized more Morrow Creek residents—people he had met tonight and then inadvertently, foolishly, left in charge of Savannah's safety.

She left to get a breath of fresh air quite a while ago…

"I organized a group to search the yard and its environs," Grace Murphy offered in a brisk tone, "but there was no sign of Savannah anywhere. Might she have gone home alone? I was just about to appoint someone to check at the telegraph station."

Looking down into Grace's competent, assured face, Adam felt awash in regret. Surely now his expression matched Mose's. He should have *never* left the party to pursue the Bedells. There must have been another way. Another *honest* way, like explaining to Savannah who he was and why he had to find the gang. It would have cost him her trust…but it might have saved her life.

"No," Adam said. "She wouldn't have gone home alone."

She left to get a breath of fresh air quite a while ago…

Molly frowned. "Then where could she be? It doesn't seem like her to simply vanish this way. We honestly didn't try to run her off, Mr. Corwin. We all liked her very much—"

"Don't be a ninny, Molly!" Sarah elbowed her way forward. "Anyone can see with a single look at Mr. Corwin's face that something is very wrong here. What is it? Please tell us."

"Yes," Grace urged. "Undoubtedly, we can help."

Adam gazed down at their trusting faces and could scarcely think at all. Choked by fear, he swallowed hard. As a detective, he was unshakably brave. As a man who loved his new wife, he was…unconscionably afraid. He clenched his fists.

She left to get a breath of fresh air quite a while ago…

"No one can help," Adam said. "I have to leave."

He turned, but Mose blocked his path.

"I'm going with you," Mose said. "They're down at the saloon. That's why I'm here early. I was worried about Savannah being in town near them. If we hurry, we might be able to—"

None of what he was saying made sense. Fraught with worry, Adam gave an impatient wave. Everyone stepped back except Mose.

"Get out of my way, Mose. I have to start searching."

Boardinghouses, hotels… Morrow Creek was small, but there had to be many of those places in town. Many to search, and many to be disappointed at. If Adam didn't hurry, he would be too late for certain. But still Mose stood in his way, arms crossed.

"I'm coming with you," the big man said again. "I'm telling you, they're at the saloon." He gestured. "I can show you."

Frustrated, Adam frowned. "*Who* is at the saloon?"

"The Bedell brothers. Ornery sons of bitches, and mean, besides. They were cheating at cards, not that I cared—"

With a sense of surreality, Adam stared at him. "You know who the Bedells are? How do you know who the Bedells are?"

Mose made a disgusted face. "They're a bunch of loud-mouthed cusses. People two territories over know who they are by now."

That was probably true, Adam realized ruefully. And yet—

"Bedells? Down at *my* saloon?" Jack Murphy moved forward, all Irish belligerence and Western toughness combined. He exchanged a glance with his wife, Grace. "I won't have it."

"Don't see how you can stop it, Murphy." The blacksmith, Daniel McCabe, moved forward, too. He was a huge man, but he seemed the most easygoing of everyone. He shrugged. "Bad men like to frequent saloons. For now, I say we find Savannah. The womenfolk are all up in arms. If we can put them at ease—"

"Finding Savannah *will* put us at ease!" Sarah exclaimed. She gave her husband a determined look. "These Bedell people must be threatening her, somehow. I don't know who they are, but—"

"I wish I could say the same." The newspaper editor, eastern born-and-bred Thomas Walsh, spoke up. Behind his spectacles, his eyes appeared somber, his expression serious. "I know who the Bedell boys are, and I wish I could forget."

By the time he'd given everyone a hasty dossier of the Bedell brothers' criminal exploits, all the partygoers were agog—including Adam. He'd had no notion how well informed the residents of a town like Morrow Creek could be. Or how eager to help. But that didn't change the fact that Savannah might, even now, be at the mercy of Roy Bedell. He had to go get her.

Just as he turned again, the mercantile owner, Jedediah Hofer, stepped up. He silenced the crowd with a piercing whistle. He waved his arms. Then, in his thick accent, he said, "Hurry! We must go to the sheriff's office and get help."

Adam paused. He shook his head. "That won't work. I already spoke with the sheriff. He won't even round up a posse."

The lumber mill owner, Marcus Copeland, stepped forward next. The partygoers moved aside to make room, as befit his stature in Morrow Creek. "If Sheriff Caffey won't assemble a posse," Copeland said, "I'd suggest we bring the posse to him."

The crowd of partygoers cheered—foolishly, Adam thought.

"He still wants proof," he argued. "I'm going alone."

He'd already wasted too much time here as it was. *Savannah…*

"Proof?" Fiona Crabtree asked. "What kind of proof?"

"Proof like this, I'd guess." Mose lifted his arm. In his grasp, two heavy items swung from side to side—items Adam hadn't noticed until now. "Maybe these will help. If we hurry."

To his surprise, Adam recognized the items in Mose's hand.

Incredibly they were *his* old saddlebags. The saddlebags filled with his official agency credentials—and with all his assembled proof of the Bedell brothers' crimes. The saddlebags he'd thought he'd lost when he'd confronted Roy Bedell…and had wound up shot and left for dead outside Savannah's station.

Unapologetically Mose caught his eye. "You didn't think I'd let you be around Savannah without checking who you were first, did you? I might not have found your horse—I reckon those Bedell boys stole it—but I did find these and everything that's in them. I was about to take them down to the sheriff. But since you're here." He shoved the bags in Adam's hands. "Let's go save Savannah instead."

Chapter Sixteen

With her mouth agape, Savannah listened as Mariana and Linus described an incredible story—a story about a foolish and naive woman who'd accidentally struck up a correspondence over the telegraph wires with a deadly confidence man…and in doing so had managed to bring that man west with the intimation of a "cash-money" windfall that would be his if he married her.

That woman couldn't have known, Savannah realized as she heard the story unfold, that the sharper in question ran a gang with his four devious brothers and one recently added female companion. She couldn't have known that he was a bad man who'd never intended to marry anyone at all, or that he'd successfully pulled off this scheme with at least a half dozen unfortunate women already…and had the ill-gotten profits to prove it.

She couldn't have known, Savannah learned to her growing consternation, that a certain strong-minded detective had pursued that same confidence man across several states and territories so far…but with limited success. She couldn't have known that the detective's unstoppable determination had riled up the confidence man so much that he'd stolen the detective's name and used it when arranging for his latest sham "marriage."

She couldn't have known any of that until tonight.

All she could have known, Savannah realized, was that a woman like her—desperate, distracted and eager to move on from bad situations in both New York City and Ledgerville—had been easy pickings for a man like Roy Bedell. But she hadn't realized any of that until it was too late. Much, *much* too late.

"If it makes you feel any better," Linus said, peering anxiously at her undoubtedly stricken face, "that detective of yours did get in a few whacks on Roy afore he went down. Roy's been laid up awhile now, on account of the fight they had."

"Fight?" Still feeling shocked, Savannah glanced up. "What fight? I thought you said Adam had never caught up with Roy."

Roy. Upon using that name, she almost shuddered. All this time, *he* had been the one she'd been corresponding with, making plans with, exchanging flirtatious telegraph messages with. In trusting him, she'd behaved beyond imprudently. Now she was paying for her actions—probably, later tonight, quite literally. If she were fortunate, all she would lose would be her savings.

Only those… Not her life. *If* she were lucky.

Understanding for the first time exactly how dangerous this situation was, Savannah clutched her shawl. *I'm leery of entrusting my savings to any bank or institution,* she'd written. But what about entrusting *herself*—and her heart—to an unknown man? At the memory of her supposed former "caution," she felt her lips give a bitter quirk. If only she'd known the truth…

And Adam! He'd pretended to be her mail-order groom readily enough. He'd romanced her and kissed her. *He'd married her!*

And for what reason? To set a trap for Roy Bedell, Savannah reasoned unhappily. Because that had been his job—to catch the confidence man he'd been chasing. As a detective, Adam had known full well he wasn't the fiancé she'd been waiting for, but he'd stepped into that duplicitous man's shoes all the same.

And she'd believed him.

It had taken a while. But in the end, she'd believed him.

"Nah." Linus shook his head. "What I said was that detective never *caught* Roy. But sure as shootin', Roy caught up with that detective, all right. He laid a trap for him but good, right outside your station. By the time me and my brothers got there and all the shootin' started—"

"Outside my station?" Shaking her head over the many bewildering details she'd heard tonight, Savannah stared at him. "Your brother met up with Adam outside my station? When?"

"When they both got shot up, that's when." Sourly, Mariana rose. She paced, her dingy skirts swinging above what appeared to be a scuffed pair of men's boots. "I thought for sure that Corwin was finally killed. But I guess he's got nine lives or somethin', 'cause it weren't long before Linus showed up with the news that *you* was nursin' that detective back to health."

"Yes." Savannah raised her head. "If you're expecting me to apologize for that, you'll have a long wait ahead of you."

"Humph." Mariana gave her a shrewd look, then shook her head in apparent consternation. "You really are dim-witted, aren't you? If a man ever done to *me* what Corwin did to you—"

"I'll thank you not to discuss my husband that way."

Savannah's response drew a hooting laugh. "Standin' by him, are you? I should have guessed as much. Dumb as a post."

Savannah shrugged. "You wouldn't understand."

Neither did she, in that moment. Her feelings *were* hurt. She definitely felt confused by all this. She was downright afraid at the dire situation she was in. But she was in no way ready to throw Adam to the wolves—or to the criminal element. She needed to hear from him before making any hasty judgments about what he'd done or—more importantly— why he'd done it.

"Nope, I guess I wouldn't understand." Mariana waved, still pacing. "But that's fine. You go on and be all prissy, if you want to. You look the type. But that detective of yours…" She wheeled around and eyed Savannah. "He lied to you. He used you like bait to capture my Roy. If you ever smarten up, you'll see—that ain't no way to treat a lady. A lady deserves better."

Coming from a woman who'd voluntarily joined up with a gang of admitted thieves, Mariana's advice should have been laughable. But to Savannah's dismay, those words held a smidgeon of truth. A lady *did* deserve better.

If Adam had deceived her for the sake of protecting her… Well, that she could almost understand. But if instead he'd coolly taken advantage of her, the way Mariana made it sound…

Well, if *that* were true, then Adam wasn't much different from Roy Bedell or Warren Scarne or any other man who'd misled her in the past, not caring about her feelings or her well-being.

Unwilling to admit even the possibility of that, Savannah

compressed her lips. Defiantly she addressed Mariana again.

"What makes you think *you'll* get any better treatment from Roy?" she asked her. "How do you know he won't take advantage of you the same way he was planning to take advantage of me?"

With her back to Savannah, Mariana gazed out the window at the darkened night, probably looking for signs of the Bedell brothers approaching. "'*Was* planning to take advantage' of you? Ha. Unless you're sittin' on a big old wad of cash instead of a bustle under that dress of yours, missy, I'd say you're deluding yourself. You're not getting out of this so easy."

"'Specially if this here turns out like Kansas City," Linus added in a doleful tone. "*That* weren't easy. Not for nobody."

Afraid to ask what had happened in Kansas City—but knowing she should—Savannah turned to face him. She opened her mouth.

But Linus kept right on speaking, having ducked his head to fiddle with his firearm, not noticing her tentative expression.

"What's worse," he said, "is after Roy's done with you, I'm bettin' he'll be goin' after Corwin next. He'll be wantin' to finish the job what he started. Plus, now Roy is awful annoyed about having been laid up. His leg was broke! That would make anybody a mite peevish, if their leg was broke."

"It was only a little broke, right by his ankle," Mariana argued. "He got plenty of pampering and whiskey for it, too."

Linus went on yammering, making his case for "a whole broke leg," but Savannah couldn't listen. All she kept hear-

ing, over and over in her head, were those first few words
he'd said.

*After Roy's done with you, I'm bettin' he'll be goin' after
Corwin next. He'll be wantin' to finish the job what he
started.*

Linus meant that Roy would *kill* Adam, she realized.
That's likely what he'd been trying to do outside her station, when he—or someone in his gang—had shot Adam in
the back and left him for dead. He'd almost succeeded that
time. She doubted he'd be so careless as to take the job's
completion for granted twice.

Next time, Roy Bedell would make certain Adam was
dead.

If that were true, Savannah's situation was even more
grave than she'd first realized. Because as soon as Adam—
or heaven forbid, *Mose*—noticed that she was gone from
the Finneys' party, one or both of them would come looking
for her.

If they found *her*… They would find Roy Bedell and
his brothers, too, waiting to get rid of the detective on their
tail.

She wasn't only here as a means to give over her nest-egg
money, Savannah realized in horror. She was also, providentially for Roy Bedell, here to function as bait to lure Adam
nearer.

*He's not running. No man would. Any man worth being
called a man would stay and fight, if he had the chance,*
she remembered Adam saying. *I would lay down my life
for you, Savannah.*

No matter what else occurred, she couldn't let that
happen. Not to Adam, not to Mose…not to anyone. Not on
account of her.

"I'll give you my money!" she blurted, startling Mariana
and Linus alike. "I'll give you all of it! We don't even have

to wait for Roy." As casually as she could, Savannah arched her brows at Linus. "You could surprise him. You could present the whole thing as a fait accompli. You'd like that, right, Linus?"

"A fate what?" Linus gulped, then shook his head. "I dunno what that is, but I don't like it. Roy don't cotton to surprises of any kind, 'specially when he don't see them comin'."

"But you said *you* never get the credit you deserve," Savannah cajoled. "You said your brothers always steal it from you. Yet *you're* the one who found me. You're the one who's been watching over me all night. Shouldn't *you* get some credit?"

Mariana gazed suspiciously at her. But Linus appeared to consider Savannah's words closely as he polished his gun barrel.

"I *would* like it if Roy thought I done good," he admitted.

"See there?" Feeling encouraged, Savannah stepped closer. "I don't mind helping you. You've been very kind to me."

Mariana scoffed. "Kind how? By lookin' at you like a dog with a big juicy bone he ain't 'et yet? That's a laugh."

Gawkily Linus jerked his head. He buffed his pistol across his trouser leg with agitated vigor. "Shut up, Mariana."

She laughed. "It's true. You wouldn't know what to do with a woman if you got a hold of one. Ain't that right?"

"Maybe I don't want to get a hold of this one." Linus pointed his gun belligerently at Savannah, as though it were a harmless toy. "Maybe I just wanted to meet her. Maybe…"

Confused by his timid tone, Savannah waited. "Maybe…?"

"Maybe see her dance a little for me, too," Linus finished

in a rush. He looked up, his red-cheeked face a study in mingled hopefulness and discomfiture. "I seen your posters, back in the city. Back when you looked all sparkly and pretty. If you would maybe dance a little dance for me, as The Seductive Sensation—"

Mariana snorted, putting her hands on her hips.

"—then maybe I'd go along with you and take your money from you. You know, like you said." Optimistically he showed her his teeth in a grayish smile. "Then we'd have ourselves a deal."

"That is a doltish idea," Mariana said. "If you think Little Miss Priss is gonna dance for the likes of you, Linus—"

But all Savannah could do was nod. If this was the only way to give over her money and skedaddle before Roy got here, she'd dance as though her life depended on it. Because it did.

Mustering her best actress's smile, she held out her hand. "Why, that's very gentlemanly of you, Linus! I accept."

He beamed, showing her even more of his discolored teeth.

"I'll dance for you," she specified as they shook hands on their agreement, "and then you'll come with me to get my money, so we can give it to Roy." Linus's nod—and his eager, glazed-eyed stare—partially reassured her. "But you won't need *that* at my show." She gestured for his firearm. "Before I start, you'll have to surrender that, please, or I simply can't begin."

By the time Adam reached the saloon, he was trailing a retinue of at least a dozen concerned Morrow Creek residents. Casting a backward glance at them as he pushed through the batwing doors into the noise and aromas and raucous piano music of Jack Murphy's popular watering hole, he shook his head.

"These people are *loco*," he told Mose in the Spanish vernacular of the region. "Will you tell them to go on home?"

"Do it yourself," Mose rumbled. He lifted his head to peer over the assembled drinkers' heads, then nodded. "I think maybe it won't hurt if someone's watching our backs tonight."

"It might hurt, if that 'someone' is a pack of well-meaning farmers and innocent townfolk," Adam pointed out. He aimed his chin at the assembly of men who trooped dutifully behind him into the saloon. "You should all go home! I can manage from here! If you want to collect the sheriff, that's fine, but—"

He came to a stop as Grace Murphy led the womenfolk into the saloon, too. Unblushing and determined, the whole pack of them strode past the men and headed for the bar. Behind it, the barkeep slung a towel over his shoulder, then crossed his arms.

Mose lifted his eyebrow. "*That's* why I'm not telling anybody anything." Dubiously he pointed at the uppity women. "Now that they're involved, we'd spend all night jawing instead of finding Savannah, if we tried to make them quit."

Mose was probably right. In no mood to dawdle, Adam approached the bar. Several cowboys looked sideways at him; a few Faro players and miners glanced his way, too. None of them bore the familiar, reviled features of the Bedell boys.

He was too late, Adam realized. *They'd already left here.*

Most likely, he knew, Roy and his brothers were with Savannah by now. Their intentions for her would not be good.

Grimly Adam pushed all the way forward to the bar,

dodging tobacco juice and sticky tequila spills as he went.

"Yep, I saw 'em," the bartender was telling Grace Murphy. "Despicable characters they were, too. Those Bedells took up one of our best tables, started a couple of fights, stiffed me on a bottle of Old Orchard—" he spied Jack Murphy in the crowd and gave him an apologetic shrug "—sorry, boss. Then they up and left, rowdy as they came."

"How long ago?" Adam asked. "Do you know where they went?"

The bartender scratched his chin. "Can't rightly say."

"Think, Harry!" Grace urged. "It's vitally important."

"Well…" The grizzled, gray-haired bartender hesitated. "I did hear the mean one, Roy, say something about that little boardinghouse that's next door to Miss Adelaide's place—"

"I know where that is," Daniel McCabe said. "It's close."

"Show me," Adam told him. "As for the rest of you—"

Thinking over his next words, he paused and looked behind him. To his disbelief, the crowd actually appeared to have grown as more Morrow Creek citizens had joined their impromptu posse. Gazing into their determined yet fretful faces, Adam could not justifiably lead them into danger. Not even if they were willing to go, as—to a man *and* woman—they undeniably appeared to be.

"The rest of you, bring the sheriff and whatever men he can spare," Adam told them. If he knew Sheriff Caffey, it would take his well-intentioned "helpers" all night to convince the lawman that he should intervene. By then, Adam would have settled the matter, once and for all. Satisfied that he'd safeguarded the citizenry as well as he could, Adam turned to Mose. "Except you," he said. "*You*, I'll need help from, if you're willing."

* * *

With an eager nod, Linus agreed. He turned his fire-arm around, then held it by the barrel. He offered it to Savannah.

Trembling wildly, she grabbed it. "Thank you."

As though expecting her to simply set it aside—and then perhaps remove her gown to reveal a spangled stage costume—Linus clasped his hands between his knees. He watched her. His gaze shone up at her with all the enthusiasm of a small boy's…if small boys had liked to watch ladies dance in skimpy attire.

"I heard about this one partic'lar dance," he said. "I think with some ostrich feather fans, or somethin' like 'em—"

"I'm afraid I won't be able to dance for you after all, Linus." Still shaking, Savannah raised the gun. She drew in a deep breath, then pointed it at him. "You see, I retired from the stage some time ago. When I did, I promised myself I'd never again be The Seductive Sensation—not for anyone."

He seemed mystified. He frowned. "But you said—"

"She was lyin', you saphead!" Mariana burst out. She shook her head. "I would've stopped you from doin' that, only I never thought even *you* was dumb enough to fall for that trick."

Her words drew Savannah's attention. Jerkily she nodded at Mariana, then gestured with the gun.

"Would you please sit down next to Linus?" she asked.

"I don't see how you can make me," Mariana retorted.

"I do." Linus's gaze skittered to his gun. "She's got my gun, Mariana! I guess you'd better just do what she says."

Reluctantly Mariana did. As she settled on the bed, she glanced out the murky window, giving Savannah new cause for concern. How much time did she have before Roy Bedell and his brothers arrived? Had Mariana already seen them coming?

Sorrowfully, Linus shook his head. "Roy ain't gonna like this one bit," he said in an agitated tone. "He's gonna know this is all my fault!" He eyed his lost weapon, still keeping his hands clasped childishly at his knees. "I'm gonna get a whalin' like no other. He'll prob'ly kill me, most likely."

Savannah felt sorry for that. But she couldn't waver. With her heart pounding, she took a cautious step toward the door.

"After I leave, there's nothing to stop you from leaving, too," she told Linus. "Just run away!" she urged. "Leave your brothers behind." Unaccountably she wished she could help him. He seemed so lost and hopeless. "You can start over. You can!"

Mariana scoffed. "That's real sweet, Miss Priss. Do you have any idea what kind of dreadful things this man's done?"

Still holding the gun level, Savannah shook her head. She didn't like the feel of the weapon or the need to use it, but she didn't have much choice. "No, I don't. I don't know what you've done, either. But if you're smart, you'll get out of here, too. Go someplace where Roy Bedell can't find you—both of you."

At that, Mariana seemed taken aback. She gazed at Savannah with the same keen acumen that Savannah had noticed earlier.

Then Mariana shook her head. "I've got some advice for you, too," she said in a cynical tone. "Take the window instead."

But Savannah had already yanked open the door. Keeping her gaze fixed on Mariana and Linus, she went on pointing the gun at them. She stepped sideways. *Almost there.*

She had to be smart, else risk having one of them rush at her and take away the gun.

Moving faster, she stepped to the left. Again. Again.

Her shoulder bumped into the doorjamb. Taking that as her signal, Savannah gripped the gun more tightly. She turned to run headlong down the hallway she expected to find.

Unfortunately the hallway was already occupied.

Savannah ran full chisel for a few steps toward freedom, then smacked straight into a man. With a grunt of surprise, she stumbled. His arms came around her to set her upright again.

Adam, she thought crazily, suddenly desperate for his reassuring presence and capable manner. But this wasn't Adam. Instead the man who'd grabbed her smelled of whiskey fumes and stale tobacco, grimy skin and unlaundered clothes. He emanated danger…and a conspicuous quantity of self-assurance, too.

"Well now." He treated her to a wholly unpleasant smile. Under other circumstances, he might have appeared boyishly handsome. As it was… He didn't. "If it ain't my dancin' fiancée, come to call on us. What do you know about that, boys?"

He had to be Roy Bedell. Before Savannah could do more than twist away from him, the other Bedell brothers were upon her.

The tall, spooky-looking one wrestled away the weapon she'd taken from Linus. The sour-faced one who'd jeered at her in the Finneys' yard snickered. The last one, muscular and grim, merely shoved her back in the room, herding her ahead of everyone else while Roy Bedell called out a greeting to "his woman," Mariana.

The door shut behind the lot of them. With a hollow feeling of despair, Savannah listened as it thudded closed,

knowing that she'd just lost her best—and probably only—
chance to get away.

I've got some advice for you, too, Mariana had said.
Take the window instead. Realizing now what she'd meant,
Savannah felt even more disheartened. It was just like a
criminal's "woman" to taunt her with the escape she couldn't
have.

Roy took his time greeting Mariana with a hearty kiss
and a leering, licentious whack to her ample backside. Mariana giggled, then leaned over and whispered something
to him. They both glanced slyly at Savannah. Appearing
pleased by whatever news Mariana had shared, Roy turned
to the others.

"You all might as well settle in." Cheerfully Roy rubbed
his palms together as he examined a fearful Savannah. "I
just decided I might as well take my own sweet time with
this one."

Chapter Seventeen

"Nope. I'm sorry." The boardinghouse owner gave Mose a rueful shake of his head. He seemed tired—which, given the late hour, was altogether appropriate. The place was otherwise deserted, with most of its occupants settled in for the evening. "I'm afraid I don't have any rooms available right now."

"You mean you don't have any rooms available for *me*. A colored man." Mose's deep, irate-sounding voice thundered through the anteroom reserved for boardinghouse business. "Isn't that right? You don't have a room for a darkie like me."

"No. No! I never said—I mean—it's just that—"

"*That,*" Mose interrupted. "Makes me...*unhappy.*"

His intimidating tone was plain—even from Adam's position in the boardinghouse hallway, where he'd crept when the owner wasn't looking as part of the plan he'd devised on the way here.

Marveling at Mose's performance now, Adam shook his

head. He wasn't sure how the big man had learned to appear so menacing, but his skills were certainly useful tonight.

"Please. That's not what I said." With clear apprehension, the man eyed Mose's burly arms and impatient expression. "I said we don't have any *rooms*. That's all."

"But I'm here specifically to meet up with my partners," Mose explained tautly. "Roy Bedell and his brother Edward Bedell. They said they'd be here. They're expecting me. You wouldn't want to...*interfere*...with our business dealings."

Something about that statement seemed to jostle loose a scrap of cooperation. The boardinghouse owner gave a jerky nod.

"Yes. I mean, no! No, I wouldn't want to interfere with any business of the Bedells. They *are* staying here, but they said—"

Adam listened while the boardinghouse owner babbled on about Roy Bedell's "explicit instructions" to him. It sounded as though Roy had, as usual, coerced everyone within earshot into cooperating with him, however undeservedly or criminally.

At the realization, Adam tensed his muscles. Impatiently he leaned around the corner to watch the proceedings. Given the bartender's description, he knew this was the right boardinghouse. He'd have liked to take the place right then—to burst into every room until he found Savannah. But he had to tread carefully. Getting her back from the Bedells would require all the wits he had. It would require Mose's help, too.

Even now, the big man was capably providing it. "Would you at least let me leave them a note?" he asked. "I'd be obliged."

"Fine." Sounding harassed, the boardinghouse owner pulled out paper and a pencil. Halfway in the process of handing over the items to Mose, he hesitated. He frowned.

"Uh… Would you rather *I* wrote the, uh, message for you, s-sir?"

Mose glowered. "Are you suggesting I can't write?"

"I'm…not sure? I only want to help," the man said.

With an exasperated exhalation, Mose grumbled. "Which room is it? I'll just put a note under the door myself."

Clearly expecting to be given the paper, he put out his massive hand. The boardinghouse owner gave it a wary glance.

Adam held his breath. Unless this worked, they would be hampered in finding Savannah and the Bedells. But then the boardinghouse owner appeared to decide that Mose's gigantic fist could just as easily smash his desk as it could write a note.

He pushed the paper and pencil at Mose's hand. "Please feel free to let yourself out after you're done." He appeared to look forward to that event. "I'll be locking up for the night soon."

The boardinghouse owner scurried away. Just as his feet touched the threshold of what appeared to be his own quarters, Mose cleared his throat. Emphatically.

"Which room?" he asked. "You never said."

Nervously the boardinghouse owner told him.

Ten seconds later, Adam and Mose were on their way there.

Trying not to tremble visibly in Roy Bedell's presence, Savannah stood with her posture poker straight as he approached her. He nodded as he examined her. His baby-faced appearance did little to soften the overall impression of cruelty he gave. As though ready to demonstrate that quality, he faced Linus.

"Linus. You been here all night, like I told you to be?"

"Yep. I sure have been." With a nervous gulp, Linus

nudged himself farther back on the bed. The mattress dipped sloppily.

"Well now." Considering that, Roy rubbed his hand over his jaw. Whatever his injuries had been, they hadn't hampered his ability to shave cleanly. Or to quaff whiskey. His voice sounded low and soft. "I guess that means that must have been *your* gun that my new lady friend, Miss Reed, was wavin' at me just now."

Stiffly Savannah shifted her gaze to Mariana. She expected the other woman to snootily point out what Savannah had specified to her earlier—that she was *Mrs. Corwin* now—but Mariana didn't. Instead she only watched Roy and Linus with rapt attention, just like the other three Bedell brothers did.

"Well…" Guiltily Linus glanced at the gun, which was currently being held by his brother. "She couldn't have waved it very threatenin', like." He tried to smile. "Look at her—she's just a wee bitty little thing, not fit to scare *you*, Roy. I—"

Lightning fast, Roy raised his arm. He hit Linus. Hard.

The impact of fist against flesh and bone made an awful sound. Savannah flinched. She recoiled, feeling sick.

Linus gave a muffled yowl. With tears in his eyes, he slapped his hand to his cheek. Above his fingers, with their clean, chewed-up nails, his gaze looked accusatory…and miserable.

"The point is," Roy said in a frighteningly patient voice, "that she shouldn't have had a chance to brandish a pistol at me at all. Now should she? Not if you were doin' your job, Linus."

"You tol' me," Linus murmured, "that you wouldn't smack me again. Not in front of—" Trying to be surreptitious, he aimed a nod in Savannah's direction, not looking at her. "You know."

Roy guffawed. He glanced at Savannah, then at Linus, his eyes wide with spiteful humor. "That's right. I forgot—you went and got yourself sweet on The Seductive Sensation, didn't you?"

The other brothers laughed, too. Mariana shook her head silently at all of them. Savannah could only cringe as Linus raised his hangdog head, bringing his wounded visage into view.

"You *promised* me that, Roy," he muttered. "You did."

Still standing over him, Roy exchanged amused glances with the other Bedell brothers. "Tell me, boys—did I promise that?"

"Nope," one of them said. "Don't reckon you did, Roy."

This time, Linus's disillusionment seemed doubled. "You know he did, Curtis! You was right there, you lyin' dog."

"You're the one who sounds like a dog, whinin' like that." Roy grinned at his comparison. "How 'bout you bark next, eh?"

"Aw, lay off him, Roy." Mariana stepped forward. She took his arm in hers, stroking it. "Linus was just tryin' to make a deal, to shortcut you gettin' your money, and it all went wrong on him. You can't fault him too much for tryin', can you?"

"A deal?" Seeming placated, Roy peered at Linus. A glimmer of near respect shone in his gaze. "That true, dimwit?"

Sullenly Linus nodded. His cheek already looked bruised.

"'Sides, can't we just get on with this?" Mariana gave Savannah an exasperated glance. She stroked Roy again. "I'd just as soon have this business over and done with. Settled."

"And rush *this?* Come on now, Mariana! You told me

you'd been tangled up in criminal dealings for half your life," Roy objected. "I can't believe you're gettin' cold feet now."

"I ain't," Mariana groused. "I just don't like *her*."

"Ah." With measured strides, Roy left Mariana. He crossed the room back to Savannah, bringing a chill with him. He lifted his hand, brushing his knuckles beneath her chin. His gaze bored into hers. "*I* like her. I like her a lot. I think we're goin' to get on famously, you and me. At least for a while, we are."

At his ominous tone, Savannah shuddered. She had no concept of what Roy Bedell meant to do to her…but she'd bet it would be at least as bad as what he'd done to his brother. Linus appeared to have endured that mistreatment many times over.

"Yep. I'd say we're going to get along real fine." Roy lowered his hand, crudely trailing his fingers down the front of her dress. "I guess I hit the bonanza with you, Miss Reed. What with you bein' famous, and all. I'm goin' to enjoy this plenty."

"Wait." Savannah lifted her head. "If you want my money—"

"Money? Yeah, I want that, all right." Roy nodded, seeming absorbed in her shawl. He rubbed its lacy texture between his fingers, making Savannah yearn to slap them away. "But now I'm thinkin', why should we quit at the money? Seein' as how you and me, we're two of a kind, I guess we should prob'ly—"

"I'm nothing like you!" Savannah burst out, unable to help herself. His comparison rubbed up against everything she wanted to deny about herself. "We are *not* two of a kind."

"We're not?" With a dubious grin, Roy raised his eyebrows. He cast a mocking glance at his brothers, then addressed her again. "Are you sure about that? Because from where I'm standin', we're *definitely* the same. In fact, I'd go so far as to say we're downright meant for each other, you and me."

Unable to fathom what he meant, Savannah stared at him. The look in his eyes scared her. If only she had left sooner...

"We're star-crossed lovers, Miss Reed. Brought together by fate and happenstance," Roy opined, sounding delighted with the idea. "*I'm* from a famous criminal family, *you're* from a famous criminal family—we're like royalty or somethin'. Damn near it."

He knew about her. He knew she was a "Ruthless Reed."

Inwardly Savannah despaired. It was bad enough that the Bedells had captured her. Bad enough that they intended to kill Adam the first chance they got. Bad enough that they would take all her savings and maybe kill her, too. But to add the fact that Roy Bedell was cognizant of her scandalous past and now meant to taunt her with it... It just piled on the agony. All that remained was for the people of Morrow Creek to learn about the same disreputable history Roy had...and shun her for it.

It was still possible, Savannah thought, that the Bedells would simply take her money and leave her alone. But even if they did, her hoped-for new beginning was crumbling before her very eyes. There was nothing she could do to stop it.

All she could do now was try to stay alive. If her skills as an actress had worked on one Bedell brother, it occurred to her, maybe they would work on a second brother, too.

Forcing a smile to her face, Savannah made herself look Roy in the eye. "Why, now that you put it *that* way... That's a downright *fascinating* idea, Mr. Bedell," she lied in her most flattering tone. "I'm so happy you pointed that out to me."

This time, Roy's grin seemed truly genuine. "I'm glad you think so." Dropping her shawl, he twisted to look at Mariana. "See? I told you she'd see the rightness of us bein' together."

Mariana scoffed. "You want a medal or somethin'?"

"Now, Mariana. Don't get all het up." Outrageously brash, Roy spread his arms. "There's enough of me to go around!"

The other Bedell brothers laughed and jostled each other.

"I'll help pick up the slack," the one called Curtis said.

"Me, too," another offered with a smirk. "Happy to help."

The prospect of being at the mercy of these ruthless men was almost more than Savannah could stand. Searching for an ally, however inadequate, she glanced at Linus. But he only kept his pitiful gaze fixed on the floor, seeming unaware of the proceedings around him. There'd be no help from that quarter.

"The only man I'm interested in is *you*, Mr. Bedell." Steeling herself, Savannah inhaled, then touched him. Roy's shirtfront felt unpleasantly stiff. The feel of his body beneath her palm made her queasy. "Can't we go someplace a little more private and talk some more about that bond we share? Please?"

At least then she'd be away from the other brothers. At least then she'd have a chance to appeal to whatever decency Roy Bedell still possessed. Maybe she could strike a deal with him.

Guilelessly Savannah batted her eyes at him, using the maneuver to survey his entire appearance. He had a gun belt, too. But if she could get him to turn slightly, if she could somehow manage to slip her hand lower without being noticed…

Never had she needed her sleight-of-hand skills more.

But with everyone watching, she could hardly perform magic.

"You can call me Roy." With a suggestive lifting of his eyebrows, the confidence man examined her, too. Not caring who was watching, he skimmed his hands over her body. "Please do."

With revulsion, Savannah shuddered. She swallowed hard, then nodded. "I didn't know you'd be so handsome, Roy."

He preened. "That's what all the ladies say." Abruptly his expression changed. His whisker-free jaw hardened. "Right afore they start beggin' me for mercy. What do you say, Missus Fancy Dancin' *Corwin*? Are you gonna beg me for mercy, too?"

Corwin. He knew she was married to Adam!

That must have been what Mariana had whispered to him, Savannah realized. Doubtless being the wife of the detective who'd sworn to track down Roy would not endear her to him.

Panic-stricken, she squirmed away. But Roy Bedell was too fast for her. He caught her in his pitiless grasp, then spun her around so her back was to him. She had a wobbly view of the other heckling Bedell brothers, of a dissatisfied-looking Mariana, of the ugly boardinghouse room with its useless window.

With his arm tight across her throat, Roy laughed. "Go on, Mrs. Corwin. Start beggin' right now, 'cause you'll need a head start. I ain't feelin' much inclined toward mercy tonight."

Choking, Savannah struggled. She kicked her foot but could not make contact. She wrenched her arms, smacking her hands against Roy's body behind her, but her efforts were useless.

"Let me go!" she cried. "I'll give you whatever you want."

Roy laughed harder. "Oh, you'll do that, all right—"

The door crashed open behind him, surprising everyone.

Taking advantage of the only opportunity she was likely to have, Savannah wrested away. She teetered, almost falling against the bed. She righted herself just in time.

Just in time to see Adam.

Hard-faced and toweringly tall, he pushed through the doorway. His gaze took in the assembled Bedell boys and Mariana, then arrowed in on Roy Bedell with unforgiving intensity.

"You never should have taken her, Bedell," Adam said. "This time—hell, every time—you went too far. Step away from her."

"Do it," a man behind Adam urged. "Right now."

Mose. Shocked, Savannah recognized her friend. Belatedly she spied the gun in his hand…and in Adam's. They'd come!

They'd come to rescue her. *And now they would want to sacrifice themselves. For her.* She couldn't let them do it.

But before she could do anything to try to change things, Mariana spoke up. "Corwin!" Oddly she laughed. "For a world-famous detective, it sure took you long enough to get here."

Adam shifted his gaze an inch sideways. "Evening, Mariana."

They knew one another? Dumbfounded, Savannah stared. Then she realized this whole gang knew one another. Even now, Linus gazed familiarly at Adam with a woeful, speculative expression.

"Kidnapping is a crime, Roy." Adam kept his gun leveled at the confidence man. "So are extortion, stealing and murder. I've got all the proof I need to put you away for good. I'd suggest you come along with me peacefully. Your brothers, too."

Strangely enough, Roy only laughed. "Now, why would I go and do somethin' like that, Detective?" He took an audacious, sauntering step forward, unbothered by the two firearms trained on him. With a sideways lunge, he grabbed Savannah. She kicked, but he held her fast, then went on crooning. "'Specially when I've got your *wife* here that I can use to make you let me go?"

Seeing Savannah in Roy Bedell's arms nearly blinded Adam with fury and fear. He'd taken too long to catch hold of her himself, he realized with a fresh surge of regret, and now Savannah was still at risk. Looking at her wide-eyed gaze and scared expression, he felt his heart beat with raw terror.

Forcibly he made himself shrug. "Do whatever you want with her. All I'm after is you, Bedell. If that means losing her…" Adam frowned in thought. "Well, that's the same as would have happened if I *hadn't* brought you in tonight, isn't it?"

Stricken, Savannah stared at Adam. Tears sprang to her eyes.

Beside him, Mose gave a growl of displeasure. Adam couldn't bear to look at him and see the disillusionment in his face.

"That's cold-blooded, Detective," Mariana observed from the other side of the room. "Even for a crazy bastard like you."

Gratefully Adam transferred his gaze to his partner. He'd been relieved to see that Mariana was safe—that she was *here* at all. Evidently, he realized, she'd gone undercover among the Bedells to try to bring them in. It was just like her to go above and beyond. Now she'd done the same to bolster his lies.

"That *is* pretty cold-blooded," Roy agreed. He kept his hands harshly on Savannah. "That's even worse than me. That's why I don't believe you, Corwin. You're too *good* to act that way."

"Good?" Adam scoffed. "What I am is fed up—fed up with chasing you and not catching you. It's downright wearisome. But this time, everything's turned out just like I wanted."

That lie was almost as outrageous as his first. But it had the desired effect. Standing a short distance from Mariana, Wyatt, Curtis and Edward exchanged glances, seeming a little more convinced. But they still kept their guns pointed at him.

"Give it up, Bedell." Adam gestured for Roy to release Savannah and come with him. "I'm not letting you sneak away this time. The sheriff's got my proof, and I've got *you,* so—"

"So that don't matter one whit," Roy interrupted. He aimed his wild-eyed glance at his brothers. "Me and my boys, I'd say we got you outnumbered, Detective. So why don't *you* give up?"

Facing Bedell, Adam tensed. Roy was right. Even with Mose and Mariana on his side, he didn't have much except authority and bravery to bolster his stance. He scowled to amplify both.

"Oh, no, you don't!" Linus suddenly yelled. He gave a maniacal laugh, then brandished a loaded firearm. He pointed it at Roy. "You ain't got nobody outnumbered, Roy. Not anymore! Not now that I got back my gun in all that melee. See there?"

He waved the gun. Everyone stepped back. As they did, Linus cast a shy, almost proud-looking glance at Savannah. To Adam's baffled amazement, he seemed to expect approval from her.

To his further surprise, she gave it. "Thank you, Linus."

But Roy only rolled his eyes. "You numskull, Linus! You can't even count. *You* plus him, plus him—" he pushed his chin toward a looming Mose "—only makes three. And there's still five of us, ain't there? 'Sides, you won't shoot your own brother."

Seeming uncertain, Linus wavered with his weapon.

"I reckon that's right," Mariana said. From the folds of her skirts, she raised a derringer. "But *I'd* shoot you, Roy."

Momentarily loosening his grip on Savannah, Roy stared at her. "Mariana? What are you talkin' about, sweetcakes?"

The expression of incredulity on his face was so complete that Adam would have laughed…had their situation not been so calamitous. As it was, he could only count silently. The numbers were evened out now, but a standoff was of no help to him. Not if it didn't result in Savannah being released safe and sound.

"I'd shoot you just for bein' such an inconsiderate pig," Mariana went on in an even tone. "You was goin' to take up with another woman whilst you were still with *me,* Roy. That's low."

This time it was Adam's turn to look askance at her. "Mariana? Tell me you didn't really get addle headed over *him.*"

"Me? 'Course not." Mariana shrugged. "I like my men full growed and capable of kindness. You ain't neither, Roy."

She nodded at Savannah. "Now let her go. You're comin' with us."

"With *you?* Hell, I ain't doin' nothin'!" Roy yelled, his gaze growing more infuriated. He jerked Savannah forcibly sideways, demonstrating his hold on her. "You're gonna do what *I* say, Corwin. And that means watchin' your little wife here die."

Savannah whimpered. Adam felt his gut twist. He wanted to reassure her, to help her feel less afraid…but he feared that if he looked into her eyes, he would break down completely. Roy would know how much she meant to him. All would be lost.

"You kill her, I kill you," Adam told Roy in a rough tone, not thinking about how much it hurt to say the words. "Either way, I don't care. She's already served her purpose to me."

"Oh, yeah?" Roy asked skeptically. "What was that?"

"Bringing you within range to be caught," Adam said. "She's done that, pretty providentially, too. Besides, I felt sorry for her. She wanted to get married pretty bad, and I was around."

Savannah gave another sob. Her wounded gaze felt palpable.

"She was *expectin'* me," Roy pointed out. "The better man."

Adam shook his head. "You'll never be the better man."

"You're both awful!" Savannah shouted. She squirmed in Roy's grasp, her skirts a blur of motion. She stomped on Roy's foot, making the floor tremble. He yelped. Somehow she got free.

The Bedell brothers lunged forward in alarm. But suddenly, Roy stiffened. He held up his hands in surrender—

because, as Adam saw to his disbelief, Savannah held a gun to his head.

Roy chuckled, signaling his brothers. "Hold tight there, boys. Let's not do anything too hasty. This here little lady—"

"Is leaving," Savannah interrupted in no uncertain terms. "And you're going to let me." Defiantly, she jerked her chin toward the rest of the gang. "Tell them to let me go, Roy."

"Yeah, Roy!" Linus crowed. "Tell 'em to let her go!"

"You seem to be forgettin' somethin'," Roy told her in an eerily calm tone. "My boys are willin' to kill *or* die for me. I don't believe you can say the same thing about your people."

"You're wrong," Savannah told him. "Tonight anything is possible. People are capable of things I'd never have expected." Her gaze flickered to Adam. Hastily he glanced away. "And you're doubly wrong, because these aren't *my* 'people.'" Her voice broke, then went hoarse as she continued. "Except one."

With his heart in his throat, Adam finally raised his gaze to hers. The situation here was still dangerous. The stakes were still much too dire. But he felt beyond proud of Savannah at that moment. Even Mariana watched her with grudging admiration.

He was her "people," Adam knew. He'd never valued the sense of belonging and salvation that Savannah gave him more than he did at that moment. But she didn't even look at him.

"Come on, Mose," she said firmly. "Let's go."

"Right behind you, girl," the big man said.

They both edged toward the door, keeping their guns high. Adam stared at them in patent disbelief. His mind whirled.

As she neared the door, Adam spoke. "Savannah, wait!"

She paused. Looked at him. Raised her wobbly chin proudly.

"You can't—" Mindlessly Adam gestured at the outlaws he and Mariana still held at gunpoint. "Without you and Mose—"

"You won't be able to nab the Bedells?" Upon finishing his statement for him, Savannah lifted her eyebrows. Her pretty face looked pale. Her voice shook with suppressed emotion, but her gun hand was steady. "Sure you will, Mr. Corwin."

Mr. Corwin. Her use of that formal address chilled him.

"After all, it's what you want most in the world, isn't it?" Savannah went on. "To catch the Bedell gang? At least that's what you said a little while ago."

"No!" Adam choked out. He glanced at a smirking Roy, then risked his biggest gamble yet. "I came here to save *you*—"

"Well, you did a mighty poor job of it, didn't you?" Savannah asked. "It looks to me as though I saved myself."

Linus nodded vigorously. "It looks that way to me, too."

Adam ignored him. Savannah's words cut him deeply, striking at the core of everything he believed himself to be: a man who saved, a man who cared, a man who *protected*.

"You're wrong, Savannah. All I wanted was to protect you—"

"Corwin, hush!" Mariana cut him off. "For the love of God, just quit talking, afore you make it all worse."

Savannah eyed him sadly. She edged closer to the door. "I never should have looked to a man again—not for anything. I swore not to. I guess forgetting that was my first mistake."

Protectively Mose hovered near her, scowling. The Bedell brothers only watched the tableau with hushed attention. Even Roy, still pinned under Savannah's filched pistol, didn't move.

Inexplicably Adam remembered his and Savannah's wedding night, when Savannah had mischievously pulled that key from his ear. That explained how she'd snatched Roy's gun from him. But it didn't explain why she was leaving Adam now. More than anything, he wanted to go back to that time, when Savannah had been proud to be married to him…and he had loved her fully.

Hello! We're Mr. and Mrs. Corwin! he recalled her saying. Wistfully he wished she'd say it again. Joyfully, too. But those days were gone, and Adam knew he could never recapture them. This time, he'd lost her for good.

"My second mistake," Savannah said, "was loving you at all."

Wounded almost beyond bearing, Adam stiffened. He knew what had happened. Savannah had gotten the wrong idea from the things he'd told Roy. Why shouldn't she have? he realized with a brutal sense of honesty. He'd gotten very good at lying to her.

He'd told her he was the man she'd been waiting for. That had been a lie. But he hadn't lied about loving her. Never that.

"Aww, buck up, Corwin," Roy Bedell piped up. "You won't be missin' much. Just an actress and a dancer and a criminal."

In the doorway, Savannah stiffened. Her gaze whipped to Bedell, then to Adam. He saw truthfulness reflected there…truthfulness and regret. In that moment, Adam recalled why the newspaper article in the sheriff's office had struck him so.

"Your woman's nothin' but a 'Ruthless Reed,'" Roy went on. "You must've heard of 'em. They was all over the city papers a while back." He laughed. "It's kinda funny, an upright type like yourself windin' up with a thievin' whore like her."

Linus quivered with rage. "You shut your mouth, Roy!"

Adam felt the same way. But an instant later, Savannah and Mose hustled out the door and all hell broke loose inside.

Chapter Eighteen

Standing safely in the street outside the boardinghouse, Savannah hugged her shawl against her, shaking uncontrollably. She couldn't seem to quit trembling—couldn't seem to get Roy's voice out of her head.

It's kinda funny, an upright type like yourself windin' up with a thievin' whore like her.

Well, in a sense, Roy Bedell was right. It *was* funny—or would have been, had Savannah felt capable of laughter… then or ever again. Because to anyone who mattered, she *was* what the tabloids had labeled her. She might as well accept it.

Adam already had. She'd seen it in his eyes.

"Are you all right?" Mose hovered concernedly. His big hand patted over her shoulders, as though seeking reassurance that she was truly unharmed. "I swear, I'll go back in there and make them all pay if they hurt you."

"No need for that." Humorlessly Savannah quirked her lips. "I think there are quite enough people in there by now, Mose."

For the past few minutes, Morrow Creek residents had been streaming toward the boardinghouse at a run, led by many of the same people whom Savannah had met at the Finneys' party…a million years ago, it felt. They'd started gathering outside the place a few minutes before Savannah had managed to take away Roy Bedell's gun. She'd glimpsed them through the window and had known she'd need to buy them a little more time to assemble.

Soon enough, she'd recognized the sheriff outside. She'd made it a point to learn his face—and his deputy's—upon coming to town, so she would be able to steel herself for the day when he asked her to move on, like the sheriff had in Ledgerville. Instead, inexplicably, he'd come to save her from the Bedells.

By the time Savannah had neared the boardinghouse room's door, almost the whole posse had managed to gather outside, with Sheriff Caffey, two of his deputies, Jack Murphy, Marcus Copeland, and big Daniel McCabe leading the way. Their arrival had eased Savannah's qualms about leaving Adam and Mariana behind with the Bedells, but it hadn't made leaving easy.

Nothing could have done that.

Heartsick and weary, Savannah turned to Mose. "Is the wagon nearby?" she asked. "Would you please take me home?"

"You sure you want to leave?" His gaze met hers. "You might have misunderstood something back there. There's a chance—"

"There's no chance. None at all." Savannah spied a few of the women headed her way, led by Sarah McCabe, Grace Murphy, Molly Copeland and Mrs. Finney. Their serious faces left little doubt of their intentions. Clearly *they* knew about her past now, too. Her hopes for Morrow Creek were dashed. "Please. Let's go."

"All right." Reluctantly Mose nodded. "We'll go for now."

"For forever," Savannah said firmly.

Then, without so much as a backward glance—a luxury she most certainly could not afford—she raced into the night, leaving behind all her hopes...and her heart at the same time.

Standing by while Sheriff Caffey and his deputies none-too-gently slapped Roy Bedell and his brothers in irons, Adam felt oddly removed from everything. Finally capturing the Bedell gang should have made him happy. But after the night he'd had, he felt as though nothing would ever make him happy again.

Not without Savannah by his side.

"Woowee!" Mariana approached him with her customary vigor. She holstered her trusty derringer without a single thought to the risqué view of her leg she offered the others in the room. "That was some snare, right, Corwin? I'm happy to see you're still alive and kicking, you stubborn ass, you."

Gleefully Mariana threw her arms around him in a hug.

Adam knew he must be dreaming. Mariana didn't like hugging. Hell, in all this time, he hadn't been one hundred percent certain she liked *him,* if he were completely truthful.

"Aww, don't look so down in the mouth." She slugged him in the arm, returning to her usual tomboyish stance. "I know that gal of yours left in a rush, but this business of ours ain't for the faint of heart. Most likely, bein' abducted was a lot for her to take, 'specially at the hands of *these* miscreants."

Mariana nodded in the general direction of the newly

arrested Bedells. Roy glared daggers at her. Edward, Wyatt and Curtis argued among themselves. Linus gabbed to Sheriff Caffey, talking at a speed that was scarcely comprehendible, doing his best to clear his conscience before it was too late.

"I can give you details of all them crimes, Sheriff," Linus hastily assured the lawman. "Dates and places and everythin'. I never thought what we was doin' was right. No sir, not at all. That's why I want to make amends for all the bad things I done."

"I think we can come to an arrangement," the sheriff said.

Linus appeared relieved, if bruised. Beside him, Jack Murphy and Marcus Copeland nodded with evident approval of the goings on. Next to them, Daniel McCabe folded his powerful arms and surveyed the room. Since a few seconds after Savannah had left, the place had been swamped with lawmen and helpful Morrow Creek residents, all of them intent on doing what was right.

After a brief but ferocious scuffle with the Bedells, the makeshift posse had done exactly that. It hadn't taken long.

Adam had rightfully pinned Roy and handcuffed him himself, but the act had given him no satisfaction. All he wanted was to turn back the clock and take back the lies he'd told—all of them, including the ones from tonight. If there'd been another way to protect Savannah from Roy, he would have done it, but—

But wasn't that always his excuse? That he had to lie? It *had* been until now. But starting tonight, Adam couldn't let himself off that easily. The truth was, he ached with needing Savannah—with loving her and not having her. And he deserved it.

He deserved every ounce of the pain he felt.

"I gotta say," Mariana said, still standing beside him, "I didn't think much of that Savannah Reed when we started—"

Adam felt newly wounded. "Don't—" he began.

But that only made Mariana brighten. "Whoops! Sorry, I mean *Mrs. Corwin*, don't I? Anyhow, I didn't think much of her when we started all this. I thought she was just another dumb female, set to get herself killed or worse. But she surprised me."

"She surprised me, too." Adam was still astounded at how much losing Savannah hurt. He guessed he always would be.

"I tried my damnedest to get her off of you," Mariana yammered on. "I told her how you was a mean, bad, ornery cuss who was just usin' her to catch the Bedells. 'That ain't no way to treat a lady,' I told her. But she did *not* take the bait," Mariana said emphatically. "She passed all my tests with flyin' colors! She stuck up for you, Corwin. You shoulda seen her."

"I wish I could." Damnation, he felt miserable.

"Not many women would've tried to *help* the people who were holdin' her captive, you know." Mariana shook her head, going on to describe how Savannah had consoled Linus and wisely advised the both of them to get away from Roy Bedell if they could. "That's why old Linus was so keen to help her—that and she's pretty, besides." Mariana chuckled. "That woman of yours has got a good heart, Corwin. You done fine. She's a keeper, I'd say."

"She is. But she's somebody else's to keep now." Adam spied several of the Morrow Creek residents headed his way, even as the sheriff and his deputies began hauling the Bedells to the jailhouse. Most likely, they wanted him to help secure the gang for good. Adam could not refuse. After all, that was his duty. He gave Mariana's shoulder a squeeze. "I'm glad you're safe, too, partner. There's nobody I'd rather be paired with."

Appearing suddenly alerted to something, Mariana blinked.

"The hell there ain't!" She grabbed him as he turned away, then stood up to him—all five feet and four inches of her. "You would rather be paired with Savannah. For life! Wouldn't you? I know she wasn't a damn pawn to you, like Roy was to me. You weren't playin' at this. You don't have it in you."

Wearily Adam yanked himself away. He gave Thomas Walsh a nod to indicate he'd be with the others shortly. "It doesn't matter what I want. I can't force myself on Savannah. She deserves better. She deserves the truth, for one thing."

"Then give her the truth!" Mariana put her hands on her hips, looking as though she'd like to yank out his hair. "That's what the Adam Corwin I know would do. Would *already* have done."

"I guess you don't know me as well as you think."

A sigh. "What's wrong with you? Every woman likes to know how her man feels. Every woman likes to hear him say it! Why do you think that lowdown Roy got so many ladies to marry him?"

Adam frowned. He didn't want to talk about this. "Because he brings out their motherly feelings with that infernal baby face of his?" His frown deepened. "Leave me alone, Mariana."

But his partner, steadfastly, would not. "You married her, didn't you? You was already half in love with her weeks ago, so why—" She broke off, gawking at him. "You don't think Savannah *believed* all that claptrap I spouted about you, do you?"

"I don't know," Adam said. "But she believed me."

"Sure, but you said a *lot* of things tonight," Mariana sensibly pointed out. "What if she believed all the wrong ones? What then? Aren't you gonna go after her or somethin'?"

She gave him an aggressive poke. Adam glared at her.

"No. I have a passel of sharpers to take to jail," he said.

Then he turned away and finally walked out of the room where he'd left his heart and soul and hopes…for now and forever.

Dispiritedly Savannah carried another load of her belongings to the wagon. Above her, the moon rode high in the sky, lighting her path between the vehicle and her station. In the morning, she would tender her official resignation to the telegraph company. She would have to stop by the neighbors', too, to make sure Penelope would be cared for after she'd gone. Most likely, Mr. Yarnell would also take her small flock of laying hens. His wife might like having the eggs to sell in town.

With a weary sigh, Savannah trod back to the station. In the moonlight, the place already appeared deserted.

The sight of it made her feel doubly sad. She'd truly loved living near Morrow Creek. Lately she'd even begun to dream that she and Adam might move into town someday, where she could take a less demanding post at the local telegraph station. After all, Grace Murphy had given her hope that they'd hire her. And Molly Copeland had allowed her to believe that working the wires needn't necessarily be incompatible with having children.

But now her last foray into Morrow Creek would not be to look for a small, snug house for her and Adam, or to attend any of the friendly get-togethers she'd shortsightedly been invited to tonight. It would be to withdraw her nest-egg savings from the Morrow Creek bank, where she'd stowed her money months ago.

I'm leery of entrusting my savings to any bank or institution, she'd truthfully written in her letters. But she'd been even more leery of leaving her money lying around at her remote territorial telegraph station. So she'd deposited everything in the bank and hadn't told a soul about it.

Unfortunately that meant her departure was delayed until she could retrieve it. Even though Savannah didn't have many hopes left about the possibility of successfully starting over, she still needed cash to move on.

Mose left the station, sweating beneath the weight of her ornate costume trunk. He heaved it in the wagon, making its springs jounce. He wiped his forehead. "Are you sure about this? You'd be better off trying to get a good night's sleep. You've been through an ordeal tonight, that's for certain."

"I'm sure." Fondly Savannah patted him. She was so glad he was safe after being in such danger. "If we get everything all packed up tonight, we can leave twice as quickly tomorrow." Mose was right—neither of them was alert enough to capably drive the wagon right now. "Besides, I couldn't sleep a wink anyway."

And staying busy keeps me from crying.

No, she couldn't say that to Mose. He'd only worry about her. So Savannah put on the most upbeat expression she could manage, then turned to go back inside. "Aren't you happy? We're finally headed to San Francisco, just like you wanted."

"I thought you liked it here," Mose grumbled behind her.

I did. Especially when Adam was here. But he'd only stayed because he'd pitied her, Savannah knew now. Not because he'd loved her. Not because he'd needed her, the way she needed him.

"I'm ready for a new adventure." She stepped inside with Mose on her heels, then surveyed the station. She didn't have many belongings left. She'd be ready to leave very soon. "And I want to stay one step ahead of the angry Morrow Creek mob."

Trying to laugh at that, Savannah looked at Mose. Although he usually indulged even her poorest attempts at humor, this time he only crossed his arms and gave her a concerned look.

"You've got those people all wrong," he said. "They couldn't do enough to help you tonight. They won't judge you."

"That doesn't matter. *I* will." Not wanting to think about that, she hoisted a bundle of clothing. She headed outside.

Arriving at the doorway, she nearly stepped on Adam's toes.

Startled, Savannah jerked backward. But she hadn't dreamed him. Adam truly *was* there, on her doorstep, with his hat in his hands and his heart in his eyes. A short distance behind him, a saddled-up horse stood in the yard, its sides heaving as it recovered from what must have been an impressively fast ride.

She looked up at Adam in shock. She felt her heart leap in her chest with all the irrational hopefulness that was her stock in trade. This situation was going to be troublesome. If she didn't watch herself closely, Savannah knew, she would make a fool of herself all over again by begging Adam to stay.

She'd never wanted anything more. To see him smile at her in the mornings over coffee, to feel him pull her close to him in bed at night, to hear her name spoken tenderly on his lips…

But she couldn't have any of that. Not anymore.

Forcing herself to be strong, Savannah raised her head.

But her whole body still quivered with hopefulness. Drat it all.

"You're going to want to do something with that horse, Mr. Corwin," she told him. "It's unconscionable to leave the poor creature standing there all tired and wet and hungry."

He turned his hat in his hands. "This won't take long."

Because he wasn't here for her, Savannah realized with a pang of despair. Likely he was here to collect his things.

"I'm not stealing all these things, if that's what you're wondering about." Proudly she gestured toward the loaded wagon. "Whatever you've left here is still here. I'm no thief."

Somberly Adam nodded. She didn't think he believed her.

"I know Roy Bedell told you about me, and some of that *is* true," she went on, admitting it for the first time. "My parents really were the 'Ruthless Reeds.' I really was on the stage. But I left that life behind me. For good! Only it just keeps…"

Her voice broke, forcing her to stop. Adam blinked down at her. He sighed. She realized he must be feeling impatient.

Doubtless, again, he didn't believe a word she said.

Why should he? Nobody else ever had.

"It just keeps following me," Savannah made herself say. "My past, I mean. But that needn't trouble you. I'm sure I can give you an annulment or just sever our ties somehow, before I—"

"Please don't do that," Adam said. He sounded hoarse, too.

Before she could reason out why, Mose shouldered past both of them. "I'll just take care of that horse," he announced.

He hurried into the yard. In the moonlight, he caught hold of the horse's bridle. He led the creature toward the barn.

"You needn't do that, Mose!" Savannah called out, her heart aching. "Mr. Corwin won't be staying."

With that painful truth said, she looked at Adam. She could not imagine what he'd come here for. Desperately she reviewed their conversation so far and could arrive at no explanation.

"Now then." Deliberately, Savannah pushed past him to add her bundled clothes to the wagon. Adam trod silently after her. "I've already assured you that your belongings are safe, even near me. I've already told you I'd be willing to set you legally free from our marriage. I've even admitted everything about my past—and if that doesn't make you want to run, I don't know what will." She gave a humorless chuckle. "You have no further obligation to me, Mr. Corwin. So if there's nothing else—"

"There is something else," he said.

With her gullible heart still pounding, Savannah watched as Adam set his hat atop a crate of cookware in the wagon. With his hands free, though, he seemed not to know what to do with them. They shook, curiously enough, as he fisted them at his sides.

"I'm sorry, Savannah," Adam said in a rough voice. "I'm sorry for everything I did. I'm sorry I misled you. I'm sorry I lied to you. I'm sorry I let you believe I was the man you'd been waiting for. I wasn't that man—that man you were dreaming of and hoping for. For a while, I thought maybe I could be, but—"

He hauled in a raspy, painful-sounding breath. Then, in a move as deliberate as any he'd ever made, Adam took her hand. He wrapped her fingers in his, then squeezed tightly.

"—but you deserve better than that," Adam said fervently. "*Better than me.* All I ever wanted was to protect you, but I did it the wrong way. You needed the truth, and I didn't give it to you. I'm sorry. But now, if you'll give me a chance... Maybe now I can make up for that."

Confused yet desperately encouraged, Savannah gazed up at him. His hand felt undeniably at home wrapped around hers. All the deepest parts of her yearned to be with him. But she didn't dare. Adam didn't understand about her, didn't truly know...

"You told me one time that all you wanted was for me to believe you—to believe *you* first, before anyone." Seeming to steel himself, Adam looked her in the eye. "So that's why I'm here. To give you a chance to tell me what I need to know."

Disconsolate, Savannah looked away. "You mean about my past."

It had come to that. Again. At least Adam was giving her a chance to deny all his worst fears about her. But she couldn't.

"It's all true," she said. "I told you a minute ago. It's—"

But Adam only blinked. "Not about your past. I figured that out tonight, yes. But if what you've been through is what's made you the woman you are right now, then I'm grateful for it."

Dubiously she stared up at him. "Grateful?"

"Because it's brought you to me," Adam said. "I can't be sorry for that!" He smiled. "If you hadn't been trying to start over, you wouldn't have been here for me to find you. If you hadn't been hopeful enough to try to love someone, you wouldn't have helped me, even though I didn't deserve it." With an air of wonder, Adam shook his head. "You put a dream within my grasp, Savannah. A dream I didn't even

know I had." He swore. "When I woke up to find all those
hopes within my reach, I just…took them. I'm a flawed
man. That's true; I can't deny it. But I—"

"What hopes?" she asked. "What dream? I don't understand."

"You." Smiling more broadly, Adam released her hand.
He cupped her face in his palms instead. *"You* were my
dream. Haven't you guessed by now? I love you, Savannah.
I've loved you nearly from the first moment I saw you. I love
your smile and your warmth and your wonderful, impeccable manners—"

She snorted. "They're far from impeccable. Just ask
Mose."

"—and I feel beyond lucky to have had any time with
you at all, much less to be asking for more now. But that's
what I'm doing." Deeply, Adam inhaled, fixing her with a
somber look. "So when I said before—that I want you to
tell me what I need to know—I meant this: Do you love me,
Savannah? Because that's *all* I need to know. Everything
else will turn out in the end."

"You—" Savannah hesitated "—*don't* think the worst
of me?"

"Of you? I never could," Adam swore. "Never, Savannah."

"And…*you love me?*" Disbelieving, Savannah realized what she'd heard a second ago. "You really love me?
Me?"

"More than anything else," Adam told her. "I love
you."

"Oh." Reeling beneath the impossibility of that, Savannah went on staring at him. She could scarcely breathe for
the rush of hopefulness that struck her. "I love you, too,
Adam."

The words hung between them, tentatively spoken, as

fragile as the moonlight. Fearful that he would not believe her, again, even about such a momentous truth, Savannah said it once more.

"I love you, Adam. I do!" she cried. "I'm sorry I didn't trust you more, but I was scared and confused, and I—I—"

She hesitated, despairing of a way to fully convince him. But as it turned out—wonder of wonders—she didn't have to.

"I believe you," Adam said with a smile in his voice.

Then he pulled her all the way in his arms and kissed her. Surrendering at last, laughing, daring to finally reach out for the new future she *truly* needed, Savannah kissed him back.

"But nobody ever believed me," she said. "Why you?"

Tenderly Adam stroked her cheek. As though unable to imagine they were finally together, he shook his head. "Why me? That's simple. I believe you because I know you. Because I love you. Because, even though I'm not the man you wanted—"

"Stop right there." Savannah laughed, then kissed him once more. "You're the man I *needed*. I won't hear another word to the contrary." Just to make sure, she kissed Adam again, with all the love and happiness and wonder that were in her heart.

Which was only fitting, really. Because all that love and happiness and wonder were theirs to share, brought into being by the unlikely combination of trust and coincidence, caring and daring and a tiny dose of necessary etiquette. And that reminded Savannah of something else—something she hadn't reckoned on.

"Are you willing to stay here in Morrow Creek?" she asked Adam, holding his hands in hers. "Because I've been running for a while now, trying to start over, and I'm starting to think—no place will ever feel right to me until I own up to who I am and go on from there. I don't want to compel you to do anything, of course, but with you by my side, I just might have the courage to stay here and try to hold my head high…no matter what."

"I'll do anything you want," Adam assured her. "Anything."

Happily Savannah agreed. She sighed. Near her, someone else did, too. *Mose,* she saw. He wiped a tear from his cheek.

"I'm powerfully glad you two got that settled," he said.

"Why, Mose!" Savannah smiled at him, overcome with affection. "Does that mean Adam has your blessing at last?"

Gruffly her friend nodded. "I'm not the only one."

Indicating as much, he angled his chin toward the road leading from Morrow Creek. To Savannah's surprise, an array of the town's residents came up that path even now, driving wagons and buggies and riding lone horses. In the summertime moonlight, their faces seemed friendly, if concerned for her well-being.

Adam noticed their approach, too. "I guess you left a mite too quickly. Everyone kept asking me about you tonight."

"They did?" She stared as her visitors approached. "Truly?"

Adam nodded. "You made a lasting impression, Savannah. On me, on everyone in Morrow Creek…on everyone you touched."

Savannah could scarcely believe it. But as Grace Murphy became the first to reach her and offer her a warmhearted hug, she started to accept it. Especially when Grace spoke up.

"I'm *so* admiring of your adventures on the stage!" she

exclaimed. "If you would come talk to the Social Equality Sisterhood about it, I'd be very grateful, Savannah."

"And to my book club!" Sarah McCabe put in. "Maybe even the schoolhouse. I've heard you can do magic tricks. I know the children would be absolutely thrilled to see them demonstrated."

"And to my bakery," Molly Copeland added with the friendliest smile of all. "The place could use a bit of sophistication. I'm betting you could provide it, Savannah."

They didn't want her to leave, Savannah realized in utter amazement. *They wanted her to stay.*

As she joined hands with Adam again, preparing to begin their *honest* future together, Savannah realized that she wanted exactly the same thing. She wanted to stay. For good this time.

Under these circumstances, she reckoned cheerfully, the only polite thing to do was to graciously agree, then fix a time for all those meetings she'd been invited to. But her heart suddenly felt too full for etiquette and propriety.

Instead, to her chagrin, all Savannah could do was nod.

Seeing her face, Adam waved his arm toward the small but welcoming station. "Everyone come inside and sit a spell! It's late, but Savannah and I want to welcome you properly."

Relieved, Savannah smiled at him. Once again, Adam had shown her another wonderful, undeniable truth. The two of them, together, made a perfect match. In the Territory or anywhere else, it just didn't get any better than that—better than her mail-order groom…and the love they'd found together.

* * * * *

*Harlequin Presents® is thrilled
to introduce the first installment of
an epic tale of passion and drama by*
**USA TODAY Bestselling Author
Penny Jordan!**

**When buttoned-up Giselle first meets
the devastatingly handsome Saul Parenti,
the heat between them is explosive....**

"LET ME GET THIS STRAIGHT. Are you actually suggesting that I would stoop to that kind of game playing?"

Saul came out from behind his desk and walked toward her. Giselle could smell his hot male scent and it was making her dizzy, igniting a low, dull, pulsing ache that was taking over her whole body.

Giselle defended her suspicions. "You don't want me here."

"No," Saul agreed, "I don't."

And then he did what he had sworn he would not do, cursing himself beneath his breath as he reached for her, pulling her fiercely into his arms and kissing her with all the pent-up fury she had aroused in him from the moment he had first seen her.

Giselle certainly *wanted* to resist him. But the hand she raised to push him away developed a will of its own and was sliding along his bare arm beneath the sleeve of his shirt, and the body that should have been arching away from him was instead melting into him.

Beneath the pressure of his kiss he could feel and taste her gasp of undeniable response to him. He wanted to devour her, take her and drive them both until they were equally satiated—even whilst the anger within him that she should make him feel that way roared and burned its resentment of his need.

She was helpless, Giselle recognized, totally unable to withstand the storm lashing at her, able only to cling to the man who was the cause of it and pray that she would survive.

Somewhere else in the building a door banged. The sound exploded into the sensual tension that had enclosed them, driving them apart. Saul's chest was rising and falling as he fought for control; Giselle's whole body was trembling.

Without a word she turned and ran.

Find out what happens when Saul and Giselle succumb to their irresistible desire in

THE RELUCTANT SURRENDER

Available January 2011 from Harlequin Presents®

HARLEQUIN®

A *Romance*

FOR EVERY MOOD™

Spotlight on

Classic

Quintessential, modern love stories
that are romance at its finest.

See the next page
to enjoy a sneak peek from
the Harlequin Presents® series.

REQUEST YOUR FREE BOOKS!

 HARLEQUIN® HISTORICAL:
Where love is timeless

2 FREE NOVELS PLUS 2 **FREE GIFTS!**

YES! Please send me 2 FREE Harlequin® Historical novels and my 2 FREE gifts (gifts are worth about $10). After receiving them, if I don't wish to receive any more books, I can return the shipping statement marked "cancel." If I don't cancel, I will receive 6 brand-new novels every month and be billed just $4.94 per book in the U.S. or $5.49 per book in Canada. That's a saving of 20% off the cover price! It's quite a bargain! Shipping and handling is just 50¢ per book.* I understand that accepting the 2 free books and gifts places me under no obligation to buy anything. I can always return a shipment and cancel at any time. Even if I never buy another book from Harlequin, the two free books and gifts are mine to keep forever.

246/349 HDN E5L4

Name	(PLEASE PRINT)
Address	Apt. #
City	State/Prov.	Zip/Postal Code

Signature (if under 18, a parent or guardian must sign)

Mail to the **Harlequin Reader Service:**
IN U.S.A.: P.O. Box 1867, Buffalo, NY 14240-1867
IN CANADA: P.O. Box 609, Fort Erie, Ontario L2A 5X3
Not valid for current subscribers to Harlequin Historical books.

Want to try two free books from another line?
Call 1-800-873-8635 or visit www.morefreebooks.com.

* Terms and prices subject to change without notice. Prices do not include applicable taxes. N.Y. residents add applicable sales tax. Canadian residents will be charged applicable provincial taxes and GST. Offer not valid in Quebec. This offer is limited to one order per household. All orders subject to approval. Credit or debit balances in a customer's account(s) may be offset by any other outstanding balance owed by or to the customer. Please allow 4 to 6 weeks for delivery. Offer available while quantities last.

Your Privacy: Harlequin Books is committed to protecting your privacy. Our Privacy Policy is available online at www.eHarlequin.com or upon request from the Reader Service. From time to time we make our lists of customers available to reputable third parties who may have a product or service of interest to you. If you would prefer we not share your name and address, please check here. ☐

Help us get it right—We strive for accurate, respectful and relevant communications. To clarify or modify your communication preferences, visit us at www.ReaderService.com/consumerschoice.

HIH10R